LETTERS TO MONTGOMERY CLIFT

*Christmas 2004
from Judy to
Uncle Michael*

LETTERS TO MONTGOMERY CLIFT

a novel

Noël Alumit

alyson books
los angeles

© 2002 BY NOËL ALUMIT. ALL RIGHTS RESERVED.

MANUFACTURED IN THE UNITED STATES OF AMERICA.

THIS TRADE PAPERBACK IS PUBLISHED BY ALYSON PUBLICATIONS,
P.O. BOX 4371, LOS ANGELES, CALIFORNIA 90078-4371.

FIRST EDITION PUBLISHED IN HARDCOVER BY MACADAM/CAGE PUBLISHING: 2002
FIRST ALYSON BOOKS EDITION (PAPERBACK): SEPTEMBER 2003

03 04 05 06 07 **a** 10 9 8 7 6 5 4 3 2 1

ISBN 1-55583-815-4
(PREVIOUSLY PUBLISHED WITH ISBN 1-931561-02-8 BY MACADAM/CAGE PUBLISHING.)

LIBRARY OF CONGRESS CATALOGING-IN-PUBLICATION DATA
    LETTERS TO MONTGOMERY CLIFT / NOËL ALUMIT.
        ISBN 1-55583-815-4
        1. FILIPINO AMERICANS—FICTION. 2. CHILDREN OF DISAPPEARED PERSONS—FICTION.
    3. CLIFT, MONTGOMERY—FICTION. 4. FOSTER HOME CARE—FICTION. 5. GAY YOUTH—
    FICTION. I. TITLE.
    PS3601.L86L47
    813'.6—DC21

CREDITS
COVER PHOTOGRAPHY FROM PHOTONICA/RIEDER PHOTOGRAPHY.
COVER DESIGN BY FRANCES BACA.

PART ONE

CHAPTER ONE
Letters to Montgomery Clift

```
dear mr montgomery clift,        december 4, 1976

i want one thing only. please bring my mama back
to me. safe. with no more bruises.

i will wait one week. if nothing bad happens then
i know it is ok to write you.

Sign

bong bong luwad
```

I didn't start seeing Montgomery Clift immediately. I didn't start to depend on him or adore him or desire him or touch him until later. I didn't know that his cinematic glow of black, white, and silver would influence me in such ways. Even now, I still wonder.

I saw him first in a movie, enthralled with his magnificent face, taken with his kindness. People can leave indelible marks, scars sometimes. That's what people do. That's what Montgomery Clift did for me. It didn't matter that he had been dead for ten years by the time I started writing him.

Montgomery Clift—"Monty"—was my first American friend. And who forgets a first anything? First kiss, first love, first date, first sex, first car, first time seeing your parents beaten up, first foster home, first job, first year in college, first betrayal, first real relationship.

Monty would be the most constant companion in my search for her, my mother. Mr. Clift has been with me for most of my life now. And, I don't care what the doctors say, he is real. As real to me as Robert or J or Amada or Logan or Mrs. Billaruz.

I started my life in America and my search for my parents—well, only my mother now—with Monty as my guide. The journey to find my mother would not be complete without him.

If I find Mama…when I find her—no, I can only say "if." If I find my mother, I'll give them to her. I'll give her my letters to Montgomery Clift. She will read them and I'll explain the parts in between. She will see what happened to me, see what I did to myself, and know that I've always loved her, even though she never came back.

In my mind, I've rehearsed my life story over and over again: piecing together parts of my life I want to tell her. I'm going to tell her about my childhood in Los Angeles (including life with her evil sister Yuna), my new family, my accident, my time in the hospital, and my falling in love with a dead movie star. My letters will be the greatest testament to that.

There is a finite moment where the events of your life lead, a moment filled with who you were and who you might be. It reminds me of a black dot, a tiny star aligned to make a constellation. From that dot, that tiny star, a rest-of-a-life is led. For some, it is a marriage or a divorce or a birth or a death. For me, it is a plane ride.

My bags are packed. Once the sun strikes this side of earth, Logan will take me to the airport and I'll fly away…back to the beginning. Some think time is a straight line that only continues forward. I don't believe that. I think the line of time can be bent backward, so far back, it'll break. And when it does, everything I know will fall apart. I'm going back to see who I was. I'm going to visit Yesterday, hoping to discover what went horribly wrong.

I look at my letters. And by doing so, I've bent the line of time backward. I see who I was: my words written in a child's scribble. Some of my letters are stained, warped spots where moisture used to be. Moisture that was my tears.

CHAPTER TWO
Balloon Strings When Wind Comes By

dear mr. montgomery clift,   december 14, 1976

I LOVED MONGOMERY CLIP she said. this is a good
sign because i do not think auntie yuna loves
very much.

I LOVED HIM auntie yuna said when i asked her
about you. i do not like to ask a lot from my
auntie yuna.

I CRIED WHEN HE DIED she said. I CRIED WHEN I
READ 1950s SCREEN IDOL MONGOMERY CLIP DIED. I WAS
A GIRL. BACK IN THE PHILIPPINES. IN 1966. HE WAS
DEAD AT 45. HEART TROUBLE she remembered reading.

Auntie Yuna took care of me while I waited for Mama to arrive. I know she wanted my mother to come as badly as I did.

"I hope she comes soon," Auntie Yuna said. "I don't know what the spirits were thinking. I didn't pray for this."

Auntie Yuna prayed all the time. She prayed the way Mama prayed, the way all the people I knew prayed. Her head was down; her eyes were up. She looked at pictures of saints and dead relatives on the shelf.

"Saints will take care of us if we take care of them," she said. She offered fruit and meat to holy ghosts. She placed the food on glass plates, honoring Saint Joan, Saint Paul, Saint John, Saint Theresa. Sometimes she lit a cigarette and left it in an ashtray for Uncle Virgillio. She said, "Uncle Virgillio likes to smoke. That's what killed him in the first place."

Auntie Yuna and I would eat the food she left for the spirits. She said the spirits touched the food and made it lucky. By eating the food, we became lucky, too.

"Praying is not enough," she said. "Better to put it on paper. Especially in America. Have everything on paper. I lost a deposit on an apartment once. The landlord said it wasn't on paper. Bastard."

She wrote letters to God and dead relatives. She put them next to a burning candle by the Jesus Christ cross on her shelf. "The spirits will read them," she said. "It's better than praying because prayers just go from your head into thin air. They become nothing. Look at all the people who have nothing. That's how far prayers got them. Letters are solid proof to the saints, to our ancestors that what I was praying just don't disappear. There are too many prayers floating around. They get tangled up like balloon strings when wind comes by. They get knotted together. The spirits don't know which string belongs to which balloon. The spirits don't know which prayer is yours. That's why I ended up with you. Probably some girl was praying for a child. The spirits answered the right prayer for the wrong person because I never wanted to be stuck with a child. For all I know, someone else got the million dollars I'd been praying for. I learned my lesson. Always put it down on paper. Never. Never! Will I pray like that again. God knows I didn't ask for you."

God knows I didn't ask for YOU, I thought to myself.

"Dead relatives are the best people to ask things," she said. "Better than God. Dead relatives already know you and you know them. People will do things for people they know. God knows everyone and treats everyone the same. I want to ask a favor from someone who will give better treatment.

"Letters have to be to saints or dead relatives. No one else. If you write to someone else the spirits will think we do not trust them."

So I wrote in secret and put the letters under the couch I slept on. I did not want to be mean to Auntie Yuna's spirits. I simply did not know them. I did not know who the saints were. I did not know my dead relatives, my ancestors.

I just knew what I saw. I saw Montgomery Clift. I saw him when I couldn't sleep. I turned on the television, watched the late night movie. When the commercials ended, a voice from the TV said, "And now we return to *The Search* starring Montgomery Clift."

In the movie, in *The Search*, Monty Clift plays a soldier. He finds and cares for a small boy whose mother was taken away by bad people. He takes the boy home. He gives him candy. He buys him shoes. He teaches him English. He keeps him safe. He guards the boy till his mama comes.

I prayed before I went to sleep. I prayed when I woke. I prayed with my eyes locked shut and my head buried deep into my pillow. I prayed with my hands clasped tightly, my knuckles turning white. I prayed until my whole body ached. Then I prayed some more. I prayed and prayed and prayed. I prayed for one thing. I prayed that my mother was okay and that she would come to get me.

It was Montgomery Clift's spirit I asked this of. It was his spirit I wrote. I ignored Auntie Yuna's painted saints on little cards. I offered my apple to Monty, not Uncle Virgilio or other dead uncles and aunts who were strange to me. I wrote hoping for no mix-up, no delay. I wrote, please bring my mama back to me.

•

Without my mother, my childhood continued. I'd started American school in 1976. My first teacher was Mrs. de Paul, a kind woman. She reminded me of Mrs. Baker in the Philippines. On the first day of school, Mrs. de Paul asked her students to tell her our first names and what street we lived on.

She picked me first. I didn't like to speak because my English wasn't very good. In the Philippines only rich kids learned English well. I was a child of the provinces, Benguet Province specifically, far away from the fast-paced capital of Manila.

Most of my education was done by missionaries in small shacks. My classmates came from the working class or those who didn't work at all, children of squatters. Squatters were those who simply occupied land, public or private.

My parents, especially my father, insisted I attend school. I learned English well enough, but not as well as I could have. After all, once school ended, the kids would stop speaking English and revert to speaking their native Illocano or Tagalog. We knew that English would serve us little; we had an idea that the rest of our lives would be spent in some low-paying capacity where English wouldn't be needed. The bosses or employers we'd work under would know

English, but not us.

In Mrs. De Paul's class, I spoke English slowly, almost like a guessing game, trying to think of what the next word might be.

"My...name...is...Bong Bong...and...I...live...on...Coronado Street."

"You sound retarded," the boy next to me said. My classmates laughed again, a stinging sound.

"Laughing is rude," said Mrs. De Paul and she put the boy in the corner. His name was Milton. Big Head Milton. Tiny ears and fat-nosed Milton. He was Filipino. There were a lot of kids in my class who were Filipino also, but they were born in the U.S. or came when they were babies. Some of them spoke Tagalog. They spoke Tagalog as well as I spoke English, which wasn't very good at all.

I spoke two languages, Tagalog and Illocano, but English was the only language that mattered.

At lunch Big Head Milton said, "I'm gonna kick your ass after school."

"Shut the fuck up," Robert said. Milton got scared and walked away. Robert Bulanan was another Filipino kid in my class. He was skinny with curly hair, parted in the middle. He was dark, dark like an old penny. We were both eight years old, but he looked older, perhaps a kid of eleven. When he smiled, dimples formed on both cheeks.

After school we'd go to his dad's store on Temple Street. Once Mr. Bulanan asked me, "Ano ang paborito mong kendi?"

I told him my favorite candy was chocolate then he handed me a Hershey bar.

Mr. Bulanan sounded important. His Tagalog was excellent, a product of some of the finest education the Philippines offered. People like Mr. Bulanan traveled from Manila to the Mountain Provinces like Benguet, vacationing in Baguio City. They walked up and down Session Road in their hand-tailored suits or wearing American finery like denim jeans by Levi Strauss. They'd sit on a bench nearby. I would run up to them and offer to shine their shoes with my box of polish and dirty rags.

Polishing shoes was better than what some of the other things kids did to earn money. I knew kids who dove off mountains to fetch coins tourists threw into the ocean below. Some died.

I would sit by the customers' feet and rub the polish into their leather shoes. They would give me a few pesos for my polishing. I would run to my mom and dad and give them the money. Mama would pat me on the head and tell me how this will buy us food for the night.

Mrs. de Paul said I needed to go to another class to speak and write better. They took me out of my class after lunchtime and put me in Mr. Lopez's class. Mr. Lopez made us write and speak English. I was the only Filipino boy in that class. There were two girls from Korea. Three boys and two girls from Mexico. One boy from Cuba. One girl and one boy from China.

We sat in a circle and he showed us pictures. "This is a cat," Mr. Lopez said. We all said CAT.

Even though I knew what a dumb old cat looked like and what it was called. I thought Pusa first, but then said CAT. It seemed everything that I had ever known didn't much matter. And whatever I learned wasn't good enough.

"It's cat with an aaaaaa sound, not an oooooh sound," said Mr. Lopez.

"Caaaaaaat," I said.

He said I was his first child from the Philippines. "All of the Filipino kids I knew never had a problem with English," he said.

I told him, "I did not practice English in the Philippines. English is what you say to Americans living there. I did not know a lot of Americans. I only knew two: Mr. and Mrs. Baker. But they wanted to learn Tagalog better. So that's what I spoke with them."

Mr. Lopez said I had to practice frequently. I practiced every day.

Robert noticed my English had improved. His approval was paramount to me. One day, I had gone to his house, a two-story California Townhouse on Rampart Boulevard. Rampart Boulevard had some of the prettiest houses in our neighborhood. Most of the homes were large with five or six bedrooms. We sat on Robert's stoop, a stoop which encircled the house, and watched the cars hum by.

We threw rocks at the Century 21 Real Estate sign on his front lawn, dent it real good.

"My folks wanna move," Robert said. "They don't like the neighborhood anymore. Want us to move to someplace else, maybe Carson."

I didn't think the neighborhood was that bad. I still don't. I'd seen some of the most awful living conditions in the Philippines. To me, that area, the Rampart District (which professed to have one of the highest crime rates in Los Angeles) was heaven compared to the squatter houses, made of metal and flimsy wood, I saw in the Philippines.

"You're moving?" I asked.

"Supposed to. But the house has been for sale for a long time, over a year. I don't think anyone wants to move in."

I was comforted slightly. I wanted Robert to stay.

Robert showed me all of his trophies and medals, the ones he'd won at various martial arts tournaments. I also noticed a wall of family photos. Robert and his two sisters at various stages of development. Robert as a babe, as a toddler, in kindergarten. The photos fell within the perimeters of a large wall rosary.

Robert had his own room and so did his sisters. Up until that time, I'd always shared a room with my parents. I slept on the couch of Auntie Yuna's one-bedroom apartment. Robert's room was filled with all the toys showered upon the only boy in a family. Two skateboards leaned against one wall, balls of various shapes—football, baseball, basketball, tennis balls—filled a wicker basket. There were Tonka trucks and Lego toys, coloring books and crayons. It was a child's paradise.

He had a basketball hoop above the garage door. We dribbled and shot. I did a great lay-up. I watched Robert shoot a basket, amazed at his accuracy. The ball went in almost every time, making a whipping sound as it swirled around the nylon net, eventually falling to the floor.

A lemon tree grew in his backyard also. I marveled at that tree with yellow orbs hanging from it. It seemed so out of place in an inner city neighborhood. From that very tree, Robert's mother pulled lemons to spice up her meals.

I stayed for dinner and Mrs. Bulanan made chicken adobo with the meat so tender that it fell off the bones when I brought it to my mouth. She brushed butter and honey on her hopia mungo. Sometimes the butter ran down my mouth and I caught it with my tongue.

It tasted better than Auntie Yuna's food. Even Auntie Yuna's rice tasted bad. It was always wet and mushy. I had to eat all of it or else she'd get mad. If I didn't eat all of my cabbage, she'd hit me in the face. I'd want to cry. She said if I cried she would hit me again. I tried not to. I covered my face with my hands so she couldn't see me. She'd hit me anyway.

She hit my ear once. I cried real hard, wailed.

"If you eat all your food, I would not have to discipline you like that," she said.

I ate all of her food. Even if I didn't like it. Auntie Yuna watched me eat until my plate was clean. Her eyes drilled me, opening holes I couldn't see.

Yes, I ate it all.

CHAPTER THREE
Black Marks

dear mr montgomery clift   february 20, 1977
we got a new neighbor downstairs. he has a 280zx
car parked in the lot. i haven't seen him yet but
i can hear him sometimes at night. he is not
speaking but he is making these sounds. real loud
sounds. BABY OH BABY he says. like he is in pain.
i hear a woman with him. GOD OH GOD she says.
like she is also in pain. but later they are
laughing.

i asked auntie yuna what is going on. IGNORE IT
she says THE MAN DOWNSTAIRS IS EVIL. HE IS DOING
EVIL THINGS THAT SHOULD BE DONE WHEN YOU ARE MAR-
RIED.

after school i sat in the parking lot waiting for
mr. evil to come home. i want to see what evil
looks like. i waited for almost till dark. then
his car came. i went to hide in the laundry room
because it is close to the lot. he came out of
his car carrying lots of papers. then he went to
his apt.

mr. clift, evil is real good-looking.

Mr. Evil was a tall Filipino man with skin the color of autumn leaves. I waited for him in the laundry room almost every day after school. The days I wasn't with Robert. I'd sit on the dryer and peer through the dusty window. I'd become real quiet, silent like a napping baby, when his car pulled into the parking lot. He always wore something pleasing like a starched white shirt, ironed paper flat.

One day, he wore a gray flannel sweater. His sleeves pulled up to the elbows. I saw veins running up and down his arm like roots bursting from soil.

I watched him walk past the laundry room. I heard his footsteps become real soft, tapering away like fleeting butterflies.

When I thought it was safe, I went back up to Auntie Yuna's apartment. I ran up the stairs so no one could see me. Mr. Evil's door was wide open. I looked in really fast. He wasn't there.

I opened the door to Auntie Yuna's apartment and there Evil stood, talking to her. She pulled me over to meet him. She acted strange, almost nice. She giggled and offered him food. I knew when she offered food, she offered loyalty. Mr. Evil smiled and said no.

"I need a favor," he said. "Do you have a stamp? I have a deadline. I need to get this in the mail. Pronto." He didn't sound Filipino. His R's didn't tremble like a kitten purring. He didn't mix up his P's and F's like identical twins. He sounded American like those people on TV who tell the news.

"Sure," she said.

Mr. Evil said he was a writer and his name was J. "Is this your son?" J asked Auntie Yuna.

"No," she said. "I am single. I have no children, just watching him till his mama comes." She giggled some more.

Evil gave me his hand. I brought it to my forehead. Mama taught me to do that when an older person gave me his hand. It meant I was asking for his blessing. I wondered if asking for a blessing from Evil was a bad thing? His hand was smooth and warm. They were the hands of someone who didn't know hard work. Mama's hands, papa's hands were rough and dry. J's hand felt good against my head. I wanted to sleep on his knuckles. Bless me, I thought, bless me.

Auntie Yuna laughed and said, "Anak, this is the States. You don't do that here."

Evil took my hand and shook it.

"Good to meet you," J said. "I really need that stamp, though."

Auntie Yuna went into the bedroom to get some stamps. It was just me and Evil. He bent down and looked me in the eye. His hair

was combed back like a slick asphalt road. He reminded me of a
Filipino Lee Majors in the six-million-dollar man, some kind of
superhero with special powers. If he flew away, I wouldn't have been
surprised.

He smelled real good. Like a department store.

"Do you have any brothers or sisters?" he asked. I shook my
head No.

"If you ever get lonely feel free to come to my apartment."

Auntie Yuna got him his stamps and he left. His department
store smell stayed. I went to sleep with it, surrounding me.

●

J came over once. Auntie Yuna straightened her housedress and
brushed the hair from her face, wiping her cheeks and nose of oil.

"Why J, another visit so soon?" She giggled, lowering her head.
"Did you want to see me about something?"

"Actually, I came to see Bong Bong."

"About what?" Auntie Yuna asked.

"I want to talk to him about his life."

"He's just nine, he hasn't had much of a life yet."

He said he wanted to talk to me anyway. He wanted to know
what life was like in the Philippines. The Marcoses were doing some
mean things to people, he said. At the time, I didn't understand
how bad the Marcoses were.

"I want the view of a little boy," J said. "I think it would make an
interesting angle."

I told him all I knew. I told him I wanted to help him. I told him
my dad would ask people things all the time, find out things. Dad
always got mad when people wouldn't talk.

I told him, "We lived in Baguio City, where I was born. My dad
wrote for a newspaper no one was supposed to know about. It told
secrets. My dad said it was a paper that told what the Marcoses were
doing. They were killing people and stealing from everyone. That's
what my dad would tell me.

"There were people in our house all the time. It was always at
night when they came. I could tell many of them were from different parts of the Philippines because they spoke so many different

languages, like Tagalog, Illocano, or Cebuano. There were languages I didn't even have a name for. I couldn't understand a lot of what they said. Sometimes the languages were so different, they had to speak English to understand each other. Some of the older people spoke Spanish. My English was not as good then as it is now. Now I can almost speak English without having to think of what the next word is supposed to be.

"Dad never allowed me to come to the meetings, but I heard what they were saying. Sometimes they yelled. They talked about gorillas in the mountains.

"Mama was not allowed to go to the meetings. She only entered to serve food. She was good at serving. She had a job as a maid for some rich Americans in Suello village. The Americans worked for the military. I don't know what they did, but they were real important. Mama took me along to help her clean. It was the most beautiful place with large bedrooms and fancy furniture they brought from America.

"Their names were Mr. and Mrs. Baker. Mr. Baker was the biggest man I had ever seen. He always wore his uniform when I saw him. He tried to speak to me in Tagalog, but he was so bad at it, I just nodded and smiled. Mrs. Baker spoke Tagalog a lot better. She had big brown eyes and wore a lot of gold jewelry. Mama loved her gold. I think it broke her heart knowing she would never be able to own any.

"Mrs. Baker and Mama would go to the marketplaces near Quezon road. They'd buy fish and chicken. Then take a jeepney to La Trinidad and buy vegetables. They would sometimes stop at the Chinese temple on the way and get their fortunes told.

"Mama was a good servant and she walked behind Mrs. Baker.

"'You're not a slave,' Mrs. Baker said. So Mama would walk next to her. I think Mama liked that, because people thought she was Mrs. Baker's friend and treated her nicer.

"Whenever the sellers would raise the prices because they thought they were selling to a rich American, Mama would get mad at them and make them sell their things at the regular price. I don't think Mrs. Baker knew what Mama was doing when she fought with them. They often spoke too fast for Mrs. Baker to understand.

"Mama helped Mrs. Baker dress for parties, too. Mama washed

her hands real clean so she wouldn't get any of Mrs. Baker's clothes dirty. Mama was real good at making Mrs. Baker look good, laying her gowns on her bed. She fluffed up the one she chose. Mama knew which rings or necklaces would go well with each dress.

"Mrs. Baker said if my mama ever needed anything to ask her. Mama never did. She said she wasn't worthy enough to ask Mrs. Baker of anything. I remember it was real hard for her to ask Mrs. Baker to get me to America.

"These men came in the middle of the night and beat up my dad. They said they would stop him from writing anything bad about the President. Mama begged them to go, but they beat her up, too.

"I love my father because he is my father. But I love my mother more. Sometimes I feel bad about this. When those men beat up my dad, I knew he would live. When they beat up my mom, I thought she would die.

"I watched from under the cot, I watched my parents' faces. They begged me with their eyes not to say a single word. To cry quietly. When those Military Boots kicked Mama in the stomach and the back and the chest and the legs, it might as well have been me.

"They picked up my dad and threw him out the door. When they left, I crawled out from under the cot toward Mama.

"'Go away,' she said. Words that stung like needles on my back. A second later, I knew why she said it. The door flew open. The Boots were back.

"'We knew the boy was hiding,' One Boot said. 'We'll do worse to him if you make more trouble.'

"The boots banged against the floor when they left, getting into a jeep then driving away.

"Mama got up, her nightdress wrinkled and torn, and told me to pack my things. I put all I had into a brown paper bag and Mama took me into the night to where the Bakers lived.

"She knocked on the door.

"'Who is it?' a real mad voice said from the dark house.

"'It's me, ma'am. Cessy Luwad.'

"'Cessy?' Mrs. Baker said unlocking the door, 'I hope I didn't sound rude, but my husband's in Manila...' the door opened, and

Mrs. Baker's eyes opened up real big. 'Oh, dear lord,' she said, leading us into the living room.

"'Ma'am,' Mama said, 'please forgive me for what I'm going to
ask.' It was hard for her to speak, because her lips were busted open,
spit and tears and blood bubbled from her face. Mama asked if Mrs.
Baker could send us to the States. Mrs. Baker gave Mama a hug and
said she would do that. She could arrange passports and citizenship
papers, too. All Mama had to do was say when.

"'As soon as possible,' Mama said, 'but just send my boy. Send
Bong.'

"'What about you, honey?' Mrs. Baker asked.

"'Not yet. I have to find my husband. I have to. I can't just leave.
I can't do that.'

"The next day, Mama took me to the airport. Black marks
appeared on her body where the boots kicked her. I touched one of
the marks, a bruise Mama called it, but she brushed my hand away.

"Before I left, Mama held me for the longest time and said,
'Bong, you know I love you. When I find your father, we'll come.'

"'When?' I said.

"'Soon. Real soon. Be good in the States.'

"I promised her I would."

Even though I didn't like Auntie Yuna, even though I didn't like
saying CAT with an AAAAA sound, I was good, because that's what
I promised. I was good when Auntie Yuna drank. I was good when I
went through foster care.

"'We'll be together real soon,' she said. I did not want to leave,
but Mama said I had to. She waved at me. I waved back. I walked
away. The last time I saw her, her hand was on her mouth and tears
were falling from her eyes, tripping over her long fingers, wetting
her blouse.

"'Go,' she said. 'You'll see us real soon. Go.'

"So I did. Then she was gone. I got on the plane. I saw water and
clouds. In my window, I saw the sun meet the moon. All the lights
were gone. Darkness only. I slept. I woke up in the States. I got out
of the plane and my Auntie Yuna called me. She took me to her
place in Los Angeles.

"I waited every day for Mama to knock on the door and show up.
But nothing. Years went by without a knock. Even today, I think I'll

open a door and there she'll be.

"Real Soon, Mama said. I learned Real Soon means different things sometimes."

When I finished my story, J's mouth was open and all he could say was, "Wow."

CHAPTER FOUR
The Color of Rust

Dear Montgomery Clift   May 17, 1977

Mr. Lopez and Mrs. de Paul took us on a field trip. We walked to Echo Park. There is a big lake there with people in little boats. Echo Park reminds me of Burnham Park in Baguio City. Mama and dad took me there when we had money. When mama found a house to clean.

Dad would rent a little boat and rowed us into the middle of the lake. I sat by mama and her arms were around my body and her long fingers rubbed my belly. I liked it best when her palm caressed my face. She smelled clean like detergent.

Dad took out sandwiches from a brown bag, sandwiches dad and me made. Mama never cooked on days like these. Dad knew how much mama worked.

What dad wrote was too dangerous. So dad started his own newspaper. It did not make any money. But he felt it was an important newspaper to have. Mama believed that, too. She worked while dad wrote.

At Echo Park, Robert let me have some of his sandwich. We played Tag and Robert was It. He chased all the kids until he tagged someone. Then that person chased someone. Over and over. I never got caught. I ran and ran until no one

could get me. I ran so fast that air became wind
blowing through me. I ran so fast I sweat. I
looked behind me and my classmates were far
behind. I couldn't be reached.

Then I saw you.

I said, "Hi."

I blinked and you was gone.

It was you, wasn't it?

I t was that quick. My first vision. I was behind a tree when I saw
someone. The sun was in my face. All I could see was the outline
of a tall man, slender. He stood straight with shoulders arched
back like he was at attention. A military cap was on his head tilted to
the side. It was Monty dressed in his soldier's uniform from *The Search*.

As soon as my lashes fluttered, he was gone. I looked this way
and that, whispering, "Mr. Clift?"

"Bong?" Mrs. de Paul said several yards away. "It's time to go."

I joined my classmates, knowing that, somehow, my life would
never be the same.

•

BABY OH BABY, J said in the morning, in the afternoon, at
night.

Robert told me what BABY OH BABY meant.

"No Way!" I said.

"Yeah. He's doing it," Robert said.

For some reason I didn't think of Filipinos having sex. I could
imagine other people having sex, but not Filipinos.

"Duh," Robert laughed. "How d'you think you got here?"

Never had I seen my parents kiss or hold hands or even stand
close together. I guess they had to sometime.

BABY OH BABY, J said. Over and over again.

The BABY was a top-heavy Filipina who bounced everywhere she
went. She bounced up the stairs to J's apartment. She bounced to
her car. Her chest bounced. I think all the boys in the neighborhood came out when she arrived. To watch her bounce and bounce

and bounce. A little bit of her nipples could be seen in the T-shirts she wore. Her long black hair, feathered back, bounced.

"Do you want to go to the movies?" J asked her.

"You bet," Baby Bounce said, nodding, her mane quivering.

"Do you want to do laundry?"

"Not today," Baby Bounce said, strands of hair flying as she flung her head no.

BABY OH BABY the boys in the neighborhood must have thought to themselves when Baby Bounce came by.

I didn't know what Auntie Yuna thought when Baby Bounce walked up those stairs, rang J's doorbell, and went inside. Auntie Yuna hissed and muttered something that must have been some kind of bad luck she wished on Baby Bounce.

Auntie Yuna shook her head imitating Baby Bounce, but her hair was too dry and brittle. It stayed in one place like the head of a broom. She tried to walk like Baby Bounce too, but Auntie Yuna couldn't bounce no matter how hard she tried. Auntie Yuna was a sturdy woman, wide shoulders and hips. Auntie Yuna was not like Baby Bounce and nothing like her sister, my mama.

Mama's hair was thick and straight and blacker than nighttime. She tried to make it bounce once. She went to sleep with pink curlers in her hair. In the morning she had holes as big as Coke cans floating around her head. By the afternoon, her hair fell down again, just below her shoulders, covering her ears and neck and cheeks, showing only a thin portion of her face. Her hair hung around her face like curtains revealing a small portion of an incredible view, straining your neck here and there to see what else the view may hold.

Mama and I have the same hair, I think. Dad's hair curled up and down, with a little bit of gray.

I have Mama's eyes. Which are Auntie Yuna's eyes, too. Round like a quarter but brown like mud. Mama's eyes were real warm. Blanket on a cold night warm. Auntie Yuna's eyes were empty and cold. Cave empty. Cave cold.

I got my skin from Dad, though. The color of rust on tin cans. Mama's skin was lighter. I'd never seen that color before except on sand at a beach.

I have Dad's nose and lips. Nose like a button with not so red lips. Faded roses Mama called them.

I never thought about what my parents looked like. Or what I looked like. But the longer they were there and I was here, I forgot sometimes.

Some days I imagined J and Baby Bounce as my new parents, but I knew I'd never look like the six-million-dollar man or have hair that always bounced. Especially now with the scars on my face.

There were moments when I thought real hard about my parents' faces, wondering if I looked like them. I would run to the mirror and try, try to remember.

•

There were times when Auntie Yuna wasn't in the apartment and I'd call Robert, telling him Baby Bounce was visiting. He'd be over immediately. We'd sit in the apartment and wait, listening…listening.

Then it would begin.

BABY OH BABY, J would say. Robert and I would freeze, our shoulders to our ears, our eyes ready to bust out of our sockets. Robert and I reveled in the sound of it: the moaning and the release. We heard furniture creaking and rocking. We heard heavy breathing and gasps of air. We heard, "Yes, YES!" and "Please, PLEASE!" The afternoon filled with sounds of agreement.

Robert and I would lie on the floor, looking up at the ceiling, craving.

We'd hear the climax. We always knew the climax; the most distinct sound of them all. The room seemed to expand, swell. The ceiling seemed to rise, bend outward.

BABY OH BABY, J said.

GOD OH GOD, Baby Bounce said.

BABY OH BABY, J said again.

Then a miraculous silence, serenity. The room shrank back into its usual form. Robert and I would lie there exhausted. He'd rest his head on my stomach. I'd giggle a bit. I touched his hair, feeling the thick strands of blackness.

"I think my parents sold the house," Robert said.

Robert was my best friend. He would be the first person in my new American life to disappear, vanish with the rest of my childhood.

I bought a book. It cost over ten dollars, which was a lot of money for a kid. I bought it because it was about Monty. His face was on the cover. BABY OH BABY. I kept *The Films of Montgomery Clift* under my pillow when I slept. I kept it in my backpack when I went to school, walking with Robert close by.

BABY OH BABY, I thought, when I thought of Mr. Clift.

"Bong, please get me some Scotch tape," Mr. Lopez said. But he had to say it three times before I heard him.

BABY OH BABY, I thought when I kissed the book, a yellow book with Monty's exquisite face on top. Monty dressed in a suit, his warm eyes staring straight at me. Two creases were on his forehead and his hair was combed back, a sheen atop his head. Even though paper was what I felt on my lips, I kissed the book anyway.

"Bong! Get out of that bathroom! Ay, sose, it doesn't take that long to do what you gotta do!" Auntie Yuna screamed. I put *The Films of Montgomery Clift* in my backpack and walked out like nothing happened.

BABY OH BABY, I thought when I pressed myself against my pillow, imagining him.

BABY OH BABY, I whispered in the dark, alone.

I held myself. I didn't know what I was doing, but it felt good. Up and down.

I pressed against my pillow.

I held myself between my fingers. Tightly. Up and down.

I felt a grinding, an unscrewing. A knot being untied. It began down there. Starting from that loose patch of skin between my legs. I shook. And shook. And shook. And shook.

My white Fruit of the Loom underwear was no longer white. More gray. From the wetness that came from me. I threw my underwear away so no one could ever know what I did. What we did.

Mr. Clift. Montgomery. Montgomery Clift.

I discovered what BABY OH BABY really meant.

CHAPTER FIVE
The Low Resonance of a Man's Voice

```
Dear Montgomery,              February 7, 1978

Mr. Clift, what should I do? I want to see my
mom's letter but I don't want J to fall in love
with Auntie Yuna. Or worse, if the love spell
fails, J will walk around Los Angeles like a
crazy man.

I'll sleep on it. Please give me an answer by
morning.
```

"I have a letter from your mom," Auntie Yuna said to me, waving a torn envelope in front of me with stamps from the Philippines covering the upper right side.

"Let me see," I said, trying to snatch the envelope from her. She hid it behind herself.

"No," she said, smelling of King Cobra Malt Liquor. "First, you do something for me."

"What?"

"Go into J's place and get me something." She stood so close to me I saw her rotted yellow teeth, wet with spit. I had grown a few inches since coming to the States, but Auntie Yuna was still taller. She had gotten fat, making her face fatter, making the anger which always showed on her face bigger.

"What do you want?"

"A sock or a shirt. Something that belongs to him."

That proved Auntie Yuna was a witch. She didn't have to say what she was going to do with that sock or that shirt. There was a guy who walked the streets of Baguio City. He talked to himself and waved at no one in particular. A love spell that went bad, people told me.

"I won't get you anything," I said.

I didn't see her hand come from behind her and grab the hairs at the very top of my head. She yanked so hard I fell to my knees.

"You get me something of his or I'll burn this letter, Stupid Boy."

I struggled to get away, but she yanked harder.

"Get me something of his!" she said. I felt hairs being separated from my scalp. She smashed her chubby fist into my face, hitting my right eye. I was dizzy, and through clenched teeth, I said, "All right, I'll get you something. I'll do it. Okay, I'll do it."

She let go, and I wondered what I had just agreed to.

•

The next day, I knocked on J's door. He was on the phone, but he let me in. Baby Bounce wasn't there. She was on the other end of the line. Even when they weren't together they were together.

"I think you should do what you think is best," he said to her.

I looked around the apartment wondering what to take. Maybe his catcher's mitt? Maybe his calculator? There really wasn't that much to take. J's apartment had a sofa and a TV set. His walls were bare and he didn't have that much of his stuff around.

"Take something easy," he said. "Take a class you know you can pass."

There was a red tie on the floor. With lines all over it. It was almost under the sofa, barely visible.

"Don't sweat it. It's no big deal. Just take it," he said. "All you need is one course then you'll have your degree."

I rolled up the tie while J's back was to me.

"I wouldn't miss it. I wouldn't miss it for anything. Your graduation is important to me, too," he said. "It's taken you five years to get that degree."

I put the tie into my pocket.

J turned around and faced me.

"There it's done. No big deal," he said. "In a few months you'll be done. Then we can be married." He hung up the phone.

"What's up, Bong?"

Looking at him, I believed J was the handsomest man I'd ever seen. His slender face always appeared kind and a lock of black hair fell across his forehead. His dark brown eyes reminded me of milk chocolate.

"What's up?" he asked again.

I kept my hands to my side, squeezing the lump that was his tie in my pocket.

"Nothing."

"What happened to your eye?"

"Nothing."

"I got a shiner like that once. Did you get into a fight at school?"

I didn't say anything, but he took it as a yes.

"Well," he said, "you know fighting's not cool sometimes. But I hope you kicked the crap out of him."

I had to smile. He smiled, too. At school all the grown-ups told me fighting was wrong. J was the first person to say it's not so bad.

He held his palms up for me.

"Hit me," he said.

"Huh?"

"Hit my hands. Let's see you fight." Then he did some karate moves that I knew he copied from a Bruce Lee movie.

"C'mon, Big Guy," he said. "Show me what you got."

That's what I liked about Americans. They called kids Big Guy or Sport or Champ.

Even though J is Filipino, he was born and raised in Stockton. I always thought Filipinos were born in the Philippines, but J was living proof that wasn't so.

"Show me whatcha got, sport?" he said, again holding his hands up, his palms facing me.

I made a fist. I hit him, making a dull slap on his palms.

"Harder," he said.

I hit him a little harder, but I wasn't in the mood. In a little while he'd be falling in love with Auntie Yuna.

"Hit me again," he said.

I hit him again. And again. And again. Putting every bit of feeling into my arms and my fists. I stopped aiming at his palms. Instead I aimed for his face or his chest. Hitting him. Over and over. If I hit him, I thought J would do something mean like slap me or tell me to get out of his apartment. I would hate him for being mean, cruel. Then I wouldn't have felt too bad about Auntie Yuna turning him into a zombie.

Instead, he caught my fists and held them tight, and asked, "Hey, champ, you OK?"

I didn't want to cry. But the more I didn't want to, the more I couldn't stop myself.

"It'll be all right," he said to me. It was a man's voice. I think I needed to hear a man's voice at that moment. I was used to hearing that from women. I was used to hearing girls in general speak soft and gentle, but sometimes I liked when a man talked that way. When my dad was kind, I knew it was a special moment, because it wasn't who he was really about. It made it more special. I needed to hear the low resonance of a man's voice. I think boys need to hear that every once in a while.

J pulled me into him. He didn't smell like a department store anymore. He smelled real. That kind of smell a hard day leaves on you: a little bit of sweat and fading deodorant.

"Whatever it is, Bong," he said, "it'll work itself out."

I didn't think voodoo spells ever worked out.

He looked at me and said, "I feel sorry for the guy who gave you that black eye, you must have put up a real good fight. You got some power in those hands."

We watched TV, laughing at Laverne and Shirley. Somewhere during a commercial J fell asleep on his sofa. His head was back and his mouth was open, a little bit of drool on the corner of his mouth. I watched him breathe, his stomach rising and falling like a trembling hill. I touched the thin line of drool crawling down his chin. A drop of his spit was on the tip of my forefinger. I wiped it onto my lips.

I took his tie out of my pocket and placed it onto the floor. I turned off the television and headed out, carefully listening to the click of the knob as I stealthily shut the door.

I went back upstairs. Auntie Yuna was waiting for me.

"Do you have anything for me?" Auntie Yuna asked.

"No, not yet."

Her lips tightened, almost creating one long line across the area that was supposed to be her mouth. She turned away from me then locked herself in the bedroom.

The next day, I found an old sock near the laundry room. I kept it, waiting for Auntie Yuna to come home. When she did, I pulled the black sock from my pocket. I pretended to be real sad. Like I was doing the most terrible thing.

She grabbed it from me, stretching it, feeling it with her hands, then with her cheek, raising it to the light.

"Now where's the letter?" I said.

She gave me a wicked little smile. The kind where her lips went sideways. The kind that didn't show her teeth. But I knew they were there.

"When the spell works, I'll give it to you."

"That's not fair. You said to get you something that belongs to J then you'll give me the letter."

"I don't remember that," she said. Then she walked into her room, slamming the door.

It was comical watching Auntie Yuna for the next few days. I didn't know what Auntie Yuna expected. She'd give J a smile whenever she saw him, but J always pretended not to notice. She would be at the bottom of the stairwell waiting for J to come home, but J would simply nod and enter his apartment. She'd make up any excuse to knock on his door. She'd ask for sugar or milk or make up some lame story like, "I seem to be missing some mail, would you mind checking if the postman didn't give you my letters by accident?" J checked, and of course there was no letter for Auntie Yuna.

The only person who noticed Auntie Yuna was our poor landlord, Mr. Boteng. Mr. Boteng must have been at least 200 years old. He was almost bald except for a few patches of hair on the sides of his head. His skin was wrinkled and leathery. He resembled a troll. Mr. Boteng began to drop by often to see if we needed anything fixed.

"No, Mr. Boteng, there is nothing wrong with the pipes. No, Mr. Boteng, the heater works just fine. No, Mr. Boteng, the toilet always flushes that way," Auntie Yuna would say.

Mr. Boteng had also offered Auntie Yuna rice cakes and soda. He'd come over and present her with a platter of fried chicken. He'd invite her over for merienda, a snack in the middle of the day.

Maybe the black sock belonged to him.

I searched all over the apartment for Mama's letter. Nothing. I searched Auntie Yuna's room, looking through her strewn clothes on the floor, examining the pockets of her jeans. I looked under the shrine to the Virgin Mary, through her piles of letters to God and saints begging for favors. I looked under her mattress, inside her pillowcases. I went through her drawers, even the ones carrying her frayed bras. Still nothing.

The only place I hadn't searched was that ratty old handbag she carried with her wherever she went.

When she came home, I handed her a cup of King Cobra.

"Why are you being so nice?" she asked.

"I just know you work really hard."

She shrugged and drank her malt liquor. When she was done, I poured her another glass. Then another. Until the bottle was empty.

She passed out on the couch.

I looked through her bag. Under the pens and pencils and lint, I found the black sock, the one I discovered in the laundry room, the one I said was J's. It was wrapped in string with a picture card of St. Raphael pinned to it. Saint Raphael, Patron Saint of Lovers, the picture card read.

I thought the sock belonged to Mr. Boteng, because he said he had been having heartburns. I untied the sock, hoping it would break the spell. I didn't want Mr. Boteng's heart to burn anymore.

I found the letter. It was addressed to Auntie Yuna from some woman I'd never heard of before. The letter was from Auntie Yuna's friend. It wasn't from my mom at all.

I put the letter back.

I didn't sleep the entire night. I watched Auntie Yuna lie there, snoring. I wanted to smother Auntie Yuna, place a cushion over her face and snuff her out. I wanted to set her hair on fire, stick needles into the bottoms of her feet. I wanted to bite her, rip some of her flesh away from her bones.

I went into the kitchen and stared at the dirty dishes in the sink. From the sink, I pulled out a knife still covered with peanut butter. It was a small knife, no longer than my palm, but it would do what I'd wanted it to do. The tip was sharp with jagged teeth. I walked over to Auntie Yuna, trembling. I didn't know if I shook from fear or anger. I wasn't going to kill her, just hurt her. I just wanted to hurt her a little, leave a small cut or jab her a bit.

I would have done something like that to her if it weren't for Montgomery Clift. He had suddenly appeared. I didn't see him, but I knew he was sitting at the kitchen table behind me. I didn't want to turn around and see him, afraid he would go away. I knew he disapproved. It was as if Montgomery Clift had strings attached to my brain, and he was pulling them ever so gently. I dropped the knife, hearing a small thud as it fell onto the shag carpet, the green shag carpet. I saw the brown peanut butter on the knife look somehow peaceful against the green. It reminded me of dirt and grass.

I knew he was there—Monty was there. Smoking. A filterless cigarette, maybe a Lucky Strike, between his fingers.

The blue cigarette smoke traveled above my head and floated around. It curled around the lamp and it curled around the sofa. It wafted through the legs of the coffee table, skimming the magazines resting on it. It hovered above Auntie Yuna and blew away from her face when she exhaled. The blue smoke created a cloud near the ceiling. I watched it move and roll, bumping into walls.

The cloud of smoke balled together then parted like waves, creating images above me. I saw a tree, a fig tree I used to sit under in the Philippines. I waited for Mama there sometimes. While she cleaned houses and I was bored, I waited for her under that tree, choosing the ripest figs. I'd bite into one and watch the pink insides ooze out, tasting the sweetness.

I saw Mama's face appear in the smoke, and I was numb. I was caught between nowhere and heaven, watching Mama watch me. Her face was pleasant, but sullen. I stared and stared into her face, my breath almost nonexistent. I don't think I blinked once, fearful my lids would provide a moment of darkness that would separate me from her. So I stood, motionless, peering upward like the children of Fatima witnessing the appearance of the Blessed Lady. I stood there till the sun rose.

When the beams of light came through the window, the smoke vanished. And so did Montgomery Clift. Rather his presence vanished. I was returned to an ordinary apartment, a ceiling void of Mama's image, made merely of plaster.

I waited for Auntie Yuna to wake up. I could see her breathing, slow and steady.

When she stirred, her head shifted from one shoulder to another, I yelled, "YOU LIED TO ME!"

She almost fell off the couch. She looked at me wondering who I was. She looked around wondering where she was. Her broomhead hair stuck out in all directions.

"What are you talking about?" she said.

"You said you had a letter from my mama, but I know you don't."

"You went through my bag, Stupid Boy?" She hissed, got up and wobbled toward the bathroom. She swayed from side to side, leaning against a wall, then against a chair, then against a wall again.

"You're a liar. You're a liar," I said over and over.

She turned and she lunged at me, hitting me so hard across my jaw, I fell down. I took the King Cobra bottle and threw it at her. I missed.

"Stupid. Stupid boy!"

She came after me again. I covered myself with my arms, burying myself so deep inside of me I couldn't breathe.

"I did get a letter from your mom," she said. "She doesn't want you. She said you could burn in hell." She slapped me from all sides, her feet digging into my back.

I knew she was lying. My mother would have never said anything like that. But still. The thought of my mother not wanting me made me feel smaller than dust balls on the floor.

I made a fist. I couldn't see anything except the darkness my body had made, and I threw my fist out, hitting something. I heard a grunt, then a groan. I hit her. I hit Auntie Yuna.

"Liar. Liar. LIAR!" I said.

She looked at me like she didn't know what to do. She laughed. She laughed as she locked herself in her room.

I looked at my hands and I realized J was right. Fighting is not so bad sometimes. I looked at my fist and I realized J was wrong. I didn't have power in my hands, only fear.

CHAPTER SIX
King Cobra

Dear Montgomery Clift,   October 7, 1978

At school my teacher wanted to know how I got my fat lip. I told her that my next door neighbor hit me. I didn't tell her that Auntie Yuna did it. I didn't tell her that Auntie Yuna drinks. I didn't tell her that Auntie Yuna wakes up in the middle of the night and tells me to clean up. I didn't tell her that Auntie Yuna hits me with her witch's broom. I didn't tell her how Auntie Yuna keeps saying she has had bad luck beginning with the very first day I arrived.

I didn't tell her that I don't feel anything when Auntie Yuna attacks me. I didn't tell her that Auntie Yuna somehow cast a voodoo spell on me. I become a zombie when Auntie Yuna comes at me like a tiger.

"Do you have any friends?" Mrs. Nice Teacher asked.

"Yes," I said. I didn't tell her that I miss my best friend Robert. I call him sometimes but he found new friends.

I didn't tell her that Big Head Milton tells everyone that I'm an orphan because he never sees my parents pick me up after school. And tells everyone that he sees drunk Auntie Yuna at Cho's Liquor store smelling like a sewer.

"I have a friend," I told Mrs. Nice Teacher.
"He's a soldier."

"He's older, then?"

I nodded. I didn't tell her any more about you.
She wouldn't understand. She wouldn't understand
about spirits.

Mrs. Nice Teacher patted my head, probably to
even out my funny haircut, which Auntie Yuna gave
me. She cuts my hair this way and that, sometimes
cutting a little too close, snagging a little of
my skin. I didn't tell her my hair will never
bounce if Auntie Yuna keeps cutting away at it.

Mrs. Nice Teacher looked at my head real close.
She looked at my face real close. I didn't tell
her that I don't want her to be that close to me.
I didn't tell her that I only want J to stand
close to me. I didn't tell her that J would
rather spend all his time with Baby Bounce (whose
real name is Belinda.) I didn't tell her that
Baby Bounce Belinda became J's fiancee, making
Auntie Yuna pissed.

"Bong?" Mrs. Nice Teacher asked. "Are you OK?"

I didn't tell her sometimes I go to school and
before I know it, the bell rings to go home. I
disappear.

"Bong? I've been talking to you for five minutes,
and it seems like you don't hear me."

I didn't tell her that I hear her. I hear her
calling my name. I hear people talking, but it's
all fuzzy.

I didn't tell Mrs. Nice Teacher anything as I
watched her go into the principal's office.

Auntie Yuna would get up in the middle of the night to get some more King Cobra. The kitchen was connected to the living room. I knew she could see me sleeping.

She'd walk into the living room, and stand over me. My face was always turned away. She'd hover there for a very long time, an eternity it seemed. The light from the kitchen would cast her shadow upon me: a big black shape of ugly. I'd see the shadow of her head in front of me. Her hair messed up like frozen snakes. That's how she mesmerized me, made me her victim. She was Medusa.

Sometimes she'd wake me and make me do things. She made me clean the apartment or she would cut my hair or talk to me. I didn't know what to expect.

I'd lie there, waiting to see what she'd do. I would be glad when her shadow pulled away like a wave going back into a dark sea. When the door to her bedroom slammed shut, I knew I was safe for the night. No cleaning. No miserable haircuts. None of her drunken stories. Especially her stories. Her When I Was Young stories.

"When I was young," she once said, "I was beautiful. Ten times more beautiful than that stupid girl J loves. When I was young, I worked in bars in Manila. Near Subic Bay. American sailors would want only me to serve them. No one else. Only me. Only me. Only me…"

Then she would cry a little bit, pindrop tears streaming down her cheeks.

"When I was young, your mom looked up to me. She couldn't wait to get older. So she could leave our province. Who could blame her? Who could blame me? You know we were born in a nipa hut. Our mother was no good. Didn't care very much. Just let us do what we wanted. She just went away after a while. God knows what happened to our father.

"When I was young no one wanted us. Except Uncle Virgilio. He let me work in his bar. But he's gone, too. Your mom worked in the bar with me. She was pretty. She could have made lots of money. No. She didn't have what it took to work in a bar. She didn't know how to play up to the men. She didn't know it was OK to let them touch you. Kiss you. Uncle Virgilio just let her clean. I would tell her that she could make a fortune in tips if she waited on men. But she didn't. She wouldn't. Stupid Girl.

"When I was young, I could have any man. Your mother could have, too. But no. She went and got hooked up with that trouble-maker writer. Your father. Met him in the bar. He came in with fly-ers to form a union of some kind. He was stupid, stupid, stupid. No one in the bar cared. Uncle Virgilio chased him out. 'No one wants to hear what you have to say,' Uncle Virgilio said. 'Get out!' So he left. Your mother followed him out. I saw them talk and talk and talk and laugh and talk.

"Your father was a troublemaker. Troublemaker. That no-good communist. Communist. Always complaining of unfair this and unfair that, over throwing the government—"

"What's a communist?" I asked.

"I don't know! But that's what people call people who hate the way things are. Troublemakers are communists! His own family told him to disappear. He was putting his own brothers in jeopardy. You don't yell about unfairness without somebody getting mad. They were both stupid. Did you hear me?"

She nodded off, then said, "When I was young, your mom did one good thing. She gave me money to go to the States. I wanted to see America. To see where all these sailors came from. To see what made them think they could do whatever they wanted. To see if American girls let American men do those things to them also.

"Your mom gave me her dumb little savings so I could come here. That shows how stupid she was. She gave up all the money she had so I could see the States. When I was young…

"I owe her a favor. But taking care of you, stupid boy, makes us even."

CHAPTER SEVEN
The Scent of Boxes and Ajax

Dear Montgomery,   January 16, 1979

"Real soon," mama said. She'd come and get me real soon. Real soon real soon real soon.

J flew to Stockton to marry Baby Bounce Belinda. Then to Hawaii for a honeymoon. Then to Washington. He got a job working for a magazine.

"As soon as we get a place, I'll write and let you know our address," he said.

I want to go with you, I thought.

"When will you write?" I asked.

"Maybe in a few months. Real soon," he said. Real soon real soon real soon.

My school had a food drive to help homeless people begin the New Year. I knocked on all the doors of all the houses on my street.

"Can you donate a can of food to the hungry?" I asked.

Everyone gave one can. Auntie Yuna didn't want to give anything. She didn't want to do much of anything.

Once, Auntie Yuna came home smelling like sour milk.

"Who are you?" she asked me. She had trouble standing, the whites of her eyes were filled with red lines.

"I'm your nephew," I said.

She nodded and went into her bedroom. She didn't come out for three days. She came out of her room yawning and scratching between her legs.

"I have to go to the liquor store," she said and left again.

I knocked on all the doors of all the houses on my street again and asked, "Can you donate a can of food to the hungry?"

Everyone gave one can. This time I kept the food for myself. Auntie Yuna stopped buying food. She just bought beer. All of her income went to booze. Our landlord Mr. Boteng knew this.

I recalled him coming into our apartment and yelling at Auntie Yuna, "Where is the rent!?!? Do you want me to kick you out? I will, you know."

"I'll get it to you," she said. "Don't worry about it."

"Bullshit. You have been saying that for months."

Auntie Yuna took a deep breath and looked at me, then looked away. "Bong," she said, "go outside."

"I have to finish my homework," I said.

"Just go," she said, massaging her forehead, looking at Mr. Boteng with a weary expression.

I gathered all my books and sat on the stairwell, noticing the door to J's apartment slightly ajar. J had been gone for several months and Mr. Boteng had trouble renting the place. No one wanted to live in our building, which seemed to decay in the two and a half years that I lived there.

I went inside J's old place and saw the emptiness he left behind: the floor barren of his shoes, his furniture. I walked into his bedroom and spread myself across the area where I thought J laid his bed, where he and Baby Bounce bounced. His closet door was wide open, no clothes, only a wooden bar with metal hangers were left.

I inhaled deeply, hoping to find J, hoping to smell his lingering department store smell, but it was gone. The scent of boxes and Ajax took over. It was the smell of change, of going away. J had left, taking his Baby.

I also thought of Robert Bulanan and his departure. I rolled over, hugging my knees. Why do people leave? I wondered. I wanted to lie with Robert on my living room floor one last time. I wanted to hear J and Baby Bounce one last time.

I began to hear noise from Auntie Yuna's apartment. Mr. Boteng was grunting and sighing and snorting. Auntie Yuna sounded like she was coughing and coughing. I closed my eyes and put my hands over my ears.

I felt the floor tremble. Someone was in J's apartment. I sat up. I saw black wingtip shoes appear at the edge of the door. I looked up and smiled. Monty chose to visit me that day. He wore his suit, the same one he wore on the cover of *The Films of Montgomery Clift*. It was a dark suit with a collegiate-looking tie, diagonal stripes ran down it.

He looked down at me. His thick brows hovered over his eyes like parachutes. I was only aware of his eyes. There was so much compassion in his eyes, so much. He knelt down before me. I worried about his well-pressed suit and how it would wrinkle if he stayed on his knees. We looked at each other, all else disappeared. I couldn't hear Auntie Yuna's coughs. I reached out to touch him, but as I drew closer, he slowly faded away.

I went back upstairs to Auntie Yuna's apartment. Mr. Boteng was leaving. A smile across his sagging face. Auntie Yuna was spitting into the sink, spitting her insides out it seemed.

CHAPTER EIGHT
A Mark on the World

Dear Montgomery,   October 11, 1979

I'm going to find mama myself. I have a plan.
I'll save enough cash to fly to the Philippines
and find her. I started collecting money, coins
and pennies I found on the street. I have two
dollars and seventy cents so far.

I looked through the travel section of the newspaper. The cheapest airfare I could find was five
hundred and sixty dollars. Holy moly. I don't know
how long it'll take me to raise that kind of cash.
I don't care. I have to find mama. I have to.

Dear Montgomery,   January 17, 1980

I wrote J a letter. I told him Auntie Yuna went
to the liquor store and never came back. I told
him Dept. of Children Services took me away. I
told him I was placed with the Webers in Encino.

Dear Montgomery,   April 26, 1981

I want something else. I don't want the Weber
Breads or Mrs. 45, but really 60 or Mr. Touchy
Feely Phelps. Please send me something else. I
want to live with J and Belinda.

J doesn't write me as often as before. I'm afraid

he's slipping away from me. For every three letters I send him, he'll send me one.

In his last letter, he told me he's writing stories on people, profiles he called them. A profile on a business man donating a million dollars
to build a park. A profile on a kid who saved a
three legged dog from a burning house. A profile
on a woman who helps other women find the right
diet for them. He calls it Fluff. But nothing
sounds fluffy about it.

Baby Bounce wants to get pregnant and J is working all the time. He wants to have enough money
to support a family. Someday there will be three
of them. There used to be three of me.

I'm wandering, Monty. I'm wandering from family
to family, knowing none of them are my own. They
don't even come close. Please Monty, let my next
home be different.

Believe it or not, I was sad when Auntie Yuna left. My parents
had gone, Robert Bulanan had gone, and J was on his way out
of my life. As much as I hated Auntie Yuna she was the only
family I'd had.

She said she was going to a friend's house and never came back.
For two months, I was a twelve-year-old bachelor.

I managed to stock the apartment with canned vegetables,
canned ham, canned chicken, canned fruit, canned tuna. I had to
be careful where I got my food.

I knocked on all the doors of my neighborhood asking for food
to help the homeless. One woman asked me, "Weren't you here last
week collecting food for St. Gregory's church?"

"Um, yeah," I stuttered, "now I'm collecting for another
church."

"Which one?"

"St. Montgomery."

"Which saint was he?"

"I think he is patron saint of lost children."

"I think that's Saint Anthony."

"I mean he is patron saint of lost children looking for their mothers."

She squinted her eyes and gave me a can of chicken soup.

•

Mr. Boteng reported me to the Department of Children's Services. It became clear to him that Auntie Yuna was never going to pay him rent and was not going to be around to provide anything else in exchange for rent.

I was placed with the Webers. The Webers kept making me Chinese food so I could feel more at home.

"Love that sweet and sour," said Mr. Weber.

I knew lots of Chinese in the Philippines. Of course we could tell who was Filipino and who was Chinese. But to the Webers if you were oriental you were Chinese.

"I'm Filipino," I said.

"That's real close to China, isn't it?" was Mr. Weber's reply.

The Webers let me stay in their guestroom. Pictures of the Grand Canyon filled the walls.

I had seven dollars saved up. The Webers started giving me an allowance. I'd never heard of such a thing. All I had to do was wash dishes every once in a while or take out the garbage. (An allowance is such a unique American idea, because children in the Philippines would never get paid money for chores they were expected to do anyway.)

The Webers had a boy two years younger than me. I didn't know how the Webers put up with that brat for ten years. His name was Nolan. He looked like one of Auntie Yuna's saints. He had the yellowest hair I'd ever seen. And eyes greener than watermelon skin. He may have looked like an angel, but he was the devil in disguise.

One day, we walked on the Santa Monica Pier. Nolan saw a white T-shirt with a picture of the band Blondie on it. He wanted it. Mrs. Weber said No. He screamed and yelled until his mother got it for him.

Once, he came into my room and said, "Let's fight."

"I'm busy," I said.

He jumped all over me anyway, hitting me. It was real soft, so it didn't hurt. It just bothered me. Then he yelled, "Air raid. Air raid!"

Grow up, I thought to myself.

He pretended he was a plane and crashed into me, making exploding sounds. He shook this way and that until I pushed him off my bed.

"Go to bed or else your parents will get mad," I said.

"C'mon, let's play," he said, hopping around my room.

"Get out of my room or I'll give you brain damage." I put on my best monster face. He hopped out.

From the TV shows I saw, I thought white families were supposed to be happy and normal. The Weber Breads showed me otherwise. They fought about money and hated their relatives and complained about getting a raw deal in life.

"It's because I'm a woman," Mrs. Weber Bread said. "They promoted two men, but I'm still waiting."

"Nepotistic bastards," Mr. Weber Bread said, "the boss's son gets the corner office, first pick of the prime accounts, and the rest of us have to pick up the ball when he drops it."

No Good Nolan chased cats around the neighborhood, setting their tails on fire. He lifted girls' dresses making them scream. He stole newspapers from people's lawns and threw them away. He caught butterflies and tossed them into spiders' webs. He burned spiders with the hot rays of the sun through a magnifying glass. He fed Alka Seltzers to birds and watched them get sick and die. He'd put firecrackers into a dog's ear and let it explode, the dog howling down the street. No Good Nolan screamed with delight. He'd put broken glass under neighbors' cars. He'd cut garden snakes in half with his dad's razor.

This was an American family.

I also stayed in Topanga with this nice old woman. Her name was Mrs. Sims. She told everyone that she was forty-five, but she looked sixty. Her house had a real old and musty smell to it.

Mrs. 45, But Really 60 welcomed kids into her home. The Weber Breads said things wouldn't work out with me.

I couldn't take No Good Nolan anymore. He kept hopping around the way he usually did.

"Let's fight. Let's fight," he constantly kept saying. He punched

me in the stomach. Real hard. I hit him back in the face, knocking
him over. The Weber Breads said they wouldn't stand violence in
their house. They had a terrorist for a son, but they kicked me out
anyway.

I was tired of living there. I had seventeen dollars saved up.

Mrs. Sims painted flowers and fruit then displayed them in her
living room.

"They don't look like flowers to me," I said. They really didn't.
They were big purple blotches or straight lines or circles within circles.

"Look closely," she said.

I did. I twisted my head every which way and they still didn't
look like flowers. I told her so.

"It's a degree of perception," she said. "That's how I'm going to
leave my mark in the world."

"What mark?"

"My mark of existence, so the world will know that I was here.
I'm going to do it through my art," she said, signing her name to a
painting. I didn't know why anyone wanted to be remembered for a
purple blotch that any five-year-old could do.

But still. I thought what she said about a "mark" was very important. Even if it was only blotches.

I felt Montgomery Clift left a mark on the world. He left all his
movies and a few books were written about him. He left a mark that
everyone could see. At the time, I didn't know how significant that
was to me.

Mrs. Sims was the nicest woman I'd met in a long time. She
treated me well, asking how school was or offering to help me with
homework. She even did a painting of me: it was a golden brown
blotch.

Mrs. 45, But Really 60 had one drawback. She was a vegetarian.
Really strict. I hadn't had a piece of meat for months. Once I came
home from school and stopped by McDonald's for a burger. As soon
as I stepped into her house she said, "You had meat, didn't you?"

"Yes, how did you know?"

"Because I can always detect the disgusting smell of a butchered
cow, having his throat slit, blood pouring from his neck until it slowly dies, then processed into rancid meat—probably with carrion

buzzing about—then cooked in pig lard."

"It was delicious."

"Bong, there is not a lot I ask of you. I like you and I think you like me, too. But please don't eat meat. I'll make you tofu burgers instead."

So she made me these terrible Toe Food burgers that I couldn't stand, but it was either that or spinach day in and day out.

I eventually moved in with Mr. Phelps. He lived in Torrance. Both he and his wife were therapists. Mr. Phelps took me in after Mrs. 45, But Really 60 threw me out.

Mrs. 45, But Really 60 had a cold, a really bad one. She had to stay in the hospital for a while. I told her I was old enough to take care of myself. She agreed. She told me where the food was and would call me every once in a while.

As soon as she left, I stocked up on some of the juiciest, meatiest burgers I'd ever had. I couldn't finish one, and left it in the refrigerator. I forgot about it. Mrs. 45, But Really 60 came home and ate it thinking it was a tofu burger. With her cold, I guess she couldn't smell it. She had an allergic reaction and broke out in hives.

"Twenty-five years of a strict vegetarian diet down the drain because of you!" she screamed.

She also had a humiliating experience at an art show, and blamed me. The allergic reaction remained for days; the hives spread to her face. An art critic asked if her "blotches" were self-portraits.

I liked Mr. Phelps, except sometimes he got too personal. He was my first therapist, although his services were unasked for.

"How are you FEELING today?" He asked.

"I'm fine."

"No, no, no. What I'm asking is how are you really feeling."

"I'm really feeling fine."

He had this habit of touching the back of my head. Which I didn't like. There was something condescending about it. To make things worse, he asked about Mama.

"I don't want to talk about it," I said.

"It's hard having parents abandon you."

"They didn't do that." I knew they didn't. My doubts would come later in life. Parentless children were always considered abandoned. Sometimes parents had to do other things with their lives, like fight for something they believed in, like pursue a dream that existed before children came into the picture, like choosing to find my father because my mother loved him just as much as she loved me. I believed that they didn't run out on me, they left for a little while. And I knew they didn't stop loving me.

"Bong," he said, patting the back of my head, "it's not your fault that they didn't come to get you."

I left him really quick. I told my social worker that Mr. Phelps touched me in a way that made me feel uncomfortable. No questions asked. I was out of there.

CHAPTER NINE
Mabuting Kapalaran

Dear Monty,   May 18, 1981
I have ninety-six dollars saved up.

I got all sorts of brochures, telling me the troubles of traveling. If you're in trouble, call the American consulate right away.

I got it into my head to call the Philippine Consulate to help me find my parents.

I called.

"Kamusta-Ka," I said.

"I'm fine," Operator Woman said.

"I'm trying to look for someone."

"Someone who works at the consulate?"

"No, I'm trying to find my parents."

"How can I help you, sir?"

"My dad was beaten up and taken away and—"

"Here in the States?"

"No, in the Philippines. He's a writer and he was beaten up by soldiers and taken away and I'm trying—"

"Hold on, sir."

She put me on hold. Then a click. Then a dial tone.

I called again.

"Hi, it's me again. We got disconnected. I'm trying—"

"Yes. I know." She took a deep breath, and was quiet for a very long time. "Sir," she said carefully. "We are not a human rights organization." She lowered her voice, almost to a whisper. "We are not a human rights organization. We are not in the position to find people. Do you understand? We are not Amnesty International."

She said it again slowly. "Do you understand? We are not Amnesty International."

I wrote down the name. And thanked her. Before she hung up, I think I heard her say Mabuting Kapalaran. Good Luck in Tagalog.

PART TWO

CHAPTER TEN
Frosty Pink Nails

Dear Monty,   September 16, 1981

Thank you for listening to me. My new foster home is with a Filipino family in Los Feliz. The Arangans. They're loaded. Auntie Yuna would die if she saw me now.

The Arangans have a daughter. Her name is Amada. She's thirteen like me. I haven't seen her yet. Mrs. Arangan said Amada is going to a Catholic girls' school near San Francisco.

I went through their family albums and Amada was always doing something weird in the photos. In one photo, Amada is at her birthday party with cake smashed into her face, white frosting dripping from her chin, grinning. Mr. and Mrs. Arangan looked kind of mad.

I peeked into Amada's room. Teddy bears lean against her pink walls like dear friends under a sky of bubble gum. A worn black leather jacket hangs from her closet doorknob, the leather dried and cracked like a desert lake. Cassette tapes of Billie Holiday and Janis Joplin sit by her stereo; I can imagine the sound of wailing women filling her room.

Two posters of Marilyn Monroe hover above her bed. One poster is of MM smearing perfume all over her chest and the other is of MM trying to keep her white dress down from wind blowing upward: a woman caught on the tip of a tornado.

Amada seems like a hoot.

Sincerely,

Bong

PS. Didn't you do a movie with Marilyn Monroe?

I met the Arangans in all their glory. It's sad how they eventually turned out, but I didn't know that then. To me, they were a breath of fresh air.

In the summer of 1981, I was exposed to the beauty of Mrs. Arangan, mesmerized by her. She sat in front of her mirror, fixing her hair, carefully placing every strand in place. She spoke to me in Tagalog, her voice both raspy and sweet. I enjoyed talking to her, her voice entering my ears, tickling my brain.

"I can tell you are a very good boy," she said, and I blushed. I watched her carefully apply lipstick. There was something precise about the way she did it. Auntie Yuna smeared it on. Mrs. Weber Bread applied it mechanically like she was cutting vegetables and Mrs. 45, But Really 60 never wore any. ("Do you know how many animals are tortured because of the cosmetics industry?" she once told me.) But Mrs. Arangan slid it onto her lips as finely as you'd caress a newborn baby's head.

"What is your most favorite dish in the world?" she said, looking up from her mirror, her face cracking a slight smile.

"Fried chicken."

"Fried chicken. Good. We'll make sure it's made at least once a week. So you can have something to look forward to." There was charm in her voice also, a seductive quality.

"What is your favorite dish?" I asked not wanting the conversation to end.

"I have lots of favorite dishes, Bong, but my most favorite is pizza with lots of anchovies," she said and laughed. "I have that once a week, too. My husband and my daughter don't like it so I order a whole pizza for myself and eat it all."

"I like pizza with anchovies."

"Good. I have someone to share with. Eating alone is a terrible thing," she said dabbing perfume onto her wrists and neck and shoulders. The smell of something sweet and strong filled the air.

"When I offered to be a foster parent with the department of children services," she said, "I told them I would prefer Filipino children. I don't know how to raise any other kind. I love all children, but I think my services would be of better use raising Filipinos.

"I wanted more children, but God wanted me to have only one, my daughter. When you came by, I was thrilled. A boy no less. My husband had always wanted a boy. If things work out, maybe we can adopt you."

I thought of what it would be like to be her son, the child of a fancy lady, the child of a woman who wore bright stones on her fingers, who smelled of Estée Lauder, who placed lace on her coffee table and barrettes with dangling pearls in her hair.

She sat still in front of her mirror, her back straight. I did not move because I knew she was looking at herself, her amazingly beautiful self. She picked up a porcelain brush and lifted it to her hair, hesitated, and placed it on the table. "I think that will do for now," she said. I knew she was not speaking to me, she was telling herself that her work in front of the mirror was accomplished, at least for the moment.

She turned around, looked up at me and said, "Bong. It is a nice name. I went to school with a lovely boy named Bong Bong. There are certainly many with that name. It is common. We will give you another name, a special name, an American name." She looked up to the ceiling; her mascara was perfect. "I know. We'll call you Bob. Yes. Bob. It sounds like your old name, but more appropriate for your life in the States."

"I like my name the way it is," I said.

"Please. Bob is a good name. It suits you." She took my hand, looked at me with a face that reminded me of summer, warm and full of light. "Please."

I nodded. I would have agreed to anything she said.

She smiled. "Good. I prayed for a good person for me to care for."

She stood up and walked into the hallway, her pink silk dress rustling with each step. She led me to my room, opening a white door with a golden knob. On my bed, was a present. I unwrapped the gift and discovered a baby blue sweater.

"I hope you like it," she said. "I'll get you more later, but I wanted to make sure you like this one. You need a good sweater to keep you warm."

"Thank you." Mrs. A was the most charming woman I'd ever met. She sat on my bed, leaning on the mattress with one hand. Her frosty pink nails made the brown bedspread look hideous.

"Maybe you would like to decorate your walls, put some posters up. You can decorate your walls any way you want. I can help. I like to decorate."

I knew she did. Her home was immaculate, precise. Everything was in its place: cream sofa angled just so, an oriental rug to match the sofa, green in the rug matching the paintings of forests and jungles on the wall, framed in oak wood to complement the brown tones of the coffee table and bookshelves.

She pointed to a wall and said, "You need a desk. Right over there. So you can do your homework."

I looked down, saddened by the way she talked.

"What's the matter, Bob? Is something wrong? Is it about your parents?"

I knew she wanted me to feel at home. I felt regret because I wanted to be Mrs. A's son. I felt guilty for this. I thought Mama was the most beautiful woman I'd known, but Mrs. A was beautiful, too.

I didn't want to talk about my parents with Mrs. A. I wanted to keep the two worlds different. I liked Mrs. A's world filled with palm trees on the sidewalk, a huge house—a French Normandy, she called it—with green awnings over the windows. I liked the stone driveway with a fountain in the middle and the backyard with weeping willows providing shade. I liked the foyer with a chandelier glimmering with light and the oriental rugs, with specks of gold, in the living room. Her world was about having dinner on time and buying sweaters and putting posters on my wall and gossiping about people she read about in the Filipino newspapers and deciding which rosary to take to church—the pearl one or the silver one? It was about a daughter in a boarding school and a successful husband who let her buy whatever she wanted.

"I know about your family," she said.

"You do?"

"Not a lot. Your social worker said your aunt disappeared, left you. I can't believe she did that. Your parents left you and then your aunt. How horrible for you."

She didn't know the whole thing. She thought I was simply abandoned like so many kids in foster care. She knew about Auntie Yuna, but not about Mama or Dad. I didn't want to tell her. My past would taint her perfect life. My past didn't fit into Mrs. A's world. To tell you the truth, I didn't want it to either.

"We won't leave you, Bob. You can stay for as long as you like."

I loved her. I loved her and all that she offered…until secrets came out and it all came crashing down.

•

Mr. Arangan came home from work one day and fell asleep in the living room, a newspaper on his face. He snored a godawful sound. Like he was sucking in air then choking on it. He sucked in so hard, he inhaled the newspaper into his mouth and almost asphyxiated himself. I pulled it out by putting one hand on his forehead and yanking the paper from his face. Mr. A coughed and heaved. He looked around the room, then at me, squinting to see my face.

"Salamat, Bob," he said.

"You're welcome," I said.

In the three months that I'd been living there, that was the first time Mr. A had ever said anything to me. He rarely spoke. Mr. A usually nodded at me when I came into the room. Then nodded when I left. I didn't think he was mean or anything, because my dad rarely spoke, too. He seemed to like me. Well, he didn't seem to dislike me. In a way, he was kind of friendly. He passed me more eggs at breakfast when he saw that I needed some. He passed me the funnies when he was done. He refilled my cup with soda when I'd slurped up the last drop. Sometimes before I left for school he slipped me a five note. I didn't tell him I stuck it with my fly-to-the-Philippines-to-search-for-my-parents cash.

He sat on the couch, his belly rolling over his belt like bread rising. His round face twitching and ticking like a pot of simmering stew. One leg was always moving up and down like a sewing machine needle going at full speed. Having to maintain three accounting offices made him a little on edge, I guess.

"You all right?" I asked.

"I'm fine. Fine. You saved my life," he said and laughed a little.

I folded the newspapers and stacked them on the coffee table. "Is school going OK?" he asked.

I realized why he never spoke. His voice sounded like it came from a throat filled with phlegm. Rough and wounded.

"School's 'kay."

"How are you in arithmetic?"

"All right."

"Maybe someday you can work for me. I'll give you your own office somewhere in West Covina. But you have to be good in arithmetic," he said grandly. Mr. A was like many Filipino men I had known, boisterous and jolly, trying to impress me with what he could do for me.

When the Arangans lived in that gorgeous home, not the little place they live in now in Pasadena, but that huge home in Los Feliz, there were photos of Mr. A on a wall as you walked up and down the staircase. Mr. A at graduation from the University of the Philippines. Mr. A at the opening of his first office in Glendale. Mr. A at his second office in Carson. He was smiling in all of them, but with every picture, his face becomes a little more weary, his stomach a little more pudgy. By the time you got to Mr. A at the opening of his third office in Alhambra, his face was caught in mid tick: one cheek raised to the sky, lips twisted like dead worms.

He got up and slapped me on the back. "Do you have a girlfriend yet?" he asked and rubbed his belly. I knew he wanted to relate to me. He and his wife had been trying so hard. I liked the attempt.

I thought of J, and how he hadn't written in a long time and said, "No. I don't have a girlfriend."

"Maybe that is best. You have plenty of time."

I watched him stagger to bed.

CHAPTER ELEVEN
Prisoner of Conscience

Dear Monty,   November 27, 1981

I spent the day in the library, looking up everything I could on Amnesty International. They had
been around for years. An independent organization. Not associated with any government. They
fight for human rights all over the world.
Amnesty International won a Nobel peace prize for
their work.

I thought of Mrs. 45, but really 60. Amnesty
International sounded like an organization that
she would have heard of. I thought of her blotches.

I put a blotch of my own—well a small dot—on page
168 of all of the books I checked out of the
library. A small mark that said, I was here.

Amnesty International has an office in Los
Angeles. I called them.

"Can I come into your office? I need your help."

"What kind of help?" Operator Man asked.

"I'm looking for someone. My parents."

"What happened to them?"

I told Operator Man the whole story.

"So, its been what five, maybe six years since
you've seen them?" he asked.

"Yes."

He heaved a deep sigh, and said, "Why don't you
come in next week."

My first of many meetings at Amnesty was in December of 1981.
I remember it being a dismal day. It took three busses to get
there. I was hoping for some quick answers but a gloom set in
in that first meeting. I met Mr. Boyd and he said some things I
didn't want to hear.

"It sounds like your father was a Prisoner of Conscience," Mr.
Boyd said. Prisoners of Conscience were people who were detained
because of their nonviolent expression of beliefs. That's what my
father was: a prisoner of conscience.

"But you and your mother got away?" Mr. Boyd asked.

"Yes. But she's missing, too. She was supposed to come to the
U.S. once she found my dad, but she never did."

"Son," he said, "I want you to know something." Mr. Boyd had
lines on his forehead, lines around his eyes, lines around his lips,
lines on his lips. His face looked like a well-detailed map, with his
nose as a famous landmark. He wasn't real old, maybe thirty-five.
"When a person disappears, the ripe time to try and find him is
within the first two weeks they're gone, okay?" He looked at me like
I was stupid. "That's usually how long they're held, guards wait to
see if anyone will make a fuss about the disappearances. To see if
whoever was taken hostage will be missed, understand?" I nodded.
"If a human rights group or a religious group doesn't say anything,
then…"

"Then what?"

"Well, they are put away in prison for a long time or…or they're
killed."

Never once did I consider my father dead. I looked out of Mr.
Boyd's window and I saw him: Monty. Despite what some of the doctors said, it was him. It had to be. He walked across the street in a
tan suit. I watched him walk away until he was a speck in the distance. Then he vanished. I was happy to have him near me.

"Son, are you OK?" a faraway voice said. It took me a second to
realize it was Mr. Boyd speaking.

"I'm fine."

"Now your mother wasn't detained, right? She could be free at this moment."

"I don't know where my mother is."

Mr. Boyd gave me some paperwork to fill out. I asked him if I could take the paperwork home with me and return it. He said that would be fine.

I tried to fill out the PRISONER DATA QUESTIONNAIRE. I picked it up and put it down. Six pages of questions. Most of them, I didn't have answers for.

I filled it out for my dad because he was the one who was taken. NAME OF PRISONER: Emil Luwad. COUNTRY WHERE IMPRISONED: Philippines. ADDRESS BEFORE ARREST: I don't remember. FAMILY DETAILS (I.E., WHETHER MARRIED, HOW MANY CHILDREN AND DEPENDENTS, ETC.) PLEASE GIVE NAME AND AGES WHERE POSSIBLE: He had one wife. Her name is Cessy Luwad. She's missing, too. One son. Me. Bong Bong Luwad. I don't remember how old Mom is. I'm thirteen. DATE AND PLACE OF BIRTH, OR APPROXIMATE AGE: I don't know. EDUCATION (NAMES OF SCHOOLS AND UNIVERSITIES ATTENDED): I don't know.

OCCUPATION(S) OR PROFESSION PRIOR TO ARREST: Writer. PAST OCCUPATIONS: I don't know.

More questions and more questions.

SPECIFIC CIRCUMSTANCES OF ARREST (ARRESTING AGENCY, ARREST WARRANT, ETC): I think it was a government agency who arrested my dad. RELATED ARRESTS: I don't know. LEGISLATION UNDER WHICH HELD: I don't know what this question means. HAS HE/SHE BEEN CHARGED? DID HE/SHE APPEAR BEFORE A JUDGE? IF THE PRISONER HAS BEEN CHARGED, CITE RELEVANT LEGISLATION (E.G., ARTICLE OF PENAL CODE) WHERE KNOWN, AND GIVE SPECIFIC DETAILS BROUGHT AGAINST THE PRISONER. SPECIFY ACTS OF WHICH THE PRISONER IS ACCUSED. IF PRISONER HAS NOT BEEN CHARGED, WHAT REASONS HAVE BEEN GIVEN BY THE AUTHORITIES FOR HIS/HER ARREST? FOR WHAT ACTIVITIES ON THE PART OF THE PRISONER DO YOU BELIEVE HE/SHE WAS DETAINED? WHAT ARRANGEMENTS HAVE BEEN MADE FOR LEGAL AID, IF NECESSARY? DOES THE PRIS-

ONER HAVE A DEFENSE LAWYER? HAS HE/SHE SEEN A
LAWYER SINCE ARREST? WHO CHOSE THE DEFENSE
LAWYER? NAME AND ADDRESS OF HIS/HER LAWYER. HAS
HE/SHE BEEN TRIED? IF SO, PLEASE GIVE THE FOLLOWING
DETAILS. DATE AND PLACE OF TRIAL. NAME OF COURT.

UNDER WHAT CONDITIONS IS THE PRISONER BEING
HELD? (E.G., SOLITARY CONFINEMENT, RIGHTS TO CORRE-
SPONDENCE AND VISITS FROM FAMILY, LAWYER?) PLEASE BE
AS SPECIFIC AS POSSIBLE. PRISONER'S STATE OF HEALTH?
HAS THE PRISONER BEEN TORTURED OR SUBJECTED TO ILL
TREATMENT? IF SO, HOW DID YOU KNOW THIS? DOES THE
PRISONER REQUIRE MEDICAL TREATMENT (PLEASE SPECI-
FY, IF KNOWN).

On and on and on and on. Less and less I knew.

I called Mr. Boyd. He said to mail the form back. They had to
send it to researchers in London and have them check on the situation.

I waited.

CHAPTER TWELVE
Wild Horses

Dear Monty,   January 8, 1982

Today is my birthday. Mrs. A gave me a cake with fourteen candles.

"Make a wish!" she said.

I wished my father, the Prisoner of Conscience, well, wherever he may be.

Dear Monty,   Feb. 25, 1982

The Arangan house has gotten a little more crowded. Amada was booted from boarding school. She's going to school with me now. I have the shitty task of walking with her.

She walks to school like a person wading through mud. She doesn't know how good she's got it. In the Philippines, I knew lots of kids who wanted to go to school, but their parents couldn't afford it. Not every child in the world has the privilege of school. In America, education is a right for every child. It amazes me when kids don't take advantage of it.

At lunchtime, I agreed to help one of my teachers grade papers. The classroom is on the third floor. I sat by the window and I saw the entire schoolyard. Amada sat by a tree sipping orange juice. I could see some kids behind her laughing.

I think it's because Amada has that weird colored
hair. I think Amada was going to cry. She got up
and sat by herself near the soda machine.

Sincerely,

Bob

saw a part of Mr. and Mrs. A I hadn't seen before. I was just home
from school when Mr. and Mrs. A came screeching up the driveway, the car heading right for me. Mr. A jammed on the brakes.

Mr. A got out of the car and slammed his door. Mrs. A stepped
out, fanning herself. A blonde girl sat in the backseat.

Mr. A pushed open the front door of the house and entered.
Mrs. A followed. I waited for the blonde to enter the house, but she
just sat there.

"GET IN HERE!" Mr. A yelled. It was a shock to hear his voice at
that decibel.

Mrs. A came outside and said, "Amada, please do what your
father said and come inside." Gone was Mrs. A's graceful demeanor,
something a little more insecure set in.

"I'm not coming in while he's screaming like that!" A voice bel-
lowed from the backseat.

"He'll stop yelling. Won't you, honey."

Mr. A didn't say anything.

The car door slowly opened and a girl with white blonde hair
emerged like a star going to a movie premiere. She sashayed into
the house.

I stood there in the driveway. Mrs. A tugged on my arm. "Go into
the house," she said, "before neighbors start looking at us like animals in a zoo."

Amada headed up the stairs, but Mr. A grabbed her by the arm
and shoved her into the living room. "How could you get expelled?"
he said, spit shooting out of his mouth.

"I don't know," Amada said meekly.

"Goddamn it. Thousands of dollars down the drain. All of that
money to send you to that school and you throw it away by running
off to San Francisco for a week."

"I'm sorry. It won't happen again."

Mr. A gave Amada a furious look, his face twitching and ticking like a firecracker on the floor. He stormed out of the room, almost knocking me over.

"Mother, don't be mad at me."

Mrs. A shook her head, pulled out a neatly folded kerchief and blew her nose. They both looked up and saw me.

Mrs. A reached for me with one hand, frail and weak, gesturing at me to come over before she fainted.

"Amada," Mrs. A said, "this is the young man I had been telling you about. This is Bong Bong."

"Bong?" Amada said, "Cool. As in Marijuana Bong?"

What a dip, I thought.

"It's Bong Bong. Two Bongs, not one. And it has nothing to do with marijuana," Mrs. A said. "Besides, his name is Bob now."

"Welcome to our happy home," Amada said with a smile and went up to her room.

Mr. and Mrs. A had one problem in their perfect life: a daughter named Amada.

•

One night, I stayed up late to watch *The Misfits*. The movie was about to start when Amada came into the room.

"What'cha watchin'?" she said.

If Mrs. A was careful about everything she did, her daughter was the exact opposite. Amada's voice wasn't like her mother's. Amada had a sing-songy way of speaking. A breathy and high-pitched sound.

"*The Misfits*."

"No shit?"

"No shit."

She sat beside me, her hair pointed straight up or bent in all sorts of directions. She decided to get rid of the blonde and dyed it a darker color: a deep purple. Along with her black sweats, she looked like a large bruise.

We watched the movie, transfixed. Monty was good, simply wonderful. Everyone in the movie was good. Marilyn Monroe was good. Clark Gable was good. I liked how all of them set out to catch wild horses, trying to catch something that was out of their reach or couldn't be tamed. Monty tried, though. He kept hoping, and chasing those wild horses.

I knew what Monty was feeling. I was chasing something, too. Sometimes, I'd wake up in the middle of the night, sweaty and nervous, my arms outstretched like I was grabbing for something. But there was nothing there.

Monty cared for Marilyn Monroe, making sure no one hurt her. It looked like Marilyn reciprocated. Monty's character gets hurt, his head bandaged up. She cradled his damaged, bandaged head in her lap while they talked of trust, of knowing people.

After the movie, Amada cried. Through her tears, she said, "Isn't she beautiful? That was Marilyn's last movie. She died in the middle of her next one. Marilyn was a goddess. She had this rough childhood, you know. When she was a kid, no one wanted her. But she became a star anyway, a great big fucking star." She said some other stuff, but she was crying so much that her words came out garbled. Before I could comfort her, she got up and went to her room.

I knew Montgomery Clift liked, maybe even loved, Marilyn Monroe. In *The Misfits*, I saw the way Monty looked at her, a dreamy admiration. I liked, no, loved Amada in the same way. She was different, no one like I'd ever met.

The next day, on our way to school, Amada asked me if I liked *The Misfits*.

"Yeah, I did. I'm a big fan of Monty Clift," I said.

"I've seen all of Marilyn's movies," she said. "I really like her. The first time I saw Marilyn was in *All About Eve* starring Bette Davis. Marilyn had a little part in that movie, she wasn't a star.

"Someday, I'm going to be just like her. I'm going to be an actress. I don't know how to act yet, but sometimes I practice in front of my mirror. I practice acting. I'll say a speech over and over to myself. If the speech is real sad, I'll feel like crying, you know. I think that's the mark of a real good actress, don't you? Feeling like crying at the sad parts?

"I think about going to school and study The Method. That's what all those great actors studied, The Method. Marlon Brando, James Dean, all those people studied The Method. I don't know what The Method exactly is, but I'm sure it's some great secret to acting.

"I'm going to learn how to sing, too. I sang at my old school. I sang in the church choir. I'm an alto. My voice needs some work. I know that much, but I know I can sing. Once the choirmaster made me sing "Amazing Grace" all by myself and he said I did a real nice job. He said I could have a real good voice if I practiced and studied.

"I'm going to sing and act. Then I'm going to learn to dance. I dance real well at parties and stuff, but I'm going to learn for real. Take ballet and jazz classes someday. Be real good. I'll be able to stand on my toes and do the splits without it hurting.

"I want to take tap classes, too. When I was a little girl, I taped little pennies to my shoes so I could make those click sounds when I walked. Click. Click. Like in those old Hollywood musicals. I'd dance around, clicking away on my mom's floors. She got mad at me, though. She said I was marking up her clean hardwood. So I had to stop.

"I'm going to be an actress. You wait and see."

I had a new friend, an earthly one. I couldn't help but feel Monty put us together.

CHAPTER THIRTEEN
The Mirror World

Dear Monty,   June 24, 1982

I dreamt about you. You told me, Not Yet Not Yet.
I thought of telling the Arangans that I'm look-
ing for my parents. You told me not to. Not Yet
Not Yet, I felt you say.

I love the Arangans. I want to tell them about my
life.

"Not yet," you said. "Do not tell them about your
parents. Do not."

"Why?" I wanted to know.

"There will be a time to tell them. Not now. Not
yet. Don't tell them about your parents." Your
voice sounded haunting, but firm.

I woke up, and decided to write this letter to you.
If you don't want me to tell Mr. and Mrs. A about
my parents, I won't. I trust you more than anyone.

Dear Monty,   July 10, 1982

Mr. Boyd said it didn't look good. There is a
team of researchers looking over the situation in
the Philippines. He told me thousands of people
have been abducted since Marcos started martial
law in 1972. Still. They haven't gotten word that
my folks are dead.

"**W**e're going to church on Easter Sunday," Mrs. A said. "The both of you need new clothes." She dragged Amada and me to the Glendale Galleria. She bought me khaki trousers, a red tie with little horses on it, penny loafers (with no pennies), and a very starched oxford shirt. I tried on a navy blue coat and a salesman said to Mrs. A, "Your son looks very handsome in double breast."

She brushed the hair away from my face, her long pink polished nails grazing my forehead. "Yes, he does," she said, "yes, he does."

I looked into the mirror and I wasn't who I was. I was just a guy trying on clothes with his family. Mrs. A was behind me; Amada, like a sister, nodded approvingly, partly distracted by clothes some distance away. In this Mirror World, I was normal, like everyone else: I worried about the pimples on my forehead; I wanted to learn how to drive; I wanted to go on a date. A Sense Of Belonging belonged to me. A spell was cast in Glendale.

The spell took further effect when I watched Amada and Mrs. A debate the kind of clothes to buy.

"Just try on one dress," Mrs. A pleaded. "Try this one on. Look. It has a pretty bow in the back, and peach is a good color for you."

"Bows are for little girls. And that color makes me look sick," Amada said.

"What do I have to do to get you to try on a dress? Any dress."

"How about this one?" Amada pointed to a strapless tight-fitting cocktail dress. BABY OH BABY.

"Oh, Amada. You're about ten years too young to wear that. Plus it isn't ladylike," Mrs. A said and picked out an orange lace dress with a satin collar.

"I told you, Mom, I don't like looking like fruit."

"Amada, you have two bags of jeans. You can't wear those to Easter Mass."

"Why not?"

"It's disrespectful. Every single time we go shopping, it's the same thing. Jeans, jeans, jeans. Can't you buy just one dress?"

"All right. But no fruit colors."

I watched them bicker like…like…well, like mother and daughter. I wanted to launch right into the conversation. I would've sided with Amada. Mrs. A may have impeccable taste, but it's not suited for a teenager. I wanted to do this; I felt like a part of this family. I wanted people in the mall, the salesmen in the department store to know. I belonged.

Dear Monty,   August 2, 1982

Sometimes in the middle of the night, just before I nod off, I'll hear crying. Far off. Far away. And I wonder who it is. It's my mom waving me off at the airport.

Sometimes I'll look at Mrs. A and think about how beautiful she is. She makes a mean fried rice. A lot of garlic, just enough soy. Sometimes she'll lay a sheet in the backyard. We'll have a little picnic under a weeping willow. Amada is nice. Mr. A is nice. Mrs. A is nice. The food is good. The weather is just right. Everything seems to fit. I seem to fit.

Sometimes I'll bite into my chicken and think this is how it's supposed to be. Sitting around and just eating. Maybe Amada will say something like There's A Guy At School Who Likes Me, But He's Not My Type. Mrs. A will say something like, Amada, You Have Plenty Of Time To Think About Boys, Concentrate On School. Mr. A will say, Pass The Salt.

And it all seems so ordinary. And Normal. And it feels right.

Mrs. A raised the question of adopting.

"Yes! I want you as my brother," Amada said.

I just smiled. I didn't want to be adopted

before. But now I kind of wonder. The
Philippines, Mama, and my dad seem to be leaving
me like a ship sailing away—no! more like a ship
sinking, disappearing under dark water.

Dear Monty,   September 2, 1982

I saw From Here to Eternity last night. You were
wonderful. Every one in the movie did a great
job. Frank Sinatra, Burt Lancaster, and Donna
Reed acted really well. I know you were nominated
for the academy award for that movie, one of four
nominations you received in your career. You
should have won. It was good to know that Frank
Sinatra and Donna Reed won best supporting oscars
for their roles.

From Here to Eternity was a difficult movie to
watch. You get beat up in that movie. You played
a soldier and your fellow soldiers beat you up. I
hated seeing you in such pain. It reminded me of
the night my parents were beat up, the night my
father was taken away.

In the movie, you go AWOL. You leave the army to
be in the arms of the prostitute Donna Reed. I
know what it's like to want to leave. So many
times I want go away, disappear. I leave, entering a fuzzy world where you live. In that fuzzy
world, I feel like I'm surrounded by gauze,
everything is buffered. Everything becomes a little more bearable. I like the fuzzy world.

Dear Monty,   September 14, 1982

Last Sunday, we went to church. I asked Mr. A if
he had anything to put in my hair to stop it from
standing straight up. Mr. A and I are about the
same height, we have the same coloring, and, I
think, he enjoyed showing me how to fix my hair.

He dabbed some pomade onto his palm, rubbed it into his hands, and applied it to his head. When I did the same, he told me to add a little more pomade because my hair was still messed up. I fixed it so it could look like yours, Monty. Combed back. Flat on the sides, fuller on top. My hair is probably coarser than yours, but I think I did a good job.

"I'd always wanted a son," Mr. A said out of nowhere, "but my wife couldn't have any more children after Amada." Then there was a silence that lasted forever. It's funny how saying nothing at all could say so much.

We attended Mass at Saint Basil, a huge cement church in the Mid-Wilshire area. Saint Basil looked like rows of raw crystals jutting into the air. Out front, a statue of the Virgin Mary presented itself to passing cars. Her arms were outstretched as if a person were running toward her, needing a long embrace. Our Lady of Perpetual Sorrow, a sign said beneath her.

The church was packed. The priest talked of Christ's resurrection and our own spiritual rising. He talked of love: "Jesus died for our sins, he died because he loved us. Love is the most important element in life, we should learn to do things out of love." Blah, blah, blah.

Something the priest talked about that got my attention was False Idols. He said Jesus is Our Savior. And praying to False Idols is a sin.

I thought about you, Monty. There's nothing false about you. I know Jesus is a good guy, but he didn't do for me what you did for me. I think people in this world need some kind of hope, any kind of hope to get them through the day. Some people can't relate to that guy on the cross. He seems so far away.

I think Jesus only takes care of certain people
anyway. Even though the Philippines is the most
Catholic country in Asia, why is most of the
country starving? Why do people disappear? I
don't think Jesus cares about Filipinos.

Dear Monty,   October 9, 1982

I sometimes wonder what I'll be when I grow up. I
don't know what I want to be yet. Maybe a jour-
nalist like J or my dad. It's odd saying that:
dad. I try not to think about him because I'll go
crazy. I don't feel like he's dead; then again,
how would it feel to have deadness around you?

I pulled some dead skin from my thumb, a small
withered piece by my nail. It lay on my desk,
unattached and alone.

A mada told me to go with her. We took the bus to Mann's
Chinese Theater near La Brea.
"Where are we going?" I asked.
"You'll see."
She took me to the Hollywood Roosevelt Hotel. As soon as I
entered, I knew Monty was there. I know that people leave impres-
sions, dents of themselves in space, like a woman's perfume when
she passes. Sometimes it's not a smell but a presence, an indelible
secret kept in the walls.
We sat in the lobby. She closed her eyes. She told me to do the
same thing.
"Why?"
"Because," she said, "try to feel them."
"Who?"
"Marilyn Monroe and Montgomery Clift. Don't you know this
hotel is famous for being haunted by dead stars? I read in a book
that Marilyn Monroe's ghost can be seen walking the halls.
Montgomery Clift stayed here when he filmed that movie *From Here
to Eternity.* Some say you could hear him blowing his bugle like he
did in the movie."

"Really?"

"Yeah. So close your eyes and listen."

I listened, waiting for Monty's horn. All I heard was noise, the useless sounds of people in the lobby. I wondered if Monty would come, spirit me away the way he did sometimes. I'd find myself in one of his movies. A black and white dream. I ran with him in the Nevada desert searching for horses in *The Misfits*. I waited for him in the rubble of war-torn Germany in *The Search*. I looked forward to seeing a new Monty Clift movie, because that meant there were new places he'd take me.

In the lobby of the Hollywood Roosevelt Hotel, I heard his horn. It was real soft at first, distant; a small pin of a sound. Then it slowly grew into a low wail, swelling louder. It was real sad sounding, like no one cared about what he was doing. I heard the horn. I heard it and I cared. A melody that transported me. I found myself in the army barracks where Monty was stationed in *From Here to Eternity*. He was fighting. Some assholes in the army picked on him and decided to beat him up. The sound of fists hitting their target was a horrid sound. I remembered my dad.

I heard his horn. He blew it when Frank Sinatra died. I remember how sad he felt. I remember the tears that streamed down his face knowing someone that mattered in his life would never come back. I remember him blowing that bugle, blowing wind from deep inside his gut, blowing everything he'd had, everything that mattered, into that piece of twisted metal. He was serenading the dead. That's what I heard at the Roosevelt Hotel: a sad sweet blare.

Before I knew it, tears were coming down my face. I wondered if people who mattered in my life would ever come back. I heard a soft sad sound of my own coming from me; it was more like a hum. Like an airplane far, far away. Or a bee buzzing around my head at night while I slept. I could feel it waking me and I thought about my mom and my dad. I thought about them blowing horns, blowing somewhere, calling me. Calling me.

I didn't know how to respond. Like somebody threw me a life preserver and I tried to grab for it, but the only thing I caught was water. I slipped and slid. All the time there was something floating above me that could carry me to safety.

I had to open my eyes. I had to. I couldn't take the different sounds coming at me. Drowning me out. I rubbed my eyes. There he was. There was Monty. I saw him enter the elevator. The sliding doors closed and he was gone.

CHAPTER FIFTEEN
Broken Girl

Dear Monty,   February 20, 1983

Amada was brilliant in The Glass Menagerie. She appeared on the stage, and I couldn't take my eyes off her. Although the character was supposed to be plain, it was clear that she was a lovely girl. Her hair was pulled back, revealing her full heart shaped face, and under the lights, her skin glowed.

I tried to get Mr. and Mrs. A to come, but they wouldn't.

"Fuck 'em," Amada said. She sounded tough, but I know she was hurt.

Amada was barely making it through the 10th grade. I had to help her a lot in order for her to get her homework done. When Mr. and Mrs. A saw her report card filled with C's and D's, they just about tore her head off.

Mr. A said, "Why can't you do better in school?"

Mrs. A said, "Amada, you're a bright girl, try harder."

"She is not a bright girl; she is a stupid, stupid, stupid girl," Mr. A chimed in.

I saw Amada's face tense up, but she kept still. I bet she let her mind wander when her parents yelled and nagged at her like that.

Then Mr. A shoved my report card in front of her. My report card was so close to her face, she could have kissed it. Amada maintained that stillness like a trapped animal that knew its only course of survival was not to run, but to remain motionless, hoping the predator will simply pass it by.

"Amada," Mrs. A began, "maybe you can be more like Bob. Just a little bit."

"I would be happy," Mr. A said, "if you worked a fraction as hard as Bob."

I felt like shit. I hated when they fought. I hated that Mr. and Mrs. A used me like a weapon to get back at their own child. I loved Amada and her parents. Mr. and Mrs. A were wonderful people and it amazed me that they couldn't see how beautiful their daughter was.

They didn't know how good they had it, they didn't. They had each other, they've always had each other. Instead they chose to have this ridiculous war of wills.

Mr. A asked Amada if she had anything to say for herself. Amada didn't say anything for a long time. Finally she said, "I want to be an actress."

Mr. and Mrs. A looked at her, perplexed.

Amada said, "I was just cast in a play at school."

I was surprised. It was news to me. I said, "That's really great."

Amada looked at me and smiled. Her eyes watered. Amada waited for her parents to say something. So did I. They didn't. They were as quiet as a heart attack in your sleep. Without saying a word, they disapproved.

Amada ran to her room. I followed her. She slammed the door. I could hear her throwing her pillows and stuffed animals against the wall.

I gave a gentle knock and asked if I could come in. She said, Yes. I walked in on her choking Winnie the Pooh, her hands throttling the poor bear.

"Why can't they be happy for me," she said. "It took all my nerve to audition for *The Glass Menagerie*. I got the lead. THE GODDAMN LEAD. I'm going to play Laura, Bob. I was really happy to get the part of Laura. She's broken. She's this broken girl. She has these delicate glass figurines, the only things more delicate than she is. She wants to be happy, but doesn't know how. She lives with this awful family. She's trying to hang on the best way she knows how...I auditioned and I got her. Laura. The lead. The broken girl..." She let go of Winnie and started pulverizing Snoopy.

After beating up all her stuffed animals, she lay on her bed. I sat beside her, stroking her hair. She fell asleep, her head melting into her pillow.

I left her bedroom and heard Mr. and Mrs. A talking.

"How can you make a living as an actress?" Mrs. A said.

"Yes, and those kind of people do drugs," Mr. A said. "She should become something else. A teacher, something professional."

I descended the stairwell, staring at Mr. and Mrs. A. in the living room.

"You should give her some credit," I whispered to them.

"What? What are you saying?" Mr. A said.

"I don't mean to be disrespectful, but I think Amada is right."

In the movie *The Misfits*, Monty protected Marilyn, loved her. Fighting for people you love is paramount. I learned that from Monty. If Marilyn Monroe were being hurt, he would have fought for her. I knew he would have.

"She really wants to be an actress, she really wants to do this," I said.

"It's dumb," Mr. A said.

"It's not dumb, sir. Dreams are never, ever dumb."

"Don't lecture us about dreams," he said, looking at his wife. She looked at me. "Dreams can ruin your life," he continued. "Dreams can take hold of you and never let you go, destroying any happiness you plan. Don't talk to us about dreams."

Mrs. A pulled herself up, wrapping her arm around her husband. I watched them ascend the staircase, leaning on each other.

CHAPTER SIXTEEN

Blood Prom at Hell High

Dear Monty,   May 22, 1983

I went to the library to read up on the Philippines. I found a stack of Amnesty International reports there. The reports talked of human rights violations from all over the world. In all of them, the Philippines has violations up the ass.

The reports said over 50,000 people have been "detained." Some simply disappeared. In 1975, delegates from Amnesty International visited the Philippines and interviewed a bunch of people who were detained. A lot of them talked of how they were tortured.

There was this interesting article about how the Marcoses are rich, stealing from the people. And how they hide it by having it laundered out of the Philippines and put into other countries. The Marcos family has people—"cronies" they were called—all over the world to exchange money for them.

I also researched where I can stay or cheap ways of eating when I return to the Philippines. If I'm going to look for Mama, I'll probably need to stay a few months. Mr. Boyd gave me some hints on what I'd have to do. I'll have to ask people in places where they were last seen. I need to spend time in Manila and Baguio City. I can stay in

hostels or crummy hotels. I have to eat as inex-
pensively as possible. I calculated it all. With
airfare and all, I'll need about 3,000 dollars. I
have about 315 bucks now. I need to make more
money. If you have any ideas, Monty, please let
me know. I put a blotch on page 168 of all the
books I came across.

O utside of school there was a flyer on a telephone pole. It said,
Extras Needed for Movie To Be Shot On Campus, Extras Must
Be Able To Pass For Students.

"Let's do it," Amada cried. "That's what we can do this summer,
make movies."

"What's an extra?" I asked.

"Those are people who you see in movies who just sit there or
stand there or walk by to make it look real. They're nobodies. They
sort of take up space while the real action takes place."

"I don't know if I want to be an extra."

"It pays."

She said the magic words. Amada called the number on the
flyer. We were supposed to report to such-n-such place at such-n-
such time.

It was for a movie called *Blood Prom at Hell High*. It was about a
bunch of kids who get massacred just before they graduated.

On the first day of shooting, people were all over, milling
around like a crowd at a car wreck. Amada meandered, looking at
the actors get made up or the crew place props. And cameras, lots
of cameras. I understood why Monty did movies. There was so much
happening.

Being an extra, though, meant having to wait around while the
next shot was being set up. I read during that time, placing a blotch
on page 168 of *Montgomery Clift*, a biography by Patricia Bosworth.

I breezed through *Monty* by Robert La Guardia. It was different
from Patricia Bosworth's book, *Montgomery Clift*. La Guardia's book
was more personal, Bosworth's book was more factual. Both agree
on one thing: Montgomery Clift was attracted to men. I found relief
in knowing that.

Amada had been prying about my sexuality. I had tried to evade the subject. Frankly, I didn't know myself. One night after shooting, Amada and I sat on the damp grass in the backyard.

"Do you think Anne Chang is pretty?" Amada asked.

"She's all right," I said.

"How about Lizzy Nguyen?"

"I don't know."

"Deanna Yamashiro?"

Amada got into one of her moods, asking me how she compared to other girls.

"Amada," I said, "you're the best-looking one in class, the most talented. You make all the other girls look like nothing."

She smiled and said, "Anne Chang gets a lot of dates, being a cheerleader and shit."

"I guess."

We both listened to the crickets, making that sad sound they sometimes make, a distant and constant chirp. It was calm, but a breeze made the night a little chilly.

"I think Anne Chang likes you," she said.

"Really?"

"Do you like her?"

"I never really thought about it."

"It's OK if you don't like her," she said. "It's OK if you don't like Anne or any other girl, Bob. I don't care. I really don't."

We were quiet for a very long time.

"Is it that obvious?" I said.

"Does it matter?"

"I guess not." For some reason, I wanted to cry and laugh at the same time.

The crickets stopped their mournful symphony. Amada moved closer to me, her body shielding me from the evening's chill.

•

In most of the shots, we sat in a classroom with a bunch of other kids. I thought it funny that Amada and I spent that summer vacation back in school.

"You're just suppose to sit!" Director Man said to Amada.

"I was," Amada said.

"Noooooo. You're blowing kisses at someone across the room. Act the way you usually do in class."

"But that is the way I usually act in class."

"Well, stop it."

They tried the scene again. We watched the teacher. She was a lead actor. The camera moved around us.

The lead actor was a glamorous woman. I'd seen her in commercials, telling us to drink this soda or buy that car. She was supposed to be teaching us Algebra. I knew in real life that she could barely count to ten.

In all my years in school, I'd never seen a teacher look like her. Her hair was teased and sprayed, looking like a poodle in shock. She had so much makeup on you could have thrown a stone at her and it would have stuck on her face, imbedded in all that goo.

She pointed to shapes on the blackboard, saying stuff like, "OK, class, this is a rectangle. As you can see, it has four sides." Duh.

All of a sudden, Director Man yelled, "CUT!"

We all froze because the scene was going pretty well. We wondered what went wrong.

"You, in the back," he said, pointing to Amada. We all turned around and Amada was crying, black mascara streaming from her eyes, her face looked like the back of a zebra.

"What the hell are you doing?" Director Man said.

"I'm crying."

"I can see that, but why?"

"Well, I was getting into my part."

"What part? You're a student. A regular student."

"I know. I'm playing a regular student who was just dumped by her boyfriend who she really loves. We made a pact to get married after we graduated, but he falls for a girl who works at this liquor store near his house. I'm stunned, because the girl's not that pretty. I find out through a letter he puts in my folder. I discover the letter just now and fall apart."

Director Man rolled his eyes, and told Amada to sit in another part of the room.

"But nobody can see me."

"Exactly."

We finally got the scene done.

•

In the final week of shooting *Blood Prom at Hell High*, we shot exteriors. We walked around, trying to make it look like a regular school day. Some of the actors had major attitude, strutting around like they were gods. I hoped Monty wasn't like that. Although I'd read he was rather arrogant.

Amada had calmed down and was willing to be a regular student just passing by. Director Man didn't like that Amada did a cartwheel down the hall in a real important scene. He wouldn't buy her explanation of being a cheerleader training for an upcoming football game.

"You pull another stunt like that, and you're fired," Director Man said.

Amada said she wouldn't do anything like that again.

"He is such a creep," she said. "I refuse to do what he says."

"You have to. Or you're canned," I said.

"Oh, I won't do anything big. But I'll still act."

So in all the scenes, Amada had this real stern look on her face, like she was concentrating. Fortunately, it wasn't distracting or anything. She was flattered that she was chosen to be a dead body in the gym.

"See. My acting paid off," she said.

"Make sure there's lots of blood on her," Director Man said. "And attach that hatchet to her head real good."

CHAPTER SEVENTEEN

The No-Name Place

Dear Monty,   September 2, 1983

I caught one of your films. Suddenly Last Summer was a real weird ass movie. Elizabeth Taylor and Katharine Hepburn were in it. Elizabeth Taylor had gone crazy after seeing her cousin Sebastian killed. Sebastian's mother, Katharine Hepburn, wanted to give her a lobotomy, erasing Elizabeth Taylor's memory of the incident. It turned out that Sebastian was gay and was murdered by the guys he lusted after. He died in the most horrible way: he was eaten, cannibalized.

You played the doctor, the guy who was supposed to perform the lobotomy. You tried to make everyone in the movie happy: caring for Elizabeth Taylor and delicately dealing with Katharine Hepburn.

The movie made me real uncomfortable because of all the crazy people in it. It was cool you were there to help them.

I understood why I had dreams of Monty telling me not to reveal anything about my parents to the Arangans. I understood in August of 1983. The television was on at full blast. Mr. and Mrs. A sat in front of the television, enchanted with the glowing blue light. Mrs. A was crying, wiping snot from her nose. Mr. A shook his head in disbelief.

"What are you watching?" I spoke in Tagalog, speaking casually.

Mrs. A corrected my pronunciation and told me to sit. I sat behind them. On Channel Seven there was a story about a Filipino Senator named Benigno Aquino, he was a political prisoner who was in exile in America. He returned to the Philippines and his welcome home gift was a bullet. With one shot, Mr. Aquino disappeared from the earth. I didn't realize how big the story was until I saw it on all the other channels, too.

"My God. My God. What's going to happen now?" Mrs. A said.

"We have to wait and see," Mr. A said. "*Tanga.* Why did he go back?"

"How will this affect business?" Mrs. A asked.

"I don't know. This may freeze money coming into the offices. But I have other clients. It'll be OK."

"But Marcos will be watched heavily now."

"I have other clients!" Mr. A said firmly.

The world stopped. Mr. and Mrs. A looked different to me.

"I have other clients. This shouldn't hurt us."

"How will what hurt?" I asked.

Mr. and Mrs. A exchanged glances.

"Nothing, Bob," Mrs. A said. She turned off the TV and went into the kitchen. I heard her turn on the stove. Mr. A went into the backyard and sat on some lawn furniture, twitching and ticking faster than usual.

Later, I asked Amada why they were worried.

"You don't know?" she said.

"Nope."

"Well, they don't know that I know this. But one summer I worked for my dad. I went through all these files. They looked kind of funny. I may not know much about accounting, but I know when something is funny. Like these dollars coming through Hawaii. I did a paper trail, turns out it's Marcos money. Isn't that a blast? It's kind of cool. Sort of like something out of a James Bond movie or something."

I stared at the ceiling. If you stare long enough, the surface can start forming shapes, faces. I saw Monty's face on the ceiling, looking down at me, frowning almost.

"Something wrong?"

"No, nothing." I went back into the living room and flipped on the boob tube.

•

I went fuzzy. My body was on earth, but my mind lingered else-where, hearing voices far, far away. That was the first time I went away.

This is what I remember. It was during breakfast. I couldn't look at Mr. and Mrs. A. I simply couldn't.

"How's school?" Mr. A asked.

"Bob, are you OK?" Mrs. A offered.

I mumbled something and left. I went to the bathroom and tried to throw up. Nothing came out. I wanted to go somewhere. Anywhere. As long as it was away from them and out of the house. I decided to go to the school library.

"Hey, wait up, Bobster," Amada said. But I didn't wait up. I sped out, down the street, around the block, into the schoolyard, up some stairs, into the library. I found the most secluded part, away from the librarian. I gathered as many books as possible. I didn't care what they were, any subject, any author, any title. I laid them in front of me. I took the first book, a mystery. I leafed through it. Page 168. I blotched it. Another book. Blotched it. Blotch blotch blotch. I blotched for hours. Book after book. I didn't bother making any of my classes.

Amada came in at lunch.

"What's up?" she said. She said something else, too, but I didn't hear. I just concentrated on my blotching.

I also concentrated on Montgomery Clift sitting at a table at the other end of the library...looking at me. Our eyes met. His eyes were blue, so blue. I could tell from the way he looked at me that he loved me. He loved me the way he loved Elizabeth Taylor in *Suddenly Last Summer*. She was going through a hellish time, locked up in some insane asylum. He was there for her. He told her to trust him. He promised to help her, to heal her. He promised. I could have stared into his face forever, but Amada touched me, pulling me away.

"Bob," she said, "did you hear me?"

"Get the fuck away from me!" I yelled. Everyone turned toward me.

I ran out, finding myself on some street. I wandered...I found a bookstore on Vermont Avenue. Again I grabbed some books and continued blotching. I tried not to look conspicuous, pretending to be interested in buying something.

A salesman eyed me. I thought he was going to tell me to quit blotching. Instead, he said, "You have ten minutes to make your purchases before we close." They closed at nine. I had been there for seven hours!

I was the last one to leave. I thought about going home, but didn't. I thought about the small library in the Arangans' home, and all the books lying on the shelves. But I had already blotched them the first week I was there.

I was on some residential street. All the homes were dead quiet, no one in them. It was a great neighborhood: immaculate lawns skirting elegant two-story houses, expensive cars in the carports.

I tried the back doors of a few of the houses—they were locked. I tried to push open some windows—they were sealed. I came across a shingled home, with arching windows. One window was open. Jackpot! I climbed inside. Even in the dark, I could see it was a fancy schmancy place, with deeply cushioned sofas and chairs, neat art-work—paintings and shit—on the walls or sculptured stuff on podiums.

I walked through the house, careful not to trip or make noise. I didn't want to wake anyone. Whoever was sleeping probably had a crappy day. I wanted to blotch their books and leave. I saw a large book on a coffee table. I made my way to it. It was a pretty book, the kind you'd expect on a coffee table. The book showcased the art of Andy Warhol. I looked for page 168. Damn! It only had 142 pages. I put the book back.

I wandered throughout the home some more. I almost gave up when I noticed a room, off to my left, a den of some kind. There, suspended on the wall, were two shelves holding thick books. I stood on a chair to get them. All of the books were on design and architecture. The first one said *All About Foundation,* another read, *The Perfect Home for You,* and another, *A Different Look for Your Living Room.* I pulled the pen from my shirt pocket and blotched.

When I marked the last book, I placed it on the shelf. The book was a boulder, sizing in at about 962 pages. I guess the shelf was flimsy because it crashed to the floor. Lights came on from upstairs. I raced through the house looking for that open window, but I couldn't find it. Turning left, then right. I felt like a mouse in a maze. I heard footsteps.

I panicked. I found the living room. The Andy Warhol book was my marker. I found the open window and jumped out. I ran down the street as fast as I could, curving down this avenue, up that boulevard.

I found myself in familiar territory with my high school in front of me. I didn't know what time it was, but it was late. I slept in the school parking lot. That way I could be the first one into the library and I'd have first pick of the books. I had been blotching books there since I began school but I knew there were whole sections that I hadn't gotten to yet.

I found some bushes to lie by. I pulled my body into the fetal position then slept. A huge screen of black covered my eyes. I woke, dusted myself, tasted the thick foam on my tongue.

I headed to the library. Amada came my way. Her lips were tight and her eyes squinty. I turned around and ran. I heard her yelling after me, but I kept running.

Then I walked. I walked for hours. I walked into Downtown. I came across a huge yellow art deco building. The sign on it said the Los Angeles Public Library. It was huge with dozens of rooms. And all of those rooms had books. Hundreds of thousands of them. I blotched encyclopedias on the first floor. I kept going until the library closed. I slept in the park nearby. I returned the next day. I had been doing this for a couple of days, sleeping in the park, waking up to blotch.

I walked in one morning, and a librarian stopped me.

"Look, son," the Library Lady said, a small black woman with pencils sticking out of her hair, "for the last three days, you've been coming back here to look at books. It's a good thing someone your age likes books so much, but every time I see you, you look a mess. Worse than the day before. Your hair's all wild and to smell you is like breathing in the dead. I don't want you back in here until you've cleaned up some. Y'hear?"

I nodded and walked away, stopping for a pee in the restroom. I looked in the mirror. In the Mirror World, I saw what I was: a nobody, a messy nobody. Library Lady was right, breathing in the dead. The Mirror World did not lie. This was my life. My father was taken away, my mother disappeared. The Arangans, the family I'd learned to cherish, wishing to be their adopted son, were Marcos cronies. The color gray became a feeling, a thick wool blanket that enveloped me.

I made my way back to the bookstore on Vermont and blotched some more. Kids from school trickled in with that what-do-we-do-with-the-rest-of-the-day look. I glanced at the clock. It was three-thirty. School was over. I decided to go back to the school library.

I had slept on asphalt the night before so my back was a little sore. My hand was cramped from holding that black pen. I heard a voice behind me, "Where the hell have you been? Mom and Dad have been going crazy."

It was Amada.

I just looked at her. I walked away from her, unable to speak. She followed me and said: "What's the matter, Bob?"

I walked out of the library, down the stairs, without saying a word. I walked to some place I had no name for—The No-Name Place. Beckoning me...beckoning...The No-Name Place, The No-Name Place.

I felt Amada's hand rest on my shoulder. I stopped. She came around and faced me. "Bob," she said, "talk to me." Talk to me talk to me talk to me. It sounded like an echo in a tunnel. Help me, Amada, I wanted to say. But I couldn't speak. My voice was gone. She placed her palm against my cheek, her soft skin slightly jarred me. "You don't look good," she said. "Come on, let's go."

She put her arm into mine, and guided me home. Home wasn't the right word. Rather, she guided me back to the place where I lived.

I entered the house, and I heard Mrs. A talking on the phone. "I don't want to see your parents," I whispered to Amada.

"Why? They're worried sick."

"I just can't see them. I can't."

She took me to my room and put me in my bed. I dozed off. I dreamt about my parents stuck in some prison somewhere, locked up with all those crazy people like the ones in *Suddenly Last Summer*. I dreamt of my father alone in a cell, deprived of light, food, and human contact. I dreamt of him hurt, wounded, huddled in a corner, lost. I dreamt of my mother sick and exhausted, rocking herself to sleep, surrounded by lost souls. I dreamt of her weeping and wailing, screaming and vomiting.

Montgomery Clift was in my dream, too. He had his hands out to me. I almost touched them, then I woke up.

•

I woke up in the morning with Mrs. A sitting at my bed, her hand caressing my forehead. I said, "Go away."

"Bob, I'm worried—"

"Go away."

"Eat something. Amada is bringing up some food—"

"Disappear. Just disappear."

"Bob, tell me—"

Amada entered with a tray of milk and cereal. I said, "Amada, please tell your mom to leave." They looked at each other. Mrs. A departed with her hand covering her eyes. Amada sat by me.

"OK, mister. What the fuck happened to you? You zoned out or something."

"I needed to think."

"My parents almost called the police. They almost called your case manager, too, but were afraid they'd take you away from us."

"It's because of your parents that I'm in this mess." Maybe it was the way Amada poured my cereal or maybe it was the way dimples appeared on her face like stars when she grinned, but I decided to tell her all about my folks.

"No fucking waaaaay!" she said. "What are you gonna do?"

"Get out of here. I can't stay."

"Don't be stupid. Where are you gonna go?"

"I don't know, but I can't stay here. I can't stay in this house."

"Bob, I know you're upset. But stay. You can hate my parents all you want. Hell, I do. You gotta be smart. Here, you get a bed, food, and a little spending cash. I can't stand my parents, but I'm not stupid enough to run off."

"You ran off to San Francisco."

"Exactly. I lived on the streets for a few days, begged for money. Despite what you think, being homeless is not a pleasant experience."

"I can't stay. I'll find another foster home to—"

"Look," she said, placing her hands on mine. "You being here is the only thing keeping me sane. If you leave, I don't know what I'd do. I can't be in this house alone with them. If you leave, I'll run away and never come back."

I knew she meant it. Life is so bizarre. There I was alone without my parents and there Amada was alone with hers.

"Hang out with me," she said. "We can hate my parents together. In the meantime, pocket the dough they give you. Use some of the money they got from Marcos to help you."

"Then we can't tell them about my parents. Promise?"

"Promise."

"I'm going back to the Philippines. I've got almost seven hundred dollars saved up. I'll find my folks someday."

"I know you will. Save the money. If you run away, you'll end up spending it on food and places to stay. Then you'll never be able to find them."

She had a point.

•

Mrs. A tried to talk to me one morning, cornering me in the kitchen before I went to school. Mr. A sat at the table drinking his coffee.

"You've been upset with us lately. Why?" said Mrs. A.

I remained quiet, unable to look at her. She was a beautiful woman, but she repulsed me.

"You still haven't told us why you ran off. Did we do something wrong?"

"Leave him alone," said Mr. A, "nothing to worry about. He's just doing what he wants. You don't know boys. You were out with friends, weren't you? I used to stay out all night, days at a time, when I was his age. Just leave him alone."

"Well, okay, then," she said. "Is it a girl? Were you with a girl?" I wanted to tell her, No, I'm not fucking my brains out. "Please be careful," she said. "You're too young to get married and we're too young to be grandparents."

"Yes," Mr. A added. "The last thing we want around here is some pregnant girl thinking she can move into this house. I saw girls like that all the time in the Philippines. Mothers without husbands. Shameful."

"I wasn't with a girl," I said and departed to my bedroom. The only person I wanted to be with was Monty, hoping he would be there, waiting for me on my bed.

Amada peered through my door. "You missed the excitement the other day," she said. "C'mon downstairs. I wanna show you something."

She led me into the living room. She pointed to a black box hooked up to the television. "It's a Video Cassette Recorder. My dad got it yesterday. Isn't it cool?"

Back then, in the early eighties, a VCR was rare. I'd heard of a few kids at school having one, but only a few. Being able to record something on television, view it later, or as many times as you wanted, was cool.

"I already taped something," she said. She turned the black box on. She fiddled with some buttons and turned on the TV. An old movie came on.

"It's *Freud,* starring your one and only Monty. It was on yesterday," she said. "I thought you might like it. Montgomery Clift plays the father of pyschotherapy. It's, um, interesting."

She let the VCR play. I sat there and watched.

CHAPTER EIGHTEEN
Monty's Grave

Dear Monty,   January 9, 1984

I'm writing this letter as I sit in front of a granite slab that bears your name. The headstone carries four rows of lettering. The first row reads Montgomery; the second reads Clift; the third marks your birth: 17 Oct 1920; the fourth marks your death: 23 Jul 1966.

The man who showed me your grave is standing about a hundred yards from me. It's you. I know it is, standing among the leafless trees. In the Philippines, I lived in a place with trees. The tiny house my parents rented was nestled in forest. I feel at peace here, calm as you watch me.

I'll put this letter along with the stack of letters I've written you over the years, but I'll distinguish it, stain it with the grass of your grave.

I went to school and spent as much time as I could in my room, avoiding Mr. and Mrs. A. I did chores around the house, took the trash out more often, or washed the cars. The way I saw it, I was trading services for room and board.

When Mrs. A wanted to go on a shopping trip in New York, wanted to go after Christmas when everything went on sale, I refused.

"C'mon, let's go to New York," Amada said. "It'll be fun. We can see shows and stuff."

"Amada, I don't want to spend time with your folks if I don't have to."

Then Amada pulled a dirty trick. She said, "Montgomery Clift loved New York. He died there. We can visit Montgomery Clift's grave. It's somewhere in Brooklyn."

I took a deep breath and said, "Okay, I'll go, but only to pay my respects to Mr. Clift."

Before we left, I did the laundry, scrubbed the floors, raked the leaves from the yard, arranged for our neighbor to pick up our mail. I carried all the luggage and waved down all the taxis and opened the doors to whatever room we entered or exited.

"What a gentleman," Mr. A said. I wasn't doing it to be a gentleman; I did it as part of my service, a way of helping to pay for the trip.

When we landed at La Guardia, Mr. A rented a limo. On our way to the hotel, we passed a gorgeous art deco building.

"That's the Crown Building," Mr. A said. "Imelda Marcos owns it. It's worth millions."

"Isn't it sad?" I said. "Countless people live in slums in the Philippines and the Marcos family has all that money. I wonder how they manage it all."

Amada gave me a look that said, Don't Start.

"People help them," Mr. A said. "People are helping the Marcos regime launder money, buy property under assumed names, through dummy companies."

"People like that shouldn't be allowed to walk this earth," I said. "They're helping the Marcos family get away with murder." I thought of my dad.

Amada put her arm around me, a gesture of support I thought, until she pinched me.

"I'm sure those people will have to live with that knowledge for the rest of their lives," Mr. A said wanly. He put his arm around his wife. She looked out into the cold New York sky, a chilly gray morning.

We stayed at the Plaza Hotel, an ornate building shimmering with light.

Amada and I had been diligently searching the city, carrying backpacks with sweaters and warm pretzels bought from street vendors. My backpack had paper and pens, ready to write Monty at any given moment.

I walked the streets of New York knowing he was there. New York was a scary city. So much noise. So much distraction. The only thing colder than the weather was the dark buildings that seemed to sprout from every corner. Still, I walked the Upper East Side, knowing Monty had lived there, wondering which brownstone he had occupied.

The only information I could find about his gravesite was that he was buried in a small Quaker cemetery in Brooklyn. I thought it would be easy to find such a place, but it wasn't. I went through phone books and maps to find it.

When we got there, the cemetery was virtually invisible, hidden behind trees. I found it by asking some joggers running by. They pointed off to the distance. Amada and I discovered a fenced-off area, and sure enough it was the cemetery. It was closed and didn't look like it would open any time soon.

I wanted to cry at coming this far and not being able to see Monty's grave. We walked along the fence, metal X's separating the living and the dead. There were hundreds of headstones. I didn't know how to find the one bearing Monty's name.

"Let's go," Amada said, "it's cold and I don't think we'll have a chance in hell of finding his grave."

"Shhhhhhh," I said.

I saw a man working in the graveyard, planting ferns. "Excuse me, but do you know where Monty Clift is buried?" I yelled to him. He pointed to another end of the cemetery.

"Who are you yelling at?" Amada asked.

"C'mon, that man is telling us where it is."

"Where? What man?"

I followed the fence until I could guess where he pointed. The man walked over to a headstone and pointed to it then walked away.

"Thanks," I said.

"Bob, you're scaring me. I don't see anyone."

"That's where it is. Monty is buried over there." I saw the headstone, but couldn't see the name. I told Amada to wait for me while I climbed the fence.

"Bob, where are you going?"

"I want to be alone, Amada. Please. Go away. Just for a moment."

She disappeared into the trees and I placed my arms around the headstone, kissing it.

CHAPTER NINETEEN

Happy Birthday, Monty

Dear Monty,   January 18, 1984

School is a drag. I'm writing this letter during third period, listening to my history teacher talk about World War II. I keep looking out the window, hoping to see you walk down the street. I wait for the class to end, wishing to see you in the hallway, leaning against the wall. In your hand: an unfiltered cigarette. On your face: a smile aimed at me. Only at me.

Dear Monty,   July 23, 1984

It is night. In my room, I have your photo on my bureau. I'm looking at it while I write this letter. I put a candle and some incense by your image. The only thing illuminating my room is that candle, giving a golden glow to the white walls. The incense taints the air with the smell of roses.

On this day, a nurse found you dead in your brownstone. Your heart failed. Some say you ruined your health by alcohol and drugs. It doesn't matter. On this day, you left your earthly form. All is quiet. This is the day you died. You were forty-five years old.

Dear Monty,   October 17, 1984

Happy Birthday. I left a piece of cake, angel
food with pink frosting, by your picture. I'll
eat it in the morning and swallow the luck you
leave behind.

Dear Monty,   December 23, 1984

I bought you a present, a blue cardigan—to match
your eyes. I keep it under my bed, wrapped in
silver. I'll put it under the Christmas tree at
the Hollywood Roosevelt Hotel. For you, for you.

Merry Christmas.

There were times in 1984 when I simply felt sad. I would walk home from school and miss her, miss Mama. I'd remember things I hadn't thought of in years, like when I was seven and had a miserable cold.

I was sleeping, barely conscious, and smelled the medicinal odor of Vicks Ointment. I felt Mama lift up my T-shirt and rub the ointment onto my chest. I didn't have to open my eyes to see it was her, I just knew. Her hand spread across my chest, rubbing Vicks into the center of my sternum. She pulled down my shirt then kissed my forehead.

There were times in 1984 when Amada tried to encourage me to be more active in school. "Join a club," she'd say. "Wanna join the Filipino club? I'll join with you." I shook my head no.

I wanted to start my own club, a fan club. The I-Love Montgomery-Clift-Because-He-Understands-Me-Like-No-Other club. Membership: one. Club Member Requirements: An intense yearning to worship a dead matinee star because he provides comfort, because he provides hope. Club Dues: Be willing to give part of your soul. Club Activities: Watch Monty movies no matter what hour his movies come on. If it means staying up till three in the morning to catch him on the late, late-night movie, that's what it means.

There were times in 1984 when I envied Amada. She may have hated her mother, but at least she had one. She may have had the most awful opinions of Mrs. A, but I also knew Amada loved her.

I saw Mrs. A fall asleep in front of the television and Amada whispered in her ear, "Mom? Mom, wake up. You have a bed for a reason."

Mrs. A groggily raised her head and let Amada lift her up and guide her to slumber.

CHAPTER TWENTY
One Filipino People

Dear Monty,   March 2, 1985

I have to rant. Mr. A is a prick. A fucking
prick. I hate him. Who the hell does he think he
is? He is a fool and a dimwit. I hope he knows
misery beyond his wildest dreams. I wish he'd eat
shit and die.

In reviewing some of my letters, it amazes me sometimes what I thought and felt about people. I began to experience anger toward Mr. A. I had attacks of rebellion, disagreeing about how he saw the world.

He had to let some of his accounting staff go, pissing him off, forcing himself to realize his business was crumbling. His facial tics could've told time. He kept hoping the whole Aquino assassination would finally blow over, and Marcos would reign supreme again. He did his part by extolling the virtues of the President.

"Marcos was a good guy," Mr. A said once during dinner. I couldn't look at him. "I voted for him," he continued. "People don't know what it was like. Do you know how Marcos won his election? He made us proud to be Filipino. He was handsome. His wife was beautiful. He stressed the importance of one Filipino people. Before we were all separated. You were of the Tagalog people or the Cebuano people. But never Filipino. He helped us realize we were one people. No more clannishness. No more 'You are from the Luzon, I am from Visaya.' We were one.

"His wife Imelda made it her passion to beautify the country. Make sure it was clean. Make sure there was art and culture. Show the world that we were as capable as any other Asian country of producing masterful pieces. We were not just brown people on some islands. We were civilized.

"They made us proud. I would vote for him again.

"Now they have those damned communists everywhere. Communists everywhere. Ruining everything. That's why Marcos has to be so tough to deal with those people. Make sure communists don't take over the country, making it worse…"

He continued in that vein. He continued speaking like that when he had to close down one of his offices later that year, when he had to sell one of the cars to make the mortgage, and when his hair began to fall out due to stress. He got an ulcer and walked the house at night unable to sleep.

Eventually, he could not deny what was to be the downfall of the Marcos regime. Mr. A could not deny that the life he had tried so hard to maintain was slipping away.

CHAPTER TWENTY-ONE

The Rock Hudson Disease

Dear Monty,   July 30, 1985

Someone you know is in the news. Someone you know is sick. He is another 1950's icon, another beautiful man: Rock Hudson. You know him. He was there for you in your time of need. He was there when your whole world went black. He pulled you from the wreckage. He helped you. Can you please help him?

Dear Monty,   October 4, 1985

Rock Hudson died this week. I'm sad. I'm not dreadfully sad like someone close died. I'm sad because a friend of yours is dead, a friend of mine once removed. I'm sad because Rock Hudson enjoyed the company of other men and so did you. And so do I. I'm afraid. I have to find my mother before I die. Protect me, Monty, protect me.

I believed I would disappear, vanish like Rock Hudson, like so many men in that period. I thought of boys in my school and how I wanted to know them better. I was seventeen and yearning. I thought about boys mostly in the mornings when I touched myself, rubbed myself. I stopped before I spilled. If I didn't spill, there was no way I could get the Rock Hudson disease.

There were times when I felt like I was going to burst. I wouldn't touch myself, rub myself for months. I'd wake up hard and throbbing, but I didn't release myself. If I didn't think about sex,

I thought I wouldn't get AIDS.

I ached for some of the guys at school, guys in magazines, guys on TV. I knew I couldn't do anything, say anything. From a distance, I admired boys at my school, indulged thoughts of loving them. I wanted to hold them the way they held their girlfriends at the entrance of the school, close and endearing. I wanted to whisper romantic words into their ears like, I'll never leave you, honey.

I took comfort in the life of Montgomery Clift. I knew he hid his sexuality, too. I think that is one of the reasons why I liked seeing Monty in his movies: he was hiding. He was visible to millions of people, but he hid. He made a part of himself disappear. I understood the importance of hiding.

CHAPTER TWENTY-TWO

The Dark of the Moon

Dear Monty,   February 26, 1986

Amada and I were extras in a music video. We sat in a crowd, cheering like we were in a rock concert, my voice growing hoarse, my hands flailing.

"Cheer louder," said the director, and we did. "Dance around like you're enjoying yourself." I did that, too. I stood on my seat shaking and jumping, my limbs loose, my hips gyrating.

"CUUUUUUT! We're done for the day."

But I didn't stop dancing. I was too caught up with the good news. Corazon Aquino kicked some Marcos ass! The Marcoses fled the Philippines, Aquino is now president.

I kept dancing, Monty. Life never felt so good.

Dear Monty,   May 2, 1986

Can tragedy and joy exist in the same place? You would know. I know about your life, Monty. When we sit together at the observatory, I know you. I wish you could speak to me, but you don't. You just sit there in black and white, glowing like a screen in a dark movie theater. That's enough for me, knowing you're there. We may sit silently, but I know you. I've read about your tragedy and joy. You had a brilliant career. At the same time, you suffered, taking booze and drugs.

> Tragedy and joy. Two words that line up like a
> solar eclipse. I don't know which word is the sun
> and which is the dark of the moon.

Amada had gone gaga over some guy she met at the video store. She looked at herself in the mirror, asking me if she was pretty enough for her date, a date with some boy named Lou. In her Mirror World was a girl with hair spray in her hair, a long clear neck ready for purple hickeys.

When we got a call to be extras on a movie, I thought Amada would jump at the chance. It was only for a day, and on a Saturday, so we wouldn't miss school.

"I can't. I'm spending the day with my boyfriend," she said. She said "boyfriend" like she just discovered the word, grand and romantic.

I did the extra gig by myself.

Amada wouldn't tell me much about the guy she met in the video store, except that he was perfect.

"I think you'd like him, he's the sweetest guy," she said. "I think my parents will like him, too. He's a nice Catholic boy, graduated from Loyola High School for boys. Now he's going to Loyola Marymount University. He wants to become a doctor someday.

"He thinks becoming an actress is the best thing in the world. He asked me to act for him, so I did a little scene from *The Glass Menagerie*. He loved it. He loves me.

"He gives me flowers and candy, tells me that I'm pretty, tells me that I'm smart and talented."

Although I continued to do extra work, saving money to fly to the Philippines, Amada didn't want to be an extra anymore. "The next time I'm on screen, I'm going to be a lead!" she said.

"It's easy money," I said. Money had been a little tight. Mr. A didn't hand out bills as easily as before.

"I don't care," Amada said. "Besides, I want to spend time with Lou."

Every once in a while, I'd call Mr. Boyd at Amnesty International, hoping for news about my folks. I think he was annoyed with me. We'd have a conversation that usually went like this:

"Bob, if we haven't heard about your parents by now—"

"They're NOT dead."

"I'm not saying they are, but it doesn't look good."

I called on April 5, 1986—I will never forget that date—and good news came.

"Bob," he said, "sometimes a prisoner is released. And if a prisoner is brave enough he'll help us find other prisoners."

"What do you mean?"

"Since Corazon Aquino became president, people are speaking out. Some were people imprisoned by Marcos. Former prisoners are a good way of finding people who disappeared. They provide names of other people who were inside with them."

"Yeah, so?"

"A woman arrived in Honolulu. She was jailed for a few years. She's been free for a while now, but was afraid to talk while she lived in Manila. She finally got her visa to leave. It took her eight years to get that visa."

"Why so long?"

"Well, the Philippines has the longest waiting list in the world to enter the U.S. Someone can wait for up to twenty years. She got off lucky waiting for eight. Now that she's here, she's talking big time. She encountered hundreds of people in political camp. But she was only able to provide names of a few dozen. She listed your father, Emil Luwad."

"You're fucking kidding me?"

"No, son, I'm not."

"I have to talk to her. I have to."

"I'll see what I can do."

Upon hearing the news, I went up to the Griffith Park Observatory and waited for Montgomery Clift to appear. I had begun to have regular meetings with Monty by then. I waited on a bench, the one closest to the bust of James Dean. Within moments he appeared and sat with me. We sat there and looked over the view of Los Angeles, watched the blue sky darken, until he slowly faded away.

•

Amada ran into my room. She was ecstatic. Before I could say hello, she said, "We slept together."

BABY OH BABY.

"Yeah," she said. "We made love. He wanted my first time to be special so he rented this hotel, and we drank champagne, and we did it." She burst into giggles.

"How was it?"

"It was all right. We did it a few times."

"When can I meet him?"

"We're supposed to go out this week. You can meet him then."

We waited for Lou at the Onyx, a cafe in Silverlake. Amada's face sparkled, a child waiting to open her gifts on Christmas day. He was supposed to arrive at 7:30, and by 8:15 Amada was biting her lower lip, glancing at her watch every ten seconds. At 9:00, she got up and made a phone call, signaling me to stay put. She returned, shrugged her shoulders, and sat down. By 10:00, she took up reading the *LA Weekly*, looking up whenever a man passed by. By 11:15, we were told that the cafe was closing. We walked home silently, her arms crossed in front of her.

She stood in the backyard, looking up at the sky. The moon was full, but there were no stars. She stood out there until Mr. A told her to go to bed.

I couldn't tell Amada what I'd suspected. If only she knew what guys talked about in the locker rooms or when they're by themselves. I heard them talk as they dressed or when they'd kill time in the library. The kind of conversation that takes place when boys are around other boys. They talked about their sexual exploits, imagined or real. Or they talked about the kind of sex they'd like to have. They talked about girls and their bodies. Referring to them only as "tits" or "pussy" or "ass."

Amada fell for one of those guys, some shithead named Lou. The kind of guy who would say anything, do anything to get a girl into bed. Then discard her as easily as old gym socks. I couldn't tell her that.

If only she had met another kind of guy. The kind of guy who didn't always talk about "getting some" or "having her." Those boys in the library who looked away embarrassed at hearing our sex demean our female classmates. Or even better, corrected them in talking that way. Those guys who cared about their girlfriends. The kind of guy who walked her home or bought her dinner out of affection, not the underlying greed for sex, sex, sex.

How could Amada know which one to choose when we looked the same. And if a boy is particularly cunning, he can appear as gracious or well meaning as the good boys.

Amada had been gloomy for weeks, thinking of the jerk that stood her up. The same jerk that never returned her phone calls.

"Let's go see *How to Marry a Millionaire*," I said. "It's playing at the Nuart. I can probably get the car and we can drive to see it. It stars Marilyn Monroe, Lauren Bacall, and Betty Grable."

"The last thing I want to see is the story of three girls who try to marry some guy with loads of cash."

I knew something was terribly wrong. Amada never missed a chance to see Marilyn on the big screen. Never. She sat on her bed, rocking herself like the pendulum of a grandfather clock. She looked out the window, her face an open wound.

"Forget about him, Amada."

"I can't."

"Try. You were too good for him."

"I can't forget about him, because I didn't get my period, y'know."

The next time I met Monty, it was for solace...for what was to come.

•

In the midst of Amada's crisis, Mr. Boyd set up a telephone conversation with Mrs. Billaruz, the woman who knew Dad in prison, but was living in Honolulu.

"My father. You saw him?"

"You are Emil's boy?"

"Yes, my dad..."

"Emil and I were picked up the same night. By assholes, those men were assholes. Sorry for my language. *Tanga.* Your dad was beat bad. Pretty bad. They pick us up in Baguio City, transport us to Manila."

"My mother. What about my mother?"

"I don't know about her."

"Tell me about my dad."

"They did things to him. I cannot talk about that. They did

things to us. I cannot talk on the phone about that."

"Where is he?"

"We were together for two years. I was let go. I want to meet you, Emil's boy. I know it is expensive, but can you fly, come to Hawaii?"

"Can you tell me more about my dad?"

"It has been a while. I cannot talk on the phone about what happened. It wouldn't be right. We can talk when you get here. Can you fly?"

"Please tell me, it's been so long. The last time I saw him, he had bruises. Did they disappear?"

"Yes, but new ones came along. When you get here, we can talk more. Can you afford it?"

I thought about the money I'd saved: almost two thousand dollars. "Yeah, sure," I said.

I was afraid. Mrs. Billaruz avoided the subject of my father. I didn't want to ask if he was dead; I didn't want to hear the answer.

•

Amada told me she went looking for Lou, went to his home. She wasn't greeted with the kind of warmth she'd hoped for.

"He doesn't want to see me," she said. "I told him I was pregnant, and he told me he didn't want to see me." She said shithead Lou won't help her.

"But he loved me. I loved him," she said. "When we made love, he told me he loved me. I opened myself up to him because he said he loved me. Love is the most important element in life, right? We should do things out of love."

She buried her head into a teddy bear, and took a deep breath. She looked at me, her sullen face transformed, her lips tightened, her eyes narrowed. "He used me. That prick used me! He used me, that fucking prick used me. I'll make him pay. I'll make that prick pay."

She asked me to leave. "I need to think," she said.

I closed the door behind me, but I could hear things being thrown around, records, dolls, pillows, glass being hurled into the air, denting, bruising the walls.

CHAPTER TWENTY-THREE

A Girl Like Me

Dear Monty,   May 9, 1986

There is a bruise on my arm. I bumped into a door, now there is a bruise. It is purple with a green circle around it. It hurt for awhile, but not so much anymore.

I thought about my parents. The last time I saw them, they had bruises. When Mama was beaten, the bruises seemed to appear like flowers on a vine. When my father's bruises went away, new ones came along, said Mrs. Billaruz. I thought of Amada, her ego, pride, self-confidence, self-love—all bruised.

I wondered how hard it would be to create a bruise. I bumped into a door, bumping my other arm. Nothing happened. I closed my eyes and walked real hard into a wall. Still nothing. I took my arm and slammed it into a bureau. I looked at my arm, and my flesh was still bare. I closed my eyes, and swung my arm around me, my forearm smashing against the edge of a closet door.

I woke up, and my arm had a purple flower. Somewhere between day and night it bloomed on my arm. My mother had bruises all over her body like a garden of purple daffodils.

```
Dear Monty,                          May 12, 1986

It seems Amada and I are having to get through
some really tough shit. I'm trying to be there
for her, but I don't know what to say to her when
she walks around the house like a Zombie, her
mind visiting the No-Name place.

She wanders the house in her bathrobe, sullen and
depressed. Yesterday, I asked her, "Amada, do you
want to go to the mall?"

"What?" she said, tugging on her bathrobe. "I
mean...I mean...I just...No, I don't want..." She
entered her room, and I could hear crying.

I don't bother her about the news of Mrs.
Billaruz, she doesn't need to hear it right now.
Thank God, I have you. No matter what, you're
always willing to listen.
```

Mrs. A had to sell some of her jewelry to pay bills. She didn't shop as much. She sat in front of the TV and gazed at soap operas.

I was an extra for a soap opera, her favorite one. Most soap operas are filmed in New York, but a few are filmed in Los Angeles, like *The Young and the Restless*. I played a guy in a homeless shelter.

"There you are!" Mrs. A shrieked. We watched the TV together waiting for my appearance. The camera swept over the entire set and I was sitting in a corner, trying to look homeless.

"You were really good," Mrs. A said. That was the first time I had seen her happy in a long time. I used to adore Mrs. A, then I hated her. I eventually grew indifferent. I didn't feel anything except the tingle of bruises on my arm, hidden by my long-sleeved shirts.

At the time, I didn't know how extensive my bruising would go. I just knew it was the right thing to do. Hurting myself seemed appropriate. There was comfort in pain, incredible comfort.

●

The sun fell when Amada came into my bedroom. She was calm, too calm. The day's shadow was creeping over, bringing with it small stars that barely twinkled. Amada told me she had decided to have an abortion.

"You can't tell my parents," she said, "they'll freak."

She sat on my bed, acting jittery. Her whole demeanor unnerved me. I looked down and noticed a stain on my Adidas shoes.

"Amada," I said, "if you want to keep the baby, that's all right, too."

"Yeah right, my parents would kill me," she said, rolling over in my bed.

"Amada, I'll marry you. We can get married right now if you want." I didn't want her to have the abortion. I would rather have taken on the responsibility of being a parent than have her do this. I was only eighteen, what did I know about being a parent.

"I'll marry you," I said again.

She sat up, looking sideways, then up and down. "Um, thanks for the offer, but no. I can't. The appointment is set. I have to go a couple of times. For counseling and stuff. Can you come with me?"

I remained quiet.

"I'll do this on my own then," she said, getting up and going to a shelf of books, skimming the titles with her forefinger, pulling one out then putting it back. "I'm going to get my life back," she said. "I believed a boy who said he loved me. You're supposed to do things for people you love." She bowed her head, her black hair falling over her face.

"I visited his parents, y'know…" She took a deep breath, looked up, her eyes red and moist. "I visited Lou's mom and dad. I told them about him, us. I thought they would help, them being Catholic and everything, talk to Lou to do the right thing, maybe make him marry me.

"Do you know what they told me? They told me I got myself into this mess, a girl like me got myself into this mess. A girl like me. They said Lou had a bright future ahead of him. He was going to be a doctor. I'd ruin his life, they said. A girl like me would ruin his life. They said they loved Lou and wouldn't let anything stop him from having a good life.

"Isn't that funny? They wouldn't let anything stop him. I'm an Anything. I'm not going to let anything stop me either. Boys can go on like nothing happened. Girls have to stop. Well, I'm not going to stop. I'll do it myself. I'll get them, Bob. Somehow, I'll make them pay.

"If you don't want to come with me, you don't have to," she said. Then, just before she left, she said, "I would have done anything for you, Bobster. Anything."

•

I drove her to the clinic on Sunset Boulevard. It was her second visit.

"They ask me questions, y'know," she said. "They ask me if I'm sure this is what I want to do."

"What did you say?"

"Yes, it is."

People stood outside the clinic and yelled at us. Anti-abortion people. I gave them The Finger.

"Don't give up your baby," some strange woman said. She lifted up her own kid and said, "See, isn't this child beautiful? You could have one, too."

Amada shook a little.

"Don't you want a baby? Someone of your own to love?" Strange Woman said as we entered the clinic.

"It is because I loved someone of my very own that got me into this mess," Amada yelled back.

I sat in the lobby waiting for Amada. I studied the faces of the anti-abortion people through the window, determined and fierce, all of them gearing their anger at girls like Amada. They didn't know how Amada had suffered through this decision. Seeing her alone in her room, not going out, not being the vital girl she was, was what made me change my mind. Amada had to come first, the girl has to come first.

I know boys get off easy. I saw men out there protesting against abortion, too. Which is the stupidest thing I'd seen. I wondered how many of those anti-abortion men have stuck their dicks in places they shouldn't have. Not a single word of hatred for boys like Lou. Those anti-abortion people should have looked to their sons and brothers before they started blaming girls. I'm sure Lou's parents, being Catholic and all, were against abortion.

We went in for the actual abortion a few days later.

In the meantime, I booked a plane for Hawaii. I paid for two seats. For me and Amada. I thought Amada needed to get away for a while. Graduation was the following month. We'd go then.

School was winding down. The teachers knew that we wouldn't be around so the seniors got to do what they wanted. I'd been doing more extra work for spending cash in Hawaii.

Amada fiddled with her hands as I drove her to the clinic on Sunset Boulevard. There was traffic. I worried if we'd make it in time for her appointment. In the distance, I saw black smoke rising. A building was burning.

A policeman directed cars to alternate routes. I tried to find streets that would take us to the clinic, but all the roads were blocked off. The smoke created a black cloud above us.

"Just park," Amada mumbled. "Park anywhere and we'll walk or something."

"Are you sure?"

"Yeah." Amada's hair was tangled and knotted. She tried to manage her hair by putting it into a ponytail. Her eyes were bloodshot from being unable to sleep.

"Everything will be okay." She didn't hear me. She looked at her hands, then out the window. Then at her hands again.

I found a parking space about five blocks from the clinic. We started walking, watching the sky darken with smoke, hearing sirens scream.

"I hope no one got hurt," I said.

We walked closer to the clinic. Crowds of people began to appear. We squeezed through strangers, jostling to make it to Amada's appointment.

"What happened?" I asked a bystander.

"The clinic. It was bombed," he said. "A few people had to go to the hospital."

Hospital? So much for pro-life. I guess the anti-abortionists really wanted to shut that place down. The fucks.

"Take me home. Take me home right now," Amada whispered into my ear.

•

This whole thing with Amada had gotten me tense. I called Mrs. Billaruz, wanting to hear her voice, a sweet escape from the last few days. I wanted her to talk to me, talk to me about my dad.

"How old are you now?" she asked.

"I'm eighteen."

"I'm sure you are very handsome, *pogi, diba?* Your father was handsome. Emil used to tell me about you."

Hearing my father's name, hearing him talked about like a real person made me high. I wanted more, I wanted her to tell me more...

"There was a girl in camp with us. Her name was Senya. She was a student who was arrested. She had never been away from home before. She used to think of different ways of breaking out. She was a little crazy. She thought of tying a note to a frog, letting the outside know what kind of terrible place camp was. Senya hoped she would be freed.

"Senya had a hard time sleeping. One night we found her searching for frogs. They tried to drag her back in so she can sleep, but I told them not to. We have to have hope. It's what keeps us going. So the entire barracks searched the grounds for a frog for her to tie a note to."

Mrs. Billaruz laughed, a hearty noise much like a low blowing tuba. It was a thrilling sound.

"I'm from Cebu," she said, "I can speak Tagalog, but I would rather speak Cebuano, you know. I remember when they were voting, deciding on a national language for the Philippines. It was down to three. Tagalog, Illocano, and Cebuano. Of course they chose Tagalog because there are more Tagalog people in the Philippines.

"I hate having to speak Tagalog, you know. *Tanga.* But still it is better than Spanish. Thank God those bastards were thrown out of the country. I have Spanish blood in my family, but not much. I know a lot of Filipinos place a lot of status on how much blood you have from Spain. Those people are—how you say? Lame brain.

"People in my province disappear. For no good reason. They were suspected of being Communists. I know those people who disappear. Bullshit. They were poor farmers. Dirt-poor farmers. But all you had to be was suspected, and you were taken away.

"I was a teacher working in Baguio. I led a prayer for my school group. I prayed for the souls of the people who disappear. They took me away for that!"

•

I never saw much of Mr. A. during that time.

"He's out working, looking for clients," Mrs. A said, watching *As the World Turns*. She wore her hair down, instead of wrapped in that tight bun on top of her head.

Mrs. A had lost some of her excitement. She had dulled a little bit, becoming a queen who has lost her kingdom. I couldn't help but feel sad for her. Regardless of everything, she did one good thing: She had Amada.

Auntie Yuna was mean and cranky, but she was a part of my family. I can't hate her completely, it's not her fault that we were accidentally bound together by blood. Mr. and Mrs. A, Amada, Auntie Yuna—all of us tried and tried. And sometimes, the best we were stuck with were mistakes.

•

Amada had another plan. A plan I didn't like at all.

"I need eight hundred dollars," she said.

"Why?"

"Because a girl at school told me where I can go to have an abortion. It'll cost me eight hundred dollars."

"Another clinic?"

"No. Someone she knows. Some guy out in Palmdale."

"Why don't you just go to another clinic?" I asked.

"I've had it with clinics. I've had it with those anti-abortionists being everywhere. I just want to get it over with."

"Amada, are you sure about this? We can find another clinic. I'll help. Just give me some time to find one."

"I am running out of time," she said. She took a deep breath, blowing away the strands of hair on her face. "My life is fucked. I don't want to be one of those girls, the kind people whisper about. I don't want to walk around for nine months with baggy clothes and carry books around my stomach so no one can tell. People'll think I'm a slut or just plain dumb for getting into this mess. My parents'll kill me. They're strict about me going to bed on time. Imagine what they'd do to me if they found out I was pregnant."

"There must be some other way."

"I thought about it every way I could." She took a deep breath. "If I could turn it all back, I would. But I'm stuck. I need your help."

I nodded and agreed to giving her the money she needed.

We left after school, hitting rush-hour traffic. It was almost dark when we got there. I imagined we'd be going to some horrible place in the boonies, but this place wasn't that bad: a brown stucco building in a shopping mall.

I opened my car door when Amada stopped me.

"Stay in the car," she said.

"Why?"

"Look out for bombers or something." She left the car, gave me one long look before entering the building.

I waited for almost three hours. It seemed the earth had rolled over a dozen times when Amada finally came out. She walked kind of funny, her hands over her abdomen.

She got into the car and said, "It's all done."

"Are you all right?"

She nodded, and buckled her seat belt. "When we're this far from the city," she said, "it's a whole different world. It doesn't even seem we're in the same state, the same country. I don't know where I am." She rolled down the window, letting the cool wind fill the car. "The guy was kind of cool. The guy who took care of it for me. He works in that doctor's office. He has keys and comes and goes when he wants. He only sees girls after closing. He was kind of funny, too. He was young. Cleancut. Preppy. He said he didn't want to be burdened with school loans when he got out of college. He's saving up for medical school. He does this on the side to pay for tuition." She turned on the radio, and couldn't find a station she liked. She turned it off. "I can't wait to graduate this year. I'll move away. We can live together. Move back to San Francisco, maybe. You'd like San Francisco. Or New York. I've always wanted to live in New York. Start brand new. Brand new. I'll study acting and become an actress like Marilyn."

There was barely any traffic. We zoomed back to the sparkling lights of the city. We saw the Hollywood Sign, we knew we were almost home.

CHAPTER TWENTY-FOUR

In the Blackness of My Mind

Dear Monty,   June 10, 1986

Amada and I didn't make graduation. We weren't up
for it. I'm still trying to make sense of the
last month. Having to rush Amada to the hospital
scared the shit out of me. I don't know what I
would have done if I'd lost her. I don't know
what I'd do if she vanished.

Living here is torture. Mr. and Mrs. A are in a
perpetual state of fury. I feel like I'm walking
around in a glass house. The only thing that kept
me going was my conversations with Mrs. Billaruz.
And I can't even do that anymore.

Amada and I have Hawaii to look forward to. And
I start college in the fall. Amada and I are
going to leave, find our own place, get away from
this house.

It was late and dark when Amada came into my room.
"Something's wrong," she said. The only thing I could see was the
outline of her body as she stood in the doorway. I switched on the
lamp beside my bed, and Amada was scared shitless. Her nightgown
was stained red. Her hands were bloody.

"Oh, God. Oh, God," I said rushing to her. She leaned against
me. Her feet were locked together, blood streamed down her legs.

"I have to get your parents. I have to," I said, laying her on the
floor.

I called for Mr. and Mrs. A. They shuffled down the hall. "What's the matter?" Mr. A asked. He saw Amada and gasped. Mrs. A ran to her, screaming: "Amada, Amada, AMADA!"

I called 911.

In my bedroom, Mr. and Mrs. A huddled around their daughter, rocking her. Amada kept hitting her stomach, yelling over and over again, "STOP! MAKE IT STOP! STOP BLEEDING!" Mr. A yelled louder: "CALM DOWN!!! GODDAMMIT CALM DOWN!!!" And Mrs. A yelled, too. She said nothing in particular.

In the distance, a siren approached, a whirring whistle—ongoing and unceasing. Dogs in the neighborhood reacted by barking, howling. All around me was noise. A cacophony of wailing.

●

At the hospital, Amada slept. She had been there for twenty-four hours. We camped out in the hospital waiting room.

"Do you know what happened?" Mr. A asked again.

I pretended not to hear. I thought about Amada and how she handled Lou going AWOL, disappearing. Disappearances are hard, I knew. Something I began to comprehend was the fleeting nature of human beings. We have the remarkable capacity of leaving others far behind, severing any or all relations. Sometimes by force like my parents. Most times by choice like Lou. Like Robert Bulanan. Like J. Like Auntie Yuna.

"What happened?" Mr. A asked again. I shook my head I don't know. Mrs. A clutched a rosary, reciting Hail Marys, praying. I wanted to tell her that prayers get tangled up like balloon strings.

I stared at the wall, desperately wanting a book. I wanted to wander the hospital, look for a thick medical book, and blotch.

A doctor walked into the room. "Your daughter will be fine," he said. "She will have to stay in the hospital for a few days. She began to hemorrhage from her abortion, but she'll be fine. If you have the name of the doctor, I'd like to have it. He did very shoddy work. He should be reported."

Silence.

"Abortion? We did not know she had one," Mr. A said.

The doctor took a deep breath realizing what he'd done.

"May we see her?" Mrs. A asked.

"Certainly, but let her rest," he said, and led us to her room.

Amada was unconscious. Her breathing was slow and even. Mrs. A caressed her face with incredible warmth. Mr. A looked solemnly at her, sitting on a chair by the bed, shaking his head. I stood against the wall, barely breathing, afraid of upsetting the quiet of the room.

I closed my eyes, letting my mind wander away, far, far away. I slid down the wall, resting my knees against my chest. I thought of Amada's face in the blackness of my mind, and I thought, It will be all right. Can you hear me, Amada? I love you. It will be all right. I love you.

I got up and quietly left the room, walking down the hall, finding a restroom. I didn't need to do anything in particular. I just wanted to get away. I looked into the mirror. In the Mirror World, I stared back at myself, seeing the pimples and the hairs sprouting from that ridge between my lips and my nose. I peered into the dark universe of my eyes. Suddenly, my eyes turned blue, and Monty appeared before me. We looked at each other, and I was comforted.

I reached out to touch him, but only felt the cold glass. I pressed my hand into the mirror, trying to break into the Mirror World, but the barrier wouldn't give.

I desperately wanted to be with him.

I washed my face, looked up, and Monty had disappeared like false hope. I screamed internally, COME BACK! COME BACK! I went to a toilet stall. I opened the door to the stall, placed my arm between the stall and the door, then slammed the door into my arm. I slammed it again and again, until welts ran up and down my arm. The welts stayed for a few days, until Amada returned home.

She stayed in her room, slumbering. When she woke, she didn't want to see anyone, not even me. Mrs. A brought her meals, staying for long periods of time.

Mr. A silently watched TV or read his newspapers. In the mornings, he drank his coffee with little sips, not speaking to me or to his wife. He didn't ask about Amada.

•

My only respite from all of this was talking to Mrs. Billaruz. But even those conversations were uneasy as she avoided talking about my father.

"What exactly happened in prison?" I'd asked.

"When you visit, we can talk," is all she'd say.

I kept calling her until Mr. A told me to stop.

"Bob, are you the one making those phone calls to Hawaii?" he asked me, pissed off.

I nodded.

"Stop it. They're too expensive."

•

I woke up one morning and Amada's bedroom door was wide open. I peered in; she was gone. I looked all over the house, but she wasn't around. Mrs. A's car wasn't in the driveway. I thought Amada had gotten up in the middle of the night and took off, not letting anyone stop her from doing what she wanted to do.

Amada's a free spirit, I thought, freer than birds, freer than the air birds glided upon. I wondered if she left me a good-bye note somewhere, letting me know that she was going to San Francisco or New York. Then again, it didn't matter, as long as she was free, like the untamed horses in *The Misfits*.

I ate my cereal. I heard Mrs. A's car pull up in the driveway. The front door opened. I went into the foyer. It was Mrs. A. Amada followed.

"What are you doing today?" Mrs. A asked me.

"I'm going to the library," I said, keeping my eyes on Amada. She didn't look at me; she kept her eyes to the ground. She wore a pink satin dress that looked like an upside-down tulip.

"Good. Wait for Amada. She'll go with you."

Amada went upstairs, and I sat in the living room. I knew it would take a while for Amada to get out of that hideous dress, and change into something else like Calvin Klein jeans with a Pendleton shirt.

"Are you ready?" It was Amada still dressed in the upside-down tulip. She tied her hair into a ponytail.

"Sure."

For most of our walk, Amada was silent. I asked her how she was.

"All right," she said.

"Where did you go this morning?"

"To church. Mom wants me to go with her to morning mass for

a while."

"How was it?"

"Okay. Mom wants me to pray every morning, go to confession, beg God to forgive me for what I did. I probably have to do what they say for a while, which includes wearing stupid dresses like this all the time."

"Are you sorry you did it? Had the abortion, I mean."

"Hell, no. I'm just pissed at that stupid butcher. I called the doctor's office he worked in and told them that a guy was using their offices for abortions. They asked me who it was, and I described the guy. Turns out it was the son of one of the doctors there. I hope he gets the shit beaten out of him, that good for nothing motherfucker."

I laughed. She put her arm in mine and we went off to the library.

•

Getting back into her parents' good graces hadn't been as easy as Amada had thought. She had been going to morning mass for two weeks.

"How long do I have to keep going?" Amada asked Mrs. A.

"Until I think it's time to stop," Mrs. A said.

"When will that happen?"

"I don't know."

"Christ, it wasn't like I murdered anyone."

"That's exactly what you did," Mrs. A quickly replied and left Amada at the breakfast table. Amada's eyes followed Mrs. A out of the kitchen.

"I hate this place," Amada said to me.

"They'll come around," I said.

"At least my mom's talking to me. Dad hasn't said shit to me."

•

Eventually, Mr. A did say something. Boy, did he. We were eating at a restaurant in Chinatown. Just eating. I didn't expect the meal to become a war.

"Did you choose a college?" Mr. A asked me.

"I'm going to USC," I said. "They gave me a great financial package, covering most of my tuition."

We ate quietly for most of the dinner, until Mr. A asked Amada what she was going to do. It was the first time Mr. A spoke to her. And Amada, in her usual style, said something to piss him off.

"I'm going to be an actress," Amada said.

"An actress? Not that again."

"I was gonna take classes."

"And who's going to pay for them?"

"I'll get a job."

"You don't know how to do anything."

"I'll learn to do something."

"Go to community college. Find something you like. Then study that. Try it our way for once."

"I'll do it my way."

"Like getting expelled. Like almost killing yourself by having an abortion?"

"It's my life."

"Let's go," Mrs. A said, "people are staring at us."

Without asking for the bill, Mr. A threw down some money, and raced to the car. The rest of us quickened our pace, trying to keep up with him.

We got into the car and as we drove, Mr. A yelled, "I'm sick and tired of this, Amada. You keep making the most stupid decisions. Stupid ideas in your head!"

"Stop yelling," Mrs. A said.

"They're not stupid!" Amada said.

"I said stop yelling," Mrs. A repeated quietly, rubbing her temples. "Amada, listen to your father. It would be a good idea to think of something else to do. Acting is a hard job."

"That's what I want to do."

"I don't want to hear any more, Amada," Mr. A said. "I'm sick and tired of you talking, always talking nonsense, always doing nonsense. Like having an abortion."

"I'd do it again," Amada said, crossing her arms.

"Amada!" Mrs. A brought her hands to her mouth.

"You do whatever you want without thinking," Mr. A said, speeding up the car. "Your mother and I tried to have other children. We tried so hard. We tried for years. After you were born, we still tried to have more. Give you brothers or sisters. We wanted more children. A house with children is blessed by God. Don't you know that? That's why we wanted Bob. A house with more children is blessed by God." Mr. A quickly braked at a red light. The car stopped halfway in the intersection. He turned around, his face shooting daggers at Amada. "And you go ahead and just get rid of children like it doesn't matter."

That was unfair. It did matter to Amada. I knew that and she knew that.

"WHAT DO YOU WANT FROM ME?!" Amada said.

Mr. A didn't have an answer, but Mrs. A did. She spoke softly, but firmly, "I want you to be sorry. I want you to want forgiveness. But you don't. You don't care. When do you start caring?"

The light turned green. We drove the rest of the way in silence. Once we got into the house, Amada said to her parents, "I'm not sorry for what I did. If I had the baby, you would have given me hell about that, too. No matter what choice I would've made, it would have been a bad one. I learned a long time ago, you will never be happy with who I am or what I do. So I decided to make whatever decision I wanted."

As Amada started her slow ascent upstairs, Mr. A hollered, "Amada, come back down here. Where are you going?"

"Mother, I'm not going to go to morning mass," was all she said.

Her bedroom door slammed shut.

In the morning, I knocked on Amada's door. I knocked a lot, but she didn't answer. I went downstairs to get some breakfast, waiting for her to come down. She didn't. I went back upstairs and knocked on her door some more. I twisted the knob; it was locked.

"Amada?" I said, "Wake up. I want to buy some things before we leave for Hawaii in a few days."

She still didn't come to the door. I said her name again and again and again, my voice rising each time. I banged on her door, but nothing. I shoved my weight against the door, yelling Amada's name. Still nothing. I kept shoving and shoving until the door gave way. I saw Amada on her bed, naked. She wasn't moving and a little brown plastic bottle was on the floor. I shook her. I held her in my arms, tears welling up in my eyes.

"Amada, please wake up. Please, please, please." I rocked her, holding her still body. Then I whispered a message in my mind to her soul: Come back, please come back.

I felt her rib cage expand. She took in a big breath. "Damn, I'm good," she said. "You really thought I was dead, didn't you. I'm going to be a great actress. My parents don't know shit."

I let her go, her body fell against the mattress. She bounced, giggling.

"Bitch," I said.

CHAPTER TWENTY-FIVE

Words Burned Into My Mind

Dear Monty,   July 25, 1986

I flew over the Pacific Ocean, the second time in my life, and landed in Honolulu. Mrs. Billaruz met us at the airport.

"Hello, my sweet boy," she said, then planted a wet kiss on my cheek. She took Amada and me to her small two-bedroom apartment. She'd been kind enough to let me and Amada crash here. Mrs. Billaruz sleeps in one room, Amada sleeps in the other bedroom and I sleep on the pullout sofa.

I wanted to talk to her about my parents right away, but Mrs. Billaruz said, "You rest first. We talk in the morning." I couldn't sleep, so I decided to write to you. Morning can't come quick enough.

There was something comforting about Mrs. Billaruz; her round barrel belly jiggled when she talked. She wore shapeless, tent-like dresses with flower prints. Amada would hang out at the beach while Mrs. Billaruz and I spent time together.

"I would pray," she said. "There was a lot of time just doing nothing. So much time. There were a lot of random executions…" She sat still for a long while, her eyes darted back and forth. "Sometimes the prisons would get full and they would have to make room somehow."

"My dad was kept alive?"

"So, the random executions. I spoke English good," she said. "I sounded smart, but anyone who knows me knows that is not true," she laughed. "They kept me alive, because I knew English good. Those guards were afraid of English. They were intimidated by it."

"But my dad?"

"They did things to some of the people," she said. "Things I do not know you should hear. How old are?"

"Eighteen. I'm old enough—"

"So young. I don't think you know how cruel people can be sometimes."

"I understand that my father was taken away and my mother is missing. Help me understand more."

"Sometimes, sweet boy, I don't understand it myself." She reached into a nearby bureau, and pulled out a pack of cigarettes. She lit one and said, "I'm sorry to have made you come all this way, but it is hard to talk about what happened." She blew a long stream of smoke into the air.

"They do things to a woman," she said. "They degrade her. Pinch her nipples, make her lie on the floor naked while men look down. They grab parts of her. They rape her, hold her down, while they take turns. She may scream, but they don't care. They like it when she screams so they can release themselves into her mouth. This is what they do. They do this. They do this for hours." She sucked on the cigarette, keeping the smoke inside her for several seconds, then let it go. "They did this to me," she said.

"Oh, god."

She put out her cigarette, puffs of smoke dissipating in the air. She straightened her dress and stretched her legs. She looked at me, providing me with a faint smile, and said, "I am tired, sweet boy." She got up and went into her room.

They do things to women, she said. I pulled out one of Mrs. Billaruz's cigarettes and lit it. I coughed on my first inhalation.

Monty smoked. I knew he did. I'd seen lots of pictures with cigarettes in his hands.

They do things to women. I went to sleep with those words burned into my mind.

•

Amada scored some weed from some German tourists. I smoked some. It was our last day in Hawaii.

"I'm going to miss this place," she said. "Have you been talking a lot with Mrs. Billaruz?"

"Yes."

"Cool. Tell me."

"My father's dead."

"No way."

I didn't say anything for a long time.

Mrs. Billaruz sat me down and said, "About your father. How badly do you want to know what happened?"

"Real bad," I said.

Then she gave me a look. In that look, I knew something was going to devastate me. She said, "If you want to know then I'll tell you."

She told me everything. She told it. From start to finish. "We were picked up," she said, "taken to a safehouse. Let me tell you something, there is nothing safe about a safehouse.

"They bent him backwards so the back of his head and the bottom of his feet faced each other. They tied his neck and feet together. The guards told him to sign a confession or else they would let him choke himself to death. Emil wouldn't sign a confession. They wanted him to admit to being a Communist. 'I am not a Communist,' he said, but the guards didn't listen. They let Emil squirm on the floor, like an animal. When Emil's legs got tired, he would try to straighten them, making himself gag. Spit came out of his mouth, tears came from his eyes, mucous came out his nose. Every opening on his face spilled liquid. After a while, the liquid turned red. I saw this happen. They wanted me to see.

"'Sign the confession,' a guard would say, 'then we can stop hurting you.'

"If he signed a confession, it meant they would have proof that he was a threat to the government and could put him away for a long time. He wouldn't sign. So they cut the rope, and beat him, kicked him. They knew he was a writer, so they stomped on his hands. They broke his hands.

"Blood covered his face. His face looked like wet turnips, bulging and red. But he still wouldn't sign. They beat him for hours. It was night when they started torturing him. It was daylight when they stopped. They quit for a while, then beat him for several more hours.

"Then they electrocuted him. They made him strip off his clothes. They tied wires to his thing, his penis. Jolted him with electricity. He screamed. He screamed. The electricity made him jump. Made his whole body shake and shake and shake. But he wouldn't sign. Then one of the guards said, 'Maybe we should go back and get your wife, get your kid. Do you think they can take as much pain?'

"When the guard said that, Emil signed. With his broken hand he signed."

I felt sick, my stomach ready to explode. I had this image of my dad, swollen and messed up. I wanted to vomit, but I sat there still.

"Your father and me were sent to a prison camp in Manila. Your father shivered a lot. He was always cold, he kept shaking. Sometimes he would be mean to the guards and spit at them. He couldn't speak anymore so he would just spit at them. Sometimes they put him in solitary confinement for it. Locked away in the dark for months at a time."

I wanted to run out of the room, scream, flailing my arms like a madman. Then I saw Monty Clift, standing beside Mrs. Billaruz. He wore a T-shirt and badly faded blue jeans. His hair looked windblown, partly falling across his forehead. He gave me a comforting nod. I was taken out of Mrs. Billaruz's apartment and transported to another place, a lodge perhaps. I wasn't in Hawaii anymore, I was in a country home. There was a ceiling with beams. Outside were trees, a squirrel ran on a branch. I didn't know where I was but I felt safe.

"Sweet boy," I heard a voice say.

In an instant I was back in Hawaii. Mrs. Billaruz' voice jarred me into reality.

"My boy, maybe I should stop. I talked too much already."

"No. Go on. Please, go on."

I stayed and listened some more. My small retreat with Monty reenergized me, but my fingernails dug into my arms. I felt my nails rip into my flesh as she continued.

"There were times when the prison was so full, they took people away, killed them. Just to make room. Your father was one of the men they took away. Executed."

The tips of my nails were imbedded in my skin.

"Don't do that," Mrs. Billaruz said, pulling my hands from me. She placed her palms over my arms, massaging the skin.

I left Mrs. Billaruz and found Amada on the beach. She handed me the joint. I inhaled, waiting for I don't know what. "I don't feel anything," I said.

"You have to wait a little while for it to take effect."

PART THREE

CHAPTER TWENTY-SIX

Peering Through Dirty Water

Dear Monty,   May 1, 1987

Freshman year at USC was a dud. The best moments
were the ones I spent with you. I rented your
movies, the ones that were available. When I
watch one of your films, I don't have to think
about anything: school disappears, my father's
death goes away, my mother's absence becomes
nothing to me. I don't want to think about my
parents or the Marcos regime. I don't want anything to do with the Philippines.

I bought that movie Lonelyhearts. (Well, I told
the video store that I lost it and was willing to
pay for it.) I wanted to see that movie over and
over until my heart wept. Lonelyhearts validated
all that I'd believed between us.

You had a job writing the Miss Lonelyhearts col-
umn, receiving letters from lost souls seeking
comfort, begging for advice. You read their letters, putting every bit of yourself into helping
these desperate people, getting entangled in
their lives.

Sometimes after my last class, I'll come home,
close my eyes and summon you. I'll call your
name: Monty, Montgomery, Mr. Clift. I'll drift
into a black and white movie; we're together.
I'll watch you work in Miss Lonelyhearts. I'll
sit next to you in your office. The walls are

gray and dreamy like peering through dirty water.
You answer letters.

I'll sit at a desk in the corner while you review
words from the unhappy. I can see the small lines
on your face, the tiny pores in your skin, your
bushy brows bunching up when you get confused.
You're older in this movie, your hair is thin-
ning, but you're still handsome, so handsome. And
fragile, delicate like a frail kitten. Every once
and awhile you'll look up at me and nod, confirm-
ing my existence.

I live for these moments, Monty. I live for them.
Nothing ever felt so good; the only thing missing
is your touch. How do I touch you, feel you?

Monty, I crave your arms around me.

I got a job at a restaurant near school. And after my last shift, I'd
walk around and study the contours of my new neighborhood.
The broken streets (probably from good ole California earth-
quakes) sprouted threads of green grass. The tips of downtown
buildings looked like giant needles, and at night, small rubies and
diamonds of light flickered from them.

It was the people that made the place; the skin tones attracted
me. They were mostly black, Latino, with a few Asians. The Asians
were mainly Koreans working in shabby liquor stores.

There was an elementary school nearby. The shades of brown
bouncing up and down in the schoolyard, hitting yellow balls tied to
metal poles, made me dizzy, drunk in a way. If I unfocused my eyes,
creating a blur in my vision, the children looked like part of the
earth. The earth danced.

I'd walk through the university at night. It looked different. It
passed for serene, romantic. I'd sit on the grass by Taper Hall and
watch the dark branches of ominous trees sway to the nudge of
wind. I'd take a swig of vodka from a small flask I carried in my back
pocket, light a cigarette, and think of my father.

I tried to conjure his face in my mind, but I didn't remember it.
I didn't remember him. He was just a blur. I hadn't cried for him.

How could I cry for a blur?

•

Mr. and Mrs. A moved into a little townhouse in Pasadena. It was nothing like the house in Los Feliz, but it was nice enough. Amada seemed to be getting along better with her folks since she and I moved out.

"Why do you want to live on your own? Why don't you move home and save that rent money?" Mrs. A asked.

"Because you and I would kill each other," Amada said. "And besides, there really isn't any room." They had a two-bedroom place, and I knew Mr. A wanted to use the other bedroom as an office to work out of. Selling the house broke Mrs. A's heart.

Mrs. A's hands and neck were bare, no more sparkling gems. She had sold most of her good jewelry to pay off debt.

Mrs. A would reach for my face, but I'd pull away. I didn't want to be around her. I didn't want to be around Mr. and Mrs. A. After what Mrs. Billaruz told me, I couldn't help but see them as contributors to my father's death. And the rapes, the horrible rapes.

Amada was not pleased with my behavior, saying, "Mom and Dad want to know why you don't come around."

"Just don't feel like it."

"They think of you as a son. As far as I'm concerned, you are their son and you're my brother."

"I'm a part of the Arangan family, because my own family disappeared. Your parents made that happen."

"Jesus Christ. They're not mass murderers, Bob. They're my folks. I know my parents can be lunatics, but nothing like you're saying."

"I just don't want to be around them. I can't."

Amada, dear sweet Amada. I loved her, but she'd been bugging the shit out of me. She had gotten nosy, asking me things she shouldn't. I almost regretted renting an apartment with her near school.

"How did you get those bruises on your legs?" Amada asked.

"I bumped into something."

"You've been acting weird all year. It's about your dad, isn't it?"

"I guess."

"You gotta get outta this funk, Bob. Somehow you gotta get out of it. All this negative energy isn't good for you. It isn't good for me."

Amada had been cranky. Her acting career hadn't taken off like she'd planned.

"You never want to go out," she said, "just come home and get drunk."

"Lay off, Amada."

"I got a lot of shit going on, too. Mom and Dad having to sell the house and everything. I can't get hired to save my life. Maybe it's my headshots. Maybe if I get new headshots. The last thing I gotta worry about is you."

"You don't gotta worry about me."

She gave me a wicked little look that said, I'm going to kill you if you give me grief. She left the room.

She didn't have to worry about me. I had Monty. I knew he was taking care of me. I spent every opportunity I could with him. I was still functioning then, still leading a life. It didn't get really bad until later.

I was able to go to school, communicate with people, send Christmas cards to professors I'd really liked. I sent a New Year's card to Mr. Boyd at Amnesty International wishing him the very best. I also thanked him for doing what he could to find my parents. I thought of sending Mrs. Billaruz a card also, but I didn't. I just wanted to forget her, forget everything.

I recalled a scene in *The Misfits*, the first scene that Monty was in. He waited by a phone booth, waiting for a call from his mother. Clark Gable and Marilyn Monroe pulled up to him in their car. His mother called and he told her his face was healing nicely. In the movie, Montgomery Clift smashed it up in a rodeo he was competing in. I knew it must have been a difficult scene to do because, in real life, he smashed up his own face in a car accident. He was never the same again.

My head fell back and my mind drifted until I was there with Monty in *The Misfits*. I stood outside that phone booth, my face pressing up against the glass walls, steaming up the window. He looked at me again. He smiled. It didn't matter that Clark Gable and Marilyn Monroe were waiting for him in a car a few yards away, it still felt like we were alone. It was just us.

I continued to do extra work. Extra work had paid for a lot of shit, like books or a movie or an extra night out. I was saving up for wheels.

I was an extra for a credit card commercial in Downtown L.A. It was supposed to be a warm summer in the commercial, but it was ball-busting winter in real life. Between the fake summer and the real winter, I'd choose the summer anytime.

"Try not to shiver," the director ordered the extras. I kept warm by smoking weed in the john between takes.

I didn't do extra work all the time, just whenever. It was a break from my regular waiter job. Amada refused to do extra work, but she worked with me at the same restaurant.

"Wait a minute," I said. "You're willing to wait tables, but you won't do extra work?"

"That's right. Waiting tables is a ritual on the way to becoming a great actress."

Amada took acting lessons in Hollywood while I finished up general education requirements at USC.

Amada had gotten her first real acting gig. It was only a student film, but Amada was psyched about it.

"I've got lines," she said. "I've got lines."

"What do you do in it?"

"I play this foreign exchange student who falls in love with this American. I kill myself because he rejects me in the end."

I was happy for her. I really was.

I hadn't declared a major yet.

CHAPTER TWENTY-SEVEN
Longing in My Heart

Dear Monty,   February 8, 1988

I bought a motorcycle. It was cheaper than a car.
The guy sold it to me for next to nothing. He
gave me some riding lessons. I almost have the
hang of it.

I'm learning to do wheelies in the parking lot.
Once, I fell. I scraped my forearm, an abrasion,
pink and white, formed on my arm. It tingled like
fizz.

I spent hours and hours in the school library. Page 168 was mine. I saw a guy in my Human Values class with a book that I knew I'd blotched. The guy was a real jerk, big loser fratboy with an I'm-better-than-you-bullshit-attitude. He'd come into class hung over, sitting with his frat brothers, joking about I didn't know what. The book I blotched sat on the portable desk in front of him. I stared at him, his blond crewcut and grubby sweatshirt with Greek letters emblazoned on the front.

Loser Frat Boy turned around and caught me staring. I think he was scared of me. He was probably from some suburb somewhere in the Midwest and got antsy when a minority looked at him. Especially since I didn't shave as much, drove a beat-up motorcycle, and wore a faded leather jacket, which kept me warm when I rode my bike.

He looked at the professor, and he looked back at me. I met his gaze every time. What the hell are you looking at, loser? I thought to him, knowing that he probably thought the same about me.

•

I told Mrs. A to leave me alone. She called and I told her I didn't
want her in my life.

"Bob?" Mrs. A said over the phone, "Amada tells me you won't
be home for New Year's Eve. You didn't come for Thanksgiving or
Christmas either."

"No. I'm busy."

"Bob, this is the third time you won't spend time with us on the
holidays. What did we do, Bob? What did we do that you don't want
to be around us anymore? Please come home. We are planning a
special dinner. My husband's business seems to be picking up. Why
do you want to be alone?"

I wasn't alone. I had Monty. Amada and I bought a pathetic little
tree and decorated it with her earrings. On Christmas Eve, Monty
sat across from me, sharing some eggnog. He wore a tuxedo. I felt
underdressed in my flannel pajamas. We looked at each other all
night, longing in my heart. I reached out to touch him, but my hand
went through his apparition. I tried repeatedly to hold his hand, but
the attempt was futile. When Christmas morning came, Monty left,
disappearing before my eyes.

"I'm not going over for Thanksgiving or Christmas or anything
else. It's because of you I don't have parents. It's because of people
like you!"

"Bob, what are you talking about?"

I told her about my folks.

"Bob," Mrs. A said, "we had nothing to do with it. We would
never hurt you."

"BUT YOU DID!" I said. I had an incredible urge to tell Mrs. A
to fuck off and eat shit. So I did: "FUCK OFF AND EAT SHIT." I
slammed the phone down.

I sobbed, pulling out a bottle of red wine. After a few glasses, I
hopped on my bike and cruised. I went down Hoover Street, then
down Alvarado. I hung out at MacArthur Park, watching homeless
guys find shelter in some bushes.

Then I was off again, jumping onto the Santa Monica Freeway,
cruising, just cruising. I went so fast the lights of the city turned into
long lines of neon blurs. Wind rushed through my hair like a furi-

ous river. I opened my mouth and screamed. My voice got lost in the wind, muffled by the sound of the freeway, falling away like dead leaves.

I swerved in front of a car, and it honked at me. I sped up some more hearing the hoooooooonk become a distant whistle. I got to the beach, and stood by the Pacific Ocean.

I waited. I waited for Monty. He walked up the shore in cuffed gray trousers, a camel hair coat hung over his shoulder. He looked romantic walking on the sand, glowing like a silver screen, shining in the dark evening.

We looked at each other, and I embraced him. My arms went right through him. I tried to embrace him again, but I ended up holding myself. I kicked the sand, getting on my hands and knees, throwing the sand everywhere, screaming. I screamed into the cold night air, into the deep purple sky. I screamed until my voice was gone.

He gave me a little smile. A smile that comforted me, that said he loved me, that said he wanted to feel me, too.

CHAPTER TWENTY-EIGHT
Our First Touch

Dear Monty,   April 17, 1989

We connected! We finally did it. Touch, kiss.
We're together. I will never forget tonight.
We're bound now. Forever, and ever and ever.

It was better than I'd expected. I know you love
me, you love me. I love you, too.

Loser Frat Boy was in the library. He saw me. I didn't feel like dealing with him; I went to a different part of the library. He followed me. He got on my nerves so I left. He followed me out. I turned around, but he looked like he was just examining the floor. I got to the parking lot. He was still behind me. I turned around and said, real annoyed, "What?!"

He looked at me funny, and motioned me to a darker part of the lot. I followed. He came up real close to me and started sniffing me. He kissed my neck. I didn't stop him. He put his lips on my mouth. He smelled of Ralph Lauren Polo cologne. And with the moon bright like a silver dollar, I thought of Monty, Montgomery Clift. He entered my head, my mind, pouring out of me, through my eyes, nose, and mouth until he was standing in front of me.

He was the one I was kissing in that parking lot, not Loser Frat Boy. It was him. He put his tongue into my mouth, tasting like Reese's Peanut Butter Cups. The breath from his nostrils blew onto my right cheek. He cupped his hands around my head, pressing against me. BABY OH BABY.

I was lost in him, feeling the width of Monty's torso: the shoulder blades writhing there; the pull of tense muscles encapsulating ridges of the rib cage; the stomach, expanding then falling back like the tides of a sea; the roots of the spine sprouting from the small of the back. I held him close because he belonged to me.

It was my very first kiss and it was with him.

I wanted more, so much more. I felt his hardness through the denim Levi's. I played with the buttons of his button fly, undoing them. I felt the cotton briefs. Then he disappeared.

"Kissing is the farthest I'll go," Loser Frat Boy said. He buttoned up his jeans, straightened his hair. I saw the glisten of my spit on his upper lip. He wiped it away, and walked toward the row of Greek houses, where he lived. Kissing is the farthest I'll go…he was afraid of the Rock Hudson disease.

I got on my bike and cruised around L.A., down Wilshire Boulevard, up Olympic. I celebrated our first touch, our first kiss, laughing all the way. I stopped next to cars and said, "How's your evening coming along?" Most rolled up their windows, stared straight ahead, praying for the light to turn green. Others said, "It's cool, bro. How's yours?"

"It's awesome, dude, just awesome," I said.

I stepped on the gas, and was off. I left the West Side and headed east, cruising downtown, up Hope Street, down Hill Street.

•

I couldn't just kiss him once. I had to kiss him again, feeling his breath blow against my upper lip. I was addicted to him.

"Where you going?" Amada asked me.

"Out."

"Again? That's all you do. Help me memorize lines. I have an audition for a soap opera tomorrow. I play a hospital patient with cancer. I choose to die so I can join my dead husband who was hit by a bus."

"I don't think so. I have to meet a friend." I was out the door, on my bike, searching.

I kissed him. Again and again and again. It got easier every time. I found him in a dark bar, where other men look for men of their dreams. In the bars, where the lights are low, and facial features shift like sand in the deep ocean, I found him. I found him in West Hollywood.

A man bought me a drink, and introduced himself as Paul. We talked about nothing. Later in his apartment, we rolled around on the floor. I summoned Monty.

Montgomery Clift held me. He told me to take off my shirt and I did. He told me to take off my pants and I did. He told me to taste his nipple and I did. We rubbed together like two sticks trying to start a fire.

"I need you," I said.

"I need you, too." And hearing him say that was sweet, sweet honey down my throat. I wanted him to need me, want me.

We lay in our wetness, sweat and semen and saliva.

"You wanna beer?" somebody said.

Monty disappeared. Paul returned, hideous Paul.

"You wanna beer? I got some beer."

"No, uh, thanks though."

"I hope I didn't give you those," he said pointing to bruises on my thigh.

"No, I got a bike. Sometimes, when I ride, I straddle my seat a little too hard." I didn't tell him that I gave those bruises to myself.

"Never been with an Asian guy before. What are you? Chinese? Vietnamese?"

"Filipino."

"You were tasty. Gimme your number."

I wrote down some made-up digits on a piece of paper and gave it to him.

I took off.

On my bike, wind brushed by me like a rude stranger. Boozed up from the bar and high from making love with Monty, I cruised home, hoping he wouldn't eat garlic next time.

I zoomed through the hills, the Hollywood Hills. I knew somewhere around there, Monty had his car accident. The accident that smashed up his beautiful face. I didn't know where the exact spot was, though. I just knew he was coming from a party at Elizabeth Taylor's house. He got a little drunk. He had gotten into heavy booze and drugs by then, some say because he couldn't accept his homosexuality. Elizabeth Taylor's husband Michael Wilding was there, Rock Hudson was there, his friend Kevin McCarthy was there. I read that he enjoyed the company of Kevin McCarthy and his wife.

Monty was supposed to follow Kevin down the canyon road. Somehow he lost control of his car, maybe blacking out. He hit a tree.

Kevin McCarthy went back to Elizabeth's house. He told her that Monty was in a car wreck. She drove down, and found the mangled car. She climbed in and saw Monty on the floor of the front passenger seat. His head was bloated beyond belief. His face split open. Blood was everywhere, on the floor, on his clothes, staining Elizabeth's white dress. Monty was choking, heaving like something needed to get out. Elizabeth thought he might die. She reached into Monty's mouth, and dug out two teeth that were lodged in his throat.

People tried to pull him from the wreckage of his car. One of those people was Rock Hudson.

I drove through the hills looking for the spot of the accident. I wanted to know all aspects of Monty's life, the tragedy and the joy. I couldn't find the exact spot where the accident occurred. I tried but couldn't.

Monty was never the same after the accident, getting addicted to painkillers on top of the other drugs and booze that became a part of his regular diet. He was slowly dying, withering away like a useless limb. And so was I.

•

I'd thought of Mrs. Billaruz, especially when the man who started it all was dead. The dictator was dead. Ferdinand Marcos died in that year of 1989. I read it in the paper. Funny. He couldn't take all of his power and his wealth with him. He spent his presidential term attaining wealth, stealing from the Philippines, billions of dollars gone. He placed people in prison who disagreed with him. He took parents away. He died and couldn't take his fortune with him. Now he was the master of dirt and dust.

I kept hearing Mrs. Billaruz's voice, sometimes retelling me what happened to my father. I didn't want to think of Mrs. Billaruz or my father, but her voice entered my mind, particularly when I slept. I'd wake up, unable to sleep, lying there and feeling nothing. The only thing that comforted me was scratching myself, breaking skin, biting what limbs I could bring to my mouth. There was a kind of release when I did it, a kind of pain that freed me. I saw the hurt on my body.

CHAPTER TWENTY-NINE
An Offering to His Spirit

Dear Monty,   December 25, 1989

Amada doesn't ask me to spend time with her for
Christmas anymore. She knows better. I'd rather
stay in the dark with a single candle illuminating the picture of you by my bed, creating a warm
glow around your face.

I like writing letters to you during moments like
these, a stillness that settles on the bones. And
the only sound I hear is the scraping tip of my
pen on paper.

I'll head out in a moment to find you, perhaps
sitting in a bar waiting for me. I'm coming. I'm
coming.

Dear Monty,   July 1, 1990

I rented A Place in the Sun last week. I know what
you went through in that movie. A regular guy from
nowhere trying to get somewhere, anywhere. You
played a man looking for someone, something to
feel complete. Now that I've graduated from college, I don't exactly know what I'll do.

Elizabeth Taylor held you close to her. Her face
pressed against your shoulder. Dancing slowly.
Severe close-ups frame your beautiful face: gentle, welcoming, hurt. There's a scene in the car
where you fall asleep on her shoulder. She cradled

you. She pretended to be your mama.

Mrs. Billaruz's voice still haunts me. Her voice
carries stories. Her stories have grown to pictures in my sleep, dreamy movies I don't want to
see. I keep seeing my father. I keep seeing him
naked. "They made him take off his clothes," Mrs.
Billaruz told me. "They made him stand there
naked. It was a common form of torture. They put
wires on him, they put—how you say—electrodes on
him, they tied the wires around his thing, around
his penis...and they shocked him. He screamed.
They didn't do it once. They did it to him again
and again..."

I woke up and couldn't sleep. I didn't want to
dream of my dad that way. I had to take sleeping
pills to feel drowsy.

I closed my eyes and whisked away to A Place in
the Sun. I was with you by the lake. You held
Elizabeth Taylor, cherishing the moments. Loving
her. You wanted to be with her, but felt you
couldn't. Elizabeth was too good for you. You
knew that. She represented everything that was
glorious. All that you aspired to be. She was
sheer perfection. Instead you had Shelley
Winters, dumpy, plain, ordinary. You wanted so
much. So much.

I've been doing as many extra gigs as I can find
to make ends meet. I go from job to job, wherever
I'm needed. I spent last week, every day, eight
hours a day pretending to be an Indian for a new
western. They put a long wig on me while I stood
around in a loincloth. Yesterday, I wore a suit
and pretended to be a businessman for a commercial pushing a construction company in Santa
Monica. And today, I sat on a bus, being a passenger for a new television series.

As an extra, Monty, I spend most of my time wait-

ing. I wait for the cameras and lights to be set.
I wait while the actors rehearse. I wait for
those few precious moments when the camera rolls,
and the director says, "Action."

Being an extra can be a mind-numbing experience.
Lately, after work, I find myself wound up. I end
up at the neighborhood bar to wind down. I sip my
gin, crunch the ice left in the glass.

I want an Elizabeth Taylor. I want someone to love.

Amada and I went to West Hollywood to celebrate her latest role. She played a woman who had just been bombed in Hiroshima. It was an experimental play in Santa Monica. At the end, she killed herself because she couldn't stand life after her home had been devastated.

We went for another reason: Amada wanted me to meet somebody in the cast.

"If you want a boyfriend," Amada said, "you have to start meeting guys."

"I don't want a boyfriend. I don't want anybody."

"Look. I know you need somebody. I hear you jacking off."

"I don't—"

"Yes, you do. Beds don't make creaking sounds by themselves."

I knew I should have bought a futon. What she didn't know was: I had Monty, and we dated on a regular basis and we made love on a regular basis. Sometimes, late at night, if I was too tired to search for Monty, too tired to hop on my bike and search Los Angeles, I dreamed of him instead, imagined him loving me, passionate love. I masturbated with him in mind.

Amada introduced me to a guy named Oliver Yen. He was a little guy, the top of his head barely reached my chin. He seemed pretty nice, though.

"Amada tells me your folks are still in the Philippines," Oliver said.

"Yeah, they live there."

"My father lives in Taiwan. He does business over there. My mother is out here. How about yours?"

"My dad is a pilot," I said, "and my mom is a stewardess. They do a lot of flying together. I haven't seen them in a while, because they're so busy. But they're a beautiful couple. They look so good in their uniforms, you know."

Oliver nodded. His chin bobbed over his polka-dotted bow tie.

"I'm sorry," I said. "I'm sorry Amada made you go on this date with me, but I already have a boyfriend."

"Oh, I see. Amada said you were single—"

"She doesn't know about him yet."

"Is your boyfriend a nice guy?"

"He's the greatest. Just the greatest. He loves me very much."

"I guess that's all you could ask for."

"I guess."

"Amada hasn't met him?"

"No, but she knows who he is."

•

I drove Amada into Hollywood. She had an audition for a movie. A callback actually.

"I play a hooker," she said, "who tries to straighten out her drugged-out life, but overdoses on Seconal and dies."

"For once," I said, "I'd love to see you in a role where you live."

"I don't know how long I'll be, so just hang out." She disappeared into a building.

I strolled Hollywood Boulevard, looking into store windows. The stores carried memorabilia from the bygone days of cinema: photos of old stars like Rudolph Valentino with that come-fuck-me stare or Shirley Temple dancing a jig or Greta Garbo showing off her perfect bone structure, Judy Garland as Dorothy toting Toto. Tourists took pictures at Mann's Chinese Theater, feebly fitting their hands and feet into John Travolta's prints, photographing Betty Grable's leg cast in cement.

I walked east on Hollywood Boulevard, checking out the Walk of Fame, recognizing the names of stars beneath my feet, gliding over Lucille Ball or Diana Ross or Bruce Lee. I discovered Monty's star. It's on the corner of Gower Street and Hollywood, behind a bus bench and in front of a gas station.

Some shithead left gum on the pink tile carrying his name. I scraped it off. I lit a cigarette and put it by his star, an offering to his spirit. I watched the cigarette dwindle away to nothing, gray ashes blowing away with the slightest gust of wind.

CHAPTER THIRTY

Flying, Flying Away

Dear Monty,   August 14, 1990

I love dancing with you, slow dancing: our bodies are together, moving like one entity, our muscle, skin, and bone melted together.

I went to a bar last night. I waited for you for hours, hoping you'd come. A few burly men hit on me, but I waited for you: handsome and slender. I don't dance with anyone until you come along.

It seems you tease me. Sometimes you show up, most times not. I wait for you, look for you. I wander through parks and alleys; I peer into dark movie theaters where one must be of a certain age to get in; I have waited hours, days until you see fit to touch me again.

I am devoted to you.

Forever Faithful

Bob

didn't mean to tell. I really didn't. Amada found out about me and Monty. I had to tell her.

"Okay," Amada said, "Who is this guy?"

"Huh?" I said.

"Oliver told me you've got a boyfriend. Who is it? Oliver said I know this mystery man. That explains a lot: Why you're always out, why I don't see you days at a time. Cough it up. Who is it? Is it the guy who lives downstairs?"

"No, it's not him." I was getting dressed to go to work. I was lucky enough to get the evening shift: good tips.

"Is he cute?"

"Yes."

Then I did something I shouldn't have: I took off my T-shirt, revealing the red marks on my back. The ones I gave to myself. Amada saw them, and said, "Oh my God. What happened?"

I threw on a sweater and said, "Nothing."

"Did this boyfriend of yours do this to you?"

"Of course not. Monty would never do anything like that." Once I mentioned his name, I couldn't take it back.

"Monty? His name is Monty?"

"Yes."

"Monty," she said. She stared at the ceiling, thinking. "I don't know a Monty. I thought it was somebody I knew."

"You know of him."

"The only Monty I know of is Montgomery Clift."

"Exactly."

"You're dating Montgomery Clift?"

"Yes."

"You mean you're dating someone like Montgomery Clift. Someone who looks like him, acts like him. Right?"

I was giddy. I thought of Amada as naive. "No. I'm seeing him, we meet every once in a while. We dance, we hold hands, and...make love." I blushed when I said Make Love.

She fell on her side laughing. I didn't see what was so funny. I was letting her in on my relationship; she didn't take it seriously. I was upset, disappointed really. My world with Monty was precious to me. If anyone would've understood, it was Amada. She kept laughing.

"You can't be serious?" she said.

"I am serious. We meet, we talk, we do lots of things together. I know a lot of people wouldn't understand, but I'm asking you to. I'm seeing Montgomery Clift. I've always seen him, here and there. But this time, I touch him also. You love Marilyn Monroe. Well, I love Monty. I know it's kind of strange. But that's the fact of the matter." Amada was obviously perplexed, but she nodded her head like she understood. "Please don't tell anyone, okay. Let's keep it a secret. Not everyone would get it. Promise me you'll keep it a secret." She was quiet. "Promise me you'll keep it a secret."

"I promise," she said meekly.

"I have to go. I'll be late for work."

Amada's head was cocked to one side, her mouth wide open.

One thing I believed: the world was unfair. I had to grab what I could get. I had Monty. I believed Amada wouldn't tell. I trusted her. Not everyone would have understood, they'd make fun. They wouldn't know that kind of love. They would be quick to judge, quick to condemn. My little world with Monty now included Amada.

Sometimes I wonder what my life would have been like if she hadn't told.

●

Amada cried when she saw me. "It's all my fault," she kept saying.

I was too tired to speak, too tired to tell her, No, it wasn't. I tried to tell her No with my eyes, sending her psychic messages.

"I should never have let you go last night," she said. The night we argued.

"You're being a real shit!" she said.

"I don't want to see your folks, not now, not ever."

"You'd rather spend time with an imaginary boyfriend—"

"He's not imaginary. He's real. He's the most real thing in my life."

"You're breaking my mother's heart."

"Fuck your mother!"

"Fuck your mother! Fuck your father, too! Where are they? These goddamn parents of yours. Where are they? They're dead, aren't they? Your father's dead. You might as well face the fact that your mother is dead, too."

"My mother is alive," I said.

"Where is she? The Marcoses are no longer in power, why hasn't she shown up? Meanwhile my parents are hurt that you don't want to see them. They're in a lot of pain."

"Your parents don't know shit about pain," I said. "My father was beaten until he was black and blue. That's pain. They hit him like this." I punched myself; I took my fist and hit my chest. "They hit him again!" I smacked my face. I felt warm liquid drip out of my nose, landing on my shirt, leaving a clean red spot there. "They hit him again and again, for hours and hours." I clawed at my arms, digging my nails into my skin, smacking myself, punching myself, grabbing my hair, falling onto the floor kicking away furniture, slamming against the ground.

Amada jumped on me holding onto my arms. "Stop it!" she yelled. "Why are you doing this to yourself? You give yourself bruises, don't you? You're doing it to yourself. Stop it stop it stop it stop it stop it stop it!" But I wouldn't. Amada and I twisted into each other, I kept punishing myself. "They hit him everywhere," I said. "They knew he was a writer, so they hit him on the hands. They stomped on his fingers. They did it over and over again. Until his joints were gone. They broke his hands! That's what Mrs. Billaruz told me. They broke his hands so he couldn't write anymore. His hands looked like old twisted branches. Then they tortured him again." I threw Amada off of me and slammed my knuckles against the floor, slamming them until they were red, until my hands were weak and the skin was broken.

Amada cried, "Stop it, Bob. Stop it."

I took off. Amada chased after me. "Don't go, Bob. Come back." She jumped on me, and we fell to the floor. She held me tight.

"I have to go, Amada, I have to go somewhere."

"You don't have to go anywhere. I'm sorry. Stay with me. I should have never talked about your mom and dad like that. Your mom is alive. She's out there. Stay."

"I can't. I can't." I broke away from her, got on my bike and sped off. I found myself in a bar in Silverlake, throwing back shots of tequila. With every gulp, it was going away, my fight with Amada was going away, what I said about my dad was going away, everything that I was was going away.

Amada was right. Where was she? Where? A little voice came to me, clear as a bell, giving me the answer, but I had another shot of tequila, and the little voice went away, too.

"Last call," the bartender said. "Suck 'em up. It's last call."

I got on my bike, cruised Franklin Boulevard, getting lost in the buzz of my bike echoing from the buildings around me. I hopped on the freeway and drove into Topanga Canyon, racing up and down the hills, thinking of the wire tied to him, shocking electricity.

I screamed into the night. I made a sharp turn, a little too sharp. My bike disappeared from under me. I went flying, flying away. I hit the sidewalk and skidded along the cement. I got up, and felt this warmth run down the side of my face. I saw my bike fifteen feet away. I heard a guy behind me say, "You OK?"

"Yeah, I'm all right, but my bike's trashed. Shit." I thought about the money I didn't have to pay for it. I would have to work double shifts at the restaurant, take every extra gig possible to fix the damage on my bike. I turned around, and the face of this guy was wild and scared. His eyes were bugged out and his jaw dropped.

"What's the matter?" I said.

"You better sit down," he said.

"I'm all right."

He took my arm and a searing pain went up my shoulder. He led me to the curb. We passed a parked car, and I saw my reflection in the car window. My leather jacket was torn up, my right shoulder busted open, the warmth on my face was blood, dripping down to my chest like thick red tears. The entire right side of my face was messed up, feeling like someone took a torch and lit it on fire. The right side of my face buzzed, a slow burn ravaged my temple, my cheek. My ear was bent, sort of hanging limp, twisted out of shape.

An ambulance zoomed in and a medic shot me up with painkillers. At the hospital, a cop ordered me to pee into a bottle. I passed out.

In the morning, Amada sat dressed in white, looking clean, antiseptic in a way. Mr. and Mrs. A were there, too, looking down at me with woeful eyes. Mrs. A handed me her compact mirror.

My face was swollen, the size of a basketball. Orange and wet. My face was lopsided, because my right side got most of the beating. There were gashes above and below my right eye. Both eyes were black because I broke my nose. Stitches kept my ear attached to my head. Dark purple lines crisscrossed my face, looking like someone slashed me this way and that.

"Aw fuck," was all I could think of to say.

•

I had this dream: my father came to visit me in the hospital. He didn't look like himself. He wasn't the man I remembered. He used to be young, his body erect, his head too high for his shoulders. He used to be strong, all guts and fury.

In my dream, he was small, too small to care about. He was frail and could barely stand. His hair was wild, tangled like barbed wire. His skin had lost its firmness, sagging like ill-fitting clothes.

Was this my father?

"Why haven't you cried for me?" he said. His voice was grainy. He walked around my bed, a slow walk. With each step, he seemed to vibrate, rattle. With each step, he resembled a small earthquake, enough to shake some buildings, but not strong enough to do any real damage, enough to make glass fall from shelves, but not enough to make the shelves themselves tumble.

This was my father.

He wore a dress shirt with an intricate design: blooming flowers: daisies, petunias, birds-of-paradise, and roses. Especially roses. More roses bloomed around his neck like a choker caked with rubies. Petals opened. He looked like a majestic garden.

He circled my bed, and I watched the flowers of his body blur, becoming liquid. The bright colors of the garden dripped from his body, leaving green marks, yellow marks, red marks on the floor, forming grotesque ponds.

The roses around his neck kept blooming, growing larger and fuller until his neck was completely red, forming a serrated line between his chin and his shoulders. His head shook, swaying this way and that. It tilted to the left, then to the right, then to the left again, eventually falling off, hitting the shoulder on its way down to the ground.

His headless body walked around my room. His arms were outstretched feeling his way.

I heard a croak, a small peep coming from below my bed. It was my father's head trying to speak. Saliva dribbled down the corners of his mouth. His lips moved up and down trying to form words, but only gagging sounds came out.

Then in a raspy voice, he asked, "Why haven't you cried for me?"

I didn't have an answer.

•

Amada told. She told people that I hurt myself. She told people about me and Monty. She told people at the hospital.

"So you don't hurt yourself?" Brainwasher asked.

"No."

"Then you didn't make those bruises on your body."

"No."

"Where did they come from?"

"From the accident."

"Those bruises don't match the bruises you got from the accident. The bruises you sustained from the accident were on your upper right side: the shoulder, the face. How did you get the bruises on your back? Your arms? Your legs?" He studied me. "As a matter of fact, I wonder if you caused the accident yourself."

"That's crazy. Why would I want to do that to myself? Why would I fuck up my face?"

"You tell me. Are you trying to kill yourself?"

"No. I swear I don't want to kill myself."

"Then why?"

"I'm clumsy. I bump into things."

"Are you always clumsy?"

"Yes."

"Are you clumsy around your boyfriend?"

Then Monty appeared. He couldn't have come at a better time. He filled the drab office with sunlight. Brainwasher's office was a shit-colored brown with furniture left over from the seventies: geometrical prints hung on his wall and a velour couch off to the side. Brainwasher sat behind a gray metal desk and I sat on a wooden chair.

"Are you clumsy around your boyfriend?" he repeated.

"No. I'm never clumsy around him. I always know what to do when I'm with him."

Brainwasher smiled. He was a round, pink man with red hair.

In the hospital, I woke up one morning and Brainwasher was standing over me. He didn't look like the other doctors who were taking care of me. He didn't wear a white coat or anything. He wore a plaid shirt. "I'd like to talk to you," he said.

"About what?"

"Your accident." I had been talking about my accident for

almost two weeks. I didn't want to talk about it anymore. "Your family asked me to come here," he said. "Especially Amada."

"They're not my family."

"Amada told me you hurt yourself. Is that true?" Brainwasher spoke with a calm, soothing voice. On any other occasion, I probably would have liked to talk to him, but this was not one of those occasions. He wore a nameplate pinned to his front shirt pocket. It read: Abraham Butterworth, Dept. of Psychiatry, St. Joan's Hospital. "Amada also told me you date a dead 1950's movie star." He couldn't help but smile. "Is that true, too?"

The door to my room opened. Amada, Mr. A and Mrs. A entered. Amada's face was to the floor. Mr. and Mrs. A stood beside her. Mrs. A's hands were on Amada's shoulders. There was something beautiful about the way they looked. It could have been a photograph, a real Kodak moment. It would have been perfect, except that I wanted to throttle Amada. I almost did.

I lunged from my bed, screaming, "What did you tell them, Amada? You promised you wouldn't tell anyone!" I almost had Amada in my grasp, but Brainwasher caught me and shoved me back. He was strong for a pudgy guy. He sat on me to keep me down. I wanted to rip Amada to shreds.

"Nurse!" Brainwasher said. A woman entered wearing a blue uniform. He yelled the fancy name of a drug then she disappeared. "Calm down, Bob," he said. "No one is going to hurt you."

"Fuck you." I couldn't reach for Amada, but my fingers tingled. My hands were out of control, they wanted to destroy something. I grabbed my face, and ripped the bandages and stitches away, feeling the sutures gripping my skin, eventually tearing away, stinging me.

Mr. A grabbed my arms and held them down. Amada watched with horror. Mrs. A flung her arms around, whispering something, praying maybe.

The nurse appeared and put a needle into my arm.

"Fuck you," I kept saying. I wondered if my dad was treated this way. All of my muscles weakened, my eyelids became heavy.

I awoke. My hands were cuffed to the bed. I was no longer in my hospital room. I was somewhere else. I was "under observation."

Brainwasher wanted to talk to me. The first thing I said was, "Amada is a back-stabbing lying motherfucking bitch."

CHAPTER THIRTY-ONE

Electricity

Dear Monty,   January 3, 1991

I have a room of my own, a blue room, with one
lamp by my bed. The lamp is tomato colored with a
white lampshade. I've been committed to this
room.

I live here now.

Dear Monty,   March 1, 1991

You come to me when I most need you. Like yesterday afternoon, during American Movie Classics on
cable. There is a common room where all patients
can read or play board games or watch TV. When I
enter the room, most of the patients leave,
because I have this fucked up face; they're
scared of me. I love having the common room all
to myself. I can flip through channels and find
you. I have watched your movies through the
years. I must have seen The Search fifteen times,
The Misfits maybe eight times, A Place in the Sun
nine times, From Here to Eternity eleven times.
But I'd only seen Freud once.

Freud came on today. You were the great psy-
chotherapist Sigmund Freud. You helped the men-
tally ill. All of your colleagues despised you,
because of your revolutionary theories in mental
illness. You were chastised because you believed

```
that we are all deeply affected by our child-
hoods, stemming from strong impressions and
attachments to our parents.

Please visit me soon.


Dear Monty,                          June 4, 1991

They came again, like they did last week and the
week before. The Arangan family. I stayed in my
room with you. I don't need them. I don't.
```

I hadn't touched Montgomery Clift in a long time, kissed him, held him. It had been months. I thought I would die. I saw Monty in my room, sitting with me when I nodded off, standing by the window when I woke. Seeing him was one thing, being unable to touch was unbearable.

A male nurse was sleeping on the couch in the common room, dead to the world. His feet were on the armrest, and his arms crossed over his belly. I knelt by the male nurse, a thick-necked guy with hairy arms. I thought of Monty, wishing him near me. Then Mr. Clift appeared, slowly covering the nurse with his cinematic glow, until it was Monty—not the nurse—lying there.

I touched his hand, caressing his knuckles. His nails were perfectly manicured, crescent moons at the cuticles. I lifted his hand, inspecting the palm, admiring the long lines that ran there. I brought his hand to my face feeling his dry warmth against my skin. I kissed his hand, licking his fingers.

I undid his belt, slowly and rhythmically. I unhinged the leather strap from the silver buckle, and unzipped his pants.

I nuzzled my face into his groin, tasting his cotton boxers, slipping my tongue through the slit of his underwear. His pubic hair smelled of sweat and darkness.

Then I felt my hair being pulled, a clump of my hair being ripped from my skull.

"What the fuck are you doing, you little shit," a voice said.

I looked up and Monty had disappeared, the pissed-off face of the nurse was what I saw. His face red and furious. His dishwater brown hair standing like forest trees.

"I said, 'What the fuck are you doing?'"

I saw his undone pants. And so did he. His mouth, a tight grin, opened into a disgusted silent scream. I felt my head hurled to the ground, my skull slapped the floor. I laid there on the rust-colored linoleum, looking up at the male nurse. He reached down and picked me up by the center of my T-shirt. He stood me up like a stuffed pillow, my feet barely touching the ground.

I saw his knuckles come at me like an asteroid, my head shooting back.

"You little faggot," he said and hit me again.

I thought of Monty, and saw the ugly face of the nurse glaring back at me. I didn't want to see him. I wanted Monty back. I wanted him to make everything better. I grabbed the face of the nurse with both hands, digging fingers into flesh. I wanted to rip his face off, tear it from his skull, hoping, praying Monty was behind it. I dug my hands into the sockets of his eyes, the nostrils, the ears, pulling until I felt a shattering pain in my groin.

"He tried to kill me," the nurse said, "the prick tried to fuck me, then he wanted to kill me."

I curled up like a baby. Other nurses came by and took me to my room.

It was worth it. I held Monty, tasted him. It was only for a little while, but it was worth it.

•

It started with an itch. That's all. I swear. Just an itch. I was asleep, dreaming of my father. Father touched me. His long bony fingers touched me. His nails scraped against my skin, leaving an itch, a slight itch. I scratched myself, but the lingering feeling of his nails on my skin stayed. So I kept scratching. I scratched with a fury until the feeling was gone.

I awoke with raw, bleeding skin. Brainwasher had me restrained when I slept. He also started me on Prozac.

"How do you keep in contact with Montgomery Clift?" Brainwasher asked me.

"I see him around sometimes. He visits me. We meet when we go out. But I keep in contact mostly through letters."

"Letters?"

"Yes. I write to him."

"Do you mail them?"

"I'm not stupid. I have no place to send them. I keep them. I'll just start writing a letter on a piece of paper and put it away."

"Does he write back?" Brainwasher said this like he was talking to a child.

"No, you moron," I said. Brainwasher, or Dr. Butterworth, thought I was psychotic; he thought I wasn't in touch with reality. He had been dispensing various anti-psychotic drugs to me. They had no effect. I told him the drugs didn't work because there was nothing wrong with me. But I had to explain myself to him, hoping he'd let me go. "Montgomery Clift tells me things, makes things happen. He makes me feel good. Is there anything wrong with that?"

"No. What would happen if you stop writing letters?"

"Don't know. I've written him for a long time."

"You've become dependent."

"Huh?"

"You can't live without this activity," he said. "Writing letters."

"I guess not."

"Maybe we should break you of this habit."

"Do you pray?"

"Yes."

"A lot of people pray. They go to church regularly. They say certain prayers, right?"

"Right."

"Would you ever tell them to stop doing that?" I asked.

"Of course not."

"Then why should I?"

"God...religion is an accepted form of spirituality."

"I'm not going to stop doing something because what you say I'm doing is wrong. What's wrong with having something, someone to believe in?"

He had to think about that. "Your religion is a 1950's movie star. There is something absurd about that."

"I wouldn't be here if I said I believed in Christ, would I? If I told you I believed in Jesus, and He works in my life, and I pray to Him,

I would be considered a good Christian person. Whether it's Jesus or Monty, they're symbols people turn to in times of crisis. I can pray to whoever I want, believe in whoever I want."

"Jesus and Montgomery Clift are two different things."

"Are they? I come from a part of the world where the dead are revered and prayed to. A dead uncle or aunt is just as precious as a saint or some other form of deity. I don't deserve to be locked up because you don't agree with my form of spirituality."

"The difference is you see and touch this Montgomery Clift."

"Other people claim to see and touch Jesus Christ all the time. They're allotted time on television, some have their own TV shows. Yet they're allowed to roam free."

Dr. Butterworth smiled at this. The West has an accepted form of religion or spirituality. Praying to ancestors is not one of them. The West thinks that once a person is dead, they're dead. Kaput. I don't believe that. I believe the Dead can choose to stay, and watch over us. That's why I saw Monty. That's why I saw my father in my dreams. I felt Monty close by, loving me.

•

I was tied to my bed for going to the No-Name Place. I struggled to get free, but only exhausted myself in the process.

It all started when I met with Brainwasher for my weekly session.

"Why are you so angry? You've been angry for months. Frankly, the staff is sick of it. You refuse meals, yell at the nurses, throw things—"

"I don't like being locked up for no reason."

"We have to do something. You won't take your medication."

"That Prozac shit makes me sick. I won't to take it anymore."

"All right. Let's change the subject. Let's discuss your attempted suicide."

"I'm not suicidal."

"You hurt yourself. I'm not convinced your accident was accidental."

"It was! I drank a little too much, I lost control of the bike."

"Montgomery Clift had an accident, didn't he? Ruining his face. Do you think you're Montgomery Clift?"

"Of course not. There was only one Monty."

"Why do you hate your parents?"

"I don't hate my parents; I worship them."

"Mr. and Mrs. Arangan have tried to visit you a number of times, but you won't see them."

"They're not my parents…"

"All right. Let's talk about your other parents…"

Silence.

"You've avoided talking about them. You won't tell me much."

"They're wonderful people."

"I understand they're dead."

"They're not dead."

"You have a knack for keeping dead people alive."

"My father is dead. He was killed in prison camp, but my mother is still alive."

"Does your father visit you like Montgomery Clift?"

"Sometimes. In my dreams."

"Is that why you refuse to sleep?"

Silence. I'd been doing that. Trying to stay awake. When my father visited, he asked me why I wouldn't cry for him. The nurses force-fed me sedatives so I could go to sleep.

"Is that why you refuse to sleep?" he said a little louder.

"Yes. My father comes to me in my sleep, because he's dead. Monty comes to me because he's dead, also. I don't want to sleep, because…"

"…because…"

"Because if I sleep I may see my mother in my dreams. If I see her, then I know she is dead, too." And I don't want to believe that.

"Is she dead?"

"No."

"Where is she?"

"Somewhere. Maybe she's sick. Or she can't get to me somehow. But she's alive."

"Could she be dead, too?"

"No."

"But she's disappeared."

"Yes."

"Could it be she doesn't want to see you?"

"She loves me. She wants to see me. She loves me." I got upset. I stood up, and Brainwasher stood up, too. He thought I was going to hurt him. We stood looking at each other. He looked at me, as if he was daring me.

I kicked over my chair, and he pressed a button on his desk. I ran to his shelf and threw books on the floor, I opened his books, searching for page 168, ripping them out. I had done this with three of his books, when someone pulled me to my feet, dragging me to my room, shooting a sedative into my arm. I watched the dim glow of the lamp by my bed, a piece of sun wrapped in glass.

•

I cried. I thought of my father and cried. I was in my bed staring into the bulb of the lamp. I put my hand over the light, grasping the glass in my hand, feeling the warm light bulb grow hot. I squeezed the light bulb and it shattered in my hand. I held the warm glow in my palm. Electricity bolted through me, like scalding water surging through my veins. I jerked, and jumped.

"Stop it," I said to no one in particular, "Stop it." And I thought of my dad. I wondered if this is what it felt like. When they electrocuted him, it wasn't enough to kill, just enough to hear himself scream. I wondered if this is what he went through.

And I cried. Because at that moment I was my father. And I saw the faded bruises on my arms, the ones I gave to myself: They were blue, no longer purple, a soft haze of green surrounded the blueness.

And I cried. It seemed the electricity chased me away, chased all the feeling from my body, chased the thoughts of my parents, chased my anger at Amada, chased the regret, chased the loneliness, making me hollow. Hollow and tired. Until all I had was my voice, a whisper, "Stop it," I said.

I thought of my father. The electricity. I was grateful. I cried. I cried for my father.

CHAPTER THIRTY-TWO
A Brilliant Hole

Dear Monty,   1992

I don't know what day it is Ever since that light
bulb incident the nurses watch me carefully, taking away anything that could cause me to hurt
myself, including pens or pencils I couldn't
write you for months

Today they let me draw using crayons I'm huddled
against a corner as I write this to you I don't
want the nurses to see, but they have to watch
over me

I just want to let you know that I love you And
I appreciate you sitting by my bed at night
guarding me

Dear Monty,   1992

During our sessions Dr. Butterworth sits and
watches me

We've spent most of our sessions just sitting
there looking at each other

I wonder what he sees It has been almost two
years since my accident My face has healed, but I
still look thrashed Does he see the scars that
run down my face Or the deep purple marks that
don't seem to go away

I like my face this way

Those days were a blur, a blotch like Mrs. 45, But Really 60's paintings. I'd sit by the window of my room entranced in my world with Monty. We didn't speak, but sat together. He wore an outfit from *From Here to Eternity*: slacks and a Hawaiian shirt.

Monty took me places without ever having to leave my room. The drab white walls transformed into boundless skies and endless acres of trees or sand or water. We'd sit on the shore of an island, our feet buried in moist sand, watching seagulls fly past us. Ocean mist wafted toward us like friendly spirits. The crashing surf was the earth's heartbeat. It seemed like the beginning of time, or the end of it.

I'd find myself with Monty in the California desert, dry and barren. We'd find a shade in a cluster of cactus trees, shaped like deformed hands. He wore a cowboy hat, jeans, and a plaid shirt. He'd pull out a cigarette and the smell of tobacco drifted past my nose, a taunting smell. The drumming hooves of horses could be heard nearby.

Sometimes, we were at a cotillion. We were dressed in tuxedos with shiny black shoes; golden cufflinks held our sleeves together. He'd serve me punch and we'd sit quietly in an ivy-embraced gazebo. I held a dance card and his name was written on it, over and over. He was to be my dance partner for all of the evening. The jumping rhythms of a piano filled the air.

I would willingly go with Monty. Hours, days, weeks seemed to pass. When I returned, I'd find liquid food crusted dry around my mouth or dripping onto my shirt. I don't remember eating or being fed.

"C'mon, Bobby boy, eat it all up," said one nurse, a spoon halfway in my mouth. I blinked and startled her. "I hate when you do that," she said, "your mind coming and going. Don't know how you'll be from one moment to the next."

I didn't know either.

•

Brainwasher wanted me to see another doctor, a new one.

"Frankly," he said, "our sessions haven't been very productive. A new doctor joined our staff recently. Perhaps she could be more helpful. She's worked with people like you, people who self-mutilate."

With that, I began my sessions with Dr. Chapman, a divine woman. We sat and talked about old movies. She was a big fan of Vivien Leigh and Alfred Hitchcock. She'd seen some Monty Clift movies, too.

"I thought he was wonderful in *The Heiress*," she said.

My sessions with Dr. Chapman ended too soon. I liked her Indian accent. She was born in Bombay and had been in the U.S. for ten years. She was a newlywed; pictures of her wedding day sat on her desk. Her elegant brown face beamed alongside the paler face of her husband.

After two months of talking about movies and music, she got serious, telling me about myself, things I didn't want to hear.

"There are things you don't want to know or feel," she said, her eyes focusing on me, her eyebrows coming together, almost creating a perfect V. "Self-injurers do that. I didn't have to read your file to know that one or both of your parents were absent in your life."

Absent. She didn't say dead, she said absent. I adored her for that.

"I also know," she said, "there was some kind of abuse when you were a child. I don't have to read your file to know that, either."

I thought of Auntie Yuna and her beatings. I never thought of what she did as abuse, but I guess that is what it was. A hole opened up in me, a brilliant hole.

"I know about your parents and how you don't want to talk about them. Not talking about them makes you not deal with it, you don't feel anything. Hurting yourself makes you feel something. Am I right?"

I couldn't say anything. I simply nodded because what she said was correct. I wanted her to shut up because it was too much. Instead she continued, "When you bruise yourself, you see how much pain you're in? If you purposely got into that motorcycle accident, you must have been suffering quite a bit."

I was quiet for a long time, wondering if she was psychic. I asked her, "How do you know this?"

"Let's just say I've known a few people like you. It's typical of people who injure themselves, cut themselves, bruise themselves."

Dr. Chapman started me on a new drug; it's for depression. It's only been out on the market for about a year. She said a lot of doctors are afraid to use it, but she thinks I might benefit from it. It was called Zoloft.

•

I saw Amada. Not in person, but on TV. She was on a show about detectives. She played a secretary in a monolithic downtown building, and told a detective to "wait here" while she got her boss. She had about five seconds of screen time.

Her hair was pulled back with a black barrette. She wore a gray suit; the collar of a white blouse peeked out from under the lapel of her jacket. Silver hoop earrings dangled from her ears like pendulums.

She looked happy, happy to have a part on a TV show, happy to have a cake of makeup on her face. If I didn't know her, I would have thought she was a lucky woman who led a charmed life. I know people believe what they see on TV sometimes. Amada came off as a self-confident, ambitious executive secretary, making a hefty salary working for a hotshot corporation.

Amada sparkled in her scene. She didn't look like the woman who betrayed me, told doctors that I went nuts. She didn't look like a struggling actress or a woman who had an abortion at seventeen. She looked like an important woman with interesting people to meet and colorful places to go. It seemed she had another life, another world where she belonged, a world that wanted her there.

•

Dr. Chapman asked about Monty. She asked how he was doing. "Is Mr. Clift obliging you?" she said.

I thought she was mocking me, mocking Monty. "He's fine," I said cautiously.

"Good. You know my mother visits me. I know she comes. I can feel her. Sometimes, I'll ask her for advice and somehow I manage to make the right decisions when I do that. Is it like that with you and Mr. Clift."

"Exactly."

"Americans," she said, writing something in my file, "why do they fear the dead so much? I had a grandmother who saw ghosts; she was the wisest woman I knew. Next time you see Mr. Clift, tell him hello from me."

"I'll do that."

She read my file and couldn't believe I'd been so troublesome. The Zoloft was really working; I'd calmed down a lot. I didn't know if the Zoloft was working or if it was Dr. Chapman. It didn't matter. I felt more comfortable, more secure.

"Were you always this rebellious?" she asked.

"I have a history of rebels in my family, Dr. Chapman."

"Meaning your parents?"

"Yes."

The room became quiet, only the sound of her wall clock ticked.

"Let's talk about your parents."

I hated it when she brought my parents up. She had tried to ease our sessions in that direction. I wanted to tell her I didn't want to talk about them. One was dead, the other was missing.

"Your father was tortured?" she asked.

"Yes."

"He had bruises all over his body, I'm sure."

I knew where this was heading.

"The marks on your body are gone."

"I don't hurt myself anymore," I said.

"I know," she said solemnly. She took a deep breath, speaking quietly. "Can you accept the fact that both your parents aren't coming back?"

"They were supposed to."

"But the reality is, they didn't."

"But they loved me. If people love you, they come back, don't they?"

"Not always."

"But they loved me, right?"

"I'm sure they did."

CHAPTER THIRTY-THREE
Discolored in Parts

Dear Monty,   June 9, 1993

Everyone is being real nice to me, telling me to
just hang out. The Zoloft is working for me,
things don't seem as dramatic or edgy. I like
this calm.

It also makes you come to me less often. I went
to the downtown library specifically to meet you.
I walked the halls for hours, pulling out books,
blotching page 168. I found some books that I had
blotched years ago. My blotch was still on page
168 in Gulliver's Travels. I had existed those
many years ago. All of the people who had checked
this book out carried me with them.

I waited for you, Monty. But you didn't come.
Don't leave me. Don't disappear.

In March of 1993, they let me out. I did outpatient therapy. I still
saw Dr. Chapman, but I didn't live there. I asked her why they
were letting me go.

She was frank. I was getting better, she said. I had stopped hurting myself. My skin is clear of marks.

She also added: the Arangans couldn't afford my room anymore.

"I didn't know they were paying for it," I said.

"Where do you think the money came from?" she asked.

"I don't know. I thought the bill was adding up and I would have
to pay it eventually."

"It doesn't work that way. The Arangans have been footing the bill since you got here."

•

Mr. and Mrs. A met me in the hospital waiting room. They looked humble, sweet. Amada stood by a candy vending machine. We looked at each other. I hadn't seen them since I was committed. Before, I didn't want to see them. Now I wanted nothing more than to have them take me away.

Amada approached me. She'd cut her hair. It was no longer past her shoulders. It hovered above her jaw. I don't know what she saw when she looked at me. My face had healed considerably, but it was still discolored in parts, and scarred.

She said, "Are you hungry?"

"Yes," I said.

"Good. We prepared a little feast for you."

We drove home, Amada and I in the backseat.

"I think you'll like your room," Mrs. A said. "We converted the den for you. It's not the house in Los Feliz, but it'll do."

Mr. A stared at me intermittently through the rearview mirror. He probably thought I might do something crazy like jump around and scream. But he didn't know that crazy behavior can just be sitting around, saying and doing nothing.

"You have to come over some time," Amada said. "I have this cute little studio apartment in Burbank."

"I'd like that," I said. I moved closer to her. I wanted her to touch me, a kind touch. I knew she loved me. She told people I was nuts because she loved me. Betrayal is a form of love, I know that now. People hurt you because they love you.

She put her arm around me. "You'll be OK," she said. "You'll be OK."

"I know," I said. I knew things were different. I had thought about my life. I had a lot of time. I was only twenty-five. There was lots to do. I thought of going back to school to get a master's degree, get a real cool job. Maybe meet somebody, fall in love. My father was dead. I came to realize maybe my life would be better if I thought my mother was dead, too.

At home, we sat around the kitchen table eating Mrs. A's food, carefully prepared lumpia, pansit, adobo, and rice. They watched me eat. No one said anything for the longest time. I had to break the silence.

"The food is really good," I said. I smiled. I wanted them to know that everything was all right. That I was all right.

"Mom spent a lot of time on the food," Amada offered. "Didn't you?"

"Not so much time, it was no trouble." Mrs. A said.

"She worked really hard," Mr. A said. "She made one batch of lumpia. She didn't like it and threw the whole thing out. Started all over again."

"I just wanted everything to be perfect when you came home," Mrs. A said.

"It is perfect," I said. "It is."

All three of them smiled.

"I'm sorry," I said, "that I didn't want to see you when you came to visit. I'm sorry if I made you unhappy. I'm sorry for everything that happened." I truly was.

"That's OK," Mrs. A said. "You were just going through a hard time, that's all. We all have hard times."

After dinner, we watched some TV. Amada decided to leave. She wanted me to see her apartment. I said I would.

•

I met with Dr. Chapman, enjoying the comfort of her office. I sat on her wingback sofa, pink like the inside of a grapefruit. I had gotten used to placing my feet on a wicker chest she used as a coffee table.

"How has living at home been?" she asked.

"All right."

"Have you hurt yourself?"

"No."

"Your face is healing nicely."

"I guess."

"Have you dreamt about your father?"

"A few times." My father was still there. He was in different states of decomposition. But I had a different dream. I told her about it: "He was young, probably the age I am now. I was younger, a boy still. We walked along the beach. We waded through the water, tiny waves hit our ankles, sheets of ocean fell at our feet.

"This belongs to us," my father said, waving his arm to the sea.

"The sea belongs to everyone," I said.

"We are a part of everyone, right?"

"Yes."

"Then the sea belongs to us." Dad walked, rather, hovered, over the water. He was going away from me.

"Where are you going?" I yelled.

"To the other side of the Pacific Ocean."

"That's so far away."

"Not so far. When you miss me, come to the beach, Santa Monica or Malibu beach, and stand in the ocean. I'll stand on a beach in the Philippines. The Pacific Ocean, green water, will connect us."

I told this to Dr. Chapman. She brought it to my attention that water is a good conductor of electricity.

•

Amada lived in an apartment complex overlooking some movie studios. Her place was a caramel brown, and posters from movies released in the past ten years or so hung on her wall. One poster was of *Blood Prom at Hell High*, the very first movie we did as extras. She had a video of it and we sat around and watched the movie, fast-forwarding to the scenes that we were in. Me in a classroom, me walking in the halls, me sitting on a bench eating lunch. We laughed at the shot of Amada with an ax in her head.

Amada showed me videotape of some of the TV shows and movies she'd done. They were quick takes of her delivering a line here and a line there. In most of her scenes, she gets killed or commits suicide.

"If I die one more time, I'll kill myself," she said.

"You're good at it."

"Why do Asian women have to die all the time? And it's usually over some white guy. She dies in *Madame Butterfly*, and she dies in that musical about Saigon. Why do white guys feel that some Asian woman is willing to die for them? Fuck. If I knew an Asian chick who was willing to die for a white guy, over any guy, I'd kill her myself."

Amada told me getting acting gigs had been rough. She'd been doing a lot of office work to get by. "I know I have what it takes to make it as an actress."

"It's such a tough field. Thought of doing something else?"

"No. This is what I want."

"What if you fail?"

"Then I fail. I don't mind that. Geez. What's so wrong about failing? So what. So many people put so much emphasis on succeeding. I would rather be a failure than someone who never tried. This is what I want. Supporting myself as an actress is what I hope for. Hope is important. What do you hope for?"

"I hope my scars go away."

"Your face doesn't look that bad. It almost looks normal. You just look like you got into some fight. You should tell people that. Your face is messed up 'cause you got into a fight defending my honor or something. Tell you the truth, the scars on your face make you look a little dangerous, a little wild. Some people like that."

"I'm not talking about the scars on my face."

CHAPTER THIRTY-FOUR
An Asphalt Tattoo

Dear Monty,   July 20, 1993

This month has seen independence, both for the U.S. and for the Philippines. On July 4th, we joined a neighbor's barbecue, watching fireworks explode in the sky like dreams bursting, rapidly falling on us like tears. On July 14, Mr. and Mrs. A celebrated the anniversary of the Philippines' Independence from Spain by driving into Glendale and having a feast at a Filipino restaurant.

I'm thinking of finding a job, maybe moving out. I don't want to be so dependent on the Arangans anymore. They've taken care of me for a long time.

What do I do next?

I applied for some jobs waiting tables. I gave some resumes to an employment agency. I was asked to explain a three-year gap in my resume. "What did you do in those years?" one employer asked. I was ill, I said.

I called up the place that used to get me jobs as an extra. I got a gig working on a movie. It was about the Vietnam war. I thought they would stick me in a crowd, my face buried among the masses.

"Perfect," Madame Director said to me. "We can use you for all the camp scenes."

This movie was about battered American soldiers and Vietnamese villagers put in a prison camp.

"Imagine everything that you've ever had has been taken away from you," Madame Director told us, "and you're devastated. Got that?"

She did a series of closeups of all the Asian extras looking sad and pathetic. I thought about my parents. I found myself crying, wondering about them—how their lives were, and how I wasn't a part of it. I remembered my dad telling me how he wanted me to have a good future and that's why he wrote against the Marcoses. I remembered my mom telling me she'd come to America and how we'd all have a life together. It all amounted to nothing. The Marcoses fell because a senator got shot and his wife took over. Did it really matter whether Dad went to prison or not? Whether my mom searched for him?

The sad thing was that maybe it was best that we never knew each other. I liked thinking of them as brave people, not broken ones. They left this world thinking that I went off to the States, am leading a great life, married maybe with kids.

"Cut! This isn't working. There's not enough light. Too much darkness. We'll have to do this again," Madame Director said. "Logan, make sure we get these same extras for the next couple of weeks. I don't want continuity fucked up with different prisoners, is that clear?"

"Gotcha," said Logan, an Asian guy who had the crappy task of making sure the extras were lined up for work. I liked his smile.

The Vietnam picture was kind of fun. I'd gotten to know some of the other extras. They were cool. All of them were aspiring actors. Some of them had heard of Monty, seen his films.

"He was a swell actor," one extra said. "Monty Clift was in the same mold as Brando or James Dean—that fifties method actor type. Really got into his parts."

Then Logan jumped in. "Saw him do *The Misfits*. Directed by John Huston. I have a thing for John Huston. Man's man."

I'd been watching Logan hang out with Madame Director, hanging on her every word, running around doing stuff for her. Logan told me he wanted to make films. He went to the American Film Institute to learn how to become a screenwriter. He was working as a production assistant waiting for his big break.

I thought that of all the extras, he liked me best. He'd call me to remind me of the call time for the next day. "Don't forget. Nine in the AM."

I thought he did this for all the extras, but I was wrong. A couple of them said Logan never called them. They just showed up depending on what Madame Director said the day before.

Logan came up to me and asked if I wanted a ride home. I'd been taking buses everywhere.

"Sure," I said.

Logan drove a beat-up Dodge hatchback. It looked like it would fall apart if a strong breeze came by. He cranked up his radio, a Stevie Nicks song played. Logan sang along with it. He really got into it, swaying and crooning. He couldn't sing worth shit, but it was fun to see. He was alive.

•

"Why do you have to buy this expensive food?" I heard Mr. A say to his wife in the kitchen.

"It's not expensive," she said.

"Get the cheap stuff. No more designer things."

"Campbell's soup is not designer."

"Buy generic brands only."

"I know things are hard, but I will not start eating differently. It's bad enough that I can't buy as much as before. It's bad enough that everything is falling apart." Then Mrs. A sighed, sounding like a bird breathing its last breath. "This is not how I pictured my life."

She sat in her bedroom and looked through family albums. Some of those albums go all the way back to the thirties. She showed me her life as a poor girl, putting herself through secretarial school. "I was not bad-looking back then," she said, winking at me, a small smile brightening her face. "Back then there were only so many things a girl could be. I met Mr. Arangan at my very first job. He had been an accountant for two years by then. I was not his secretary. I was the boss's secretary. I could tell Mr. Arangan had eyes for me. A girl could tell that, you know.

"We started dating. He was so tender, like a gentleman. Even back then we wanted to go to the States. Have a home in Los Angeles. San Francisco maybe. But how? We applied to go to the

United States. We had waited for six years. We had friends who had waited close to twelve years to go to America. We thought we would have to wait forever.

"The boss said he could help us. He knew men at immigration and could help us get to the U.S. within a year. All we would have to do is help him with some finances, help him with money matters. We were barely into our twenties. We didn't know what we were doing. The boss said he would even give us money to start a business if we wanted. We said Yes. We wanted to leave our province, leave all that poverty.

"We didn't know the money matters he wanted us to take care of were for dirty politicians…"

"You could have stopped taking money, stopped—"

"You say it so easy. Have you ever been indebted to someone for giving you a wonderful life? We just took what cash they gave us, changed it into American dollars for them. Put it into an account somewhere. That's how we got into this mess. It kept getting worse."

She closed her albums, placing them in the far end of her closet. "This is not how I pictured my life," she said again.

I felt a little sorry for her and her husband. I hated them for helping out the Marcos regime, but they were just people, I guess. They're not my parents, but they got beat up in other ways.

•

Logan invited me up to his apartment.

"Can I touch it? Your face I mean," he said. I knew he meant my scars, but it was weird to talk about my face like it was disjointed from my body.

I nodded.

His finger slowly traced my longest scar, which runs from my right temple to my jaw. His hand was so close to my mouth I could smell the residue of the burrito he had for lunch. Then he placed his palm against my cheek so his thumb touched the lingering bruise under my eye.

"Does it hurt?"

"Not really. The swelling has gone down a lot. You should have seen me before. I have to go in for an operation soon. When my face hit the street, a lot of dirt and shit got imbedded into my skin, leaving these green/purple marks on my face. An asphalt tattoo they call it. Doctors had to scrape some of the dirt caught in my skin."

His hand never left my face. He came closer, his face inches from mine, his eyes touring my scars like an astronaut examining the deep craters of the moon. His other hand lifted my face, tilted it this way and that. He was incredibly close to me. I heard our clothes rustling together as he maneuvered the angle of my body to see my scars better.

He had a little apartment, about the size of a large walk-in closet. He had to share a bathroom with other people down the hall. Straw hats and posters of tropical flowers adorned his walls. He had a bed frame made of bamboo bleached the color of wheat.

A small formica table with two crates for chairs sat near his kitchen, a little cubbyhole with a hot plate. Burlap cloth rested on the table. A wooden Polynesian statue, a miniature version of the towering ones you'd see in postcards from Tahiti or Hawaii, was on the table.

His closet door was wide open. Names like Ocean Pacific and Lightning Bolt were embroidered into his clothes. All his shirts had a surfing motif: men on surfboards, waves crashing onto rocks, palm trees swaying to a tropical breeze.

I imagined him wearing these shirts, the exotic and mysterious plastered across his chest. His shorts were corduroy, thin lines of brazen fabric running up and down his thighs. He had at least a dozen pairs of shoes, all Vans, designed like checker or backgammon boards, solid colors and muted ones, with thick multicolored laces—shades you would see on a clown's face. He had a circus at his feet.

He told me he was born in Maui and his folks moved to San Francisco when he was sixteen. He studied economics for a while at U.C. Berkeley, but dropped out to lead a more artistic life. He has two brothers and a sister. His parents blamed themselves for his being gay. They believed that if they stayed in Hawaii instead of moving to San Francisco, which has a large gay community, they would have never had a gay son.

Logan got even closer to me, his body pressing against me. He kissed my scars. He put his lips to my face and kissed the discoloration, kissed the grooves in my skin. I closed my eyes, and I thought of summoning Monty. I really did. If I wanted to, he would have appeared and I would have been kissing him instead of Logan. But I didn't.

I wanted to kiss Logan. I wanted to kiss another man besides Monty.

I felt dirty somehow, like I had been unfaithful. I ran out of his apartment as fast as I could.

•

Logan cornered me on the set the next day.

"Hey, what happened to you?" he said. "You shot out of my apartment, you never let me explain. I'm sorry, I shouldn't have kissed you. I just thought we connected—"

"I like you and all, but—"

"You're not gay. Right? Sorry, I just assumed."

"You assumed right, it's just...well, I'm not ready for anything yet."

"Ready for what? I'm not asking you to move in or anything. I just thought we could spend time together. Hang out or something. I think you're kinda cute s'all."

I couldn't believe he thought I was cute. He actually thought that. Logan was real handsome, slender with a spiky haircut. I was flattered.

"Cool," I said. "Let's hang out."

"We're wrapping up early. Why don't we go into West Hollywood."

"That sounds good."

We drove to a coffee shop on Robertson Boulevard. He had a latte; I had a cup of coffee. He slid his foot next to mine. I felt the rubber soles of his Vans rub against my ankle. My penis flinched.

We went for a walk down Santa Monica Boulevard. We held hands. We danced a little bit then he took me home. He walked me to the Arangans' door, and before I entered the house, Logan kissed me. A long, deep kiss. I thought of Monty, summoning his presence. I opened my eyes, but he wasn't there. I was befuddled. I mean Monty always came to me, always. I took it as a sign:

Montgomery Clift wanted me to kiss Logan.

Under the maple trees, beneath the glow of a crescent moon, amidst the music of crickets, I kissed Logan. And what a kiss that was. I was blown away, I could have kissed him forever, if the porch light didn't turn on, and Mrs. A didn't open the door and ask, "Why don't you boys come inside?"

"I'll be in in a minute," I said. I sent Mrs. A a psychic message, Go away, can't you see I'm busy. She must have heard it, because she closed the door immediately.

"I'll call you tomorrow," Logan said. And he was off.

I remember thinking: Monty, I like him. I really do.

•

Mrs. Billaruz was in town. I read in one of the Filipino newspapers that she was making appearances around the country talking about politics in the Philippines. A group of attorneys, both American and Filipino, decided to sue the Marcos family for human rights violations. Mrs. Billaruz was touring trying to raise awareness about the case. I met her at the Filipino American Community Center.

"What happened to your face, Sweet Boy?" Mrs. Billaruz asked.

"I got into a motorcycle accident."

"Thank God," she said, laughing her tuba laugh. "You look like we did when we were taken away, beaten by guards."

Mrs. Billaruz told me ten thousand victims were suing the Marcoses. It was the first case of its kind in the world.

She said I could be eligible to sign on as a victim, because my parents were one of the many who were affected by the Marcos regime. I told her No. Enough was enough. I needed to end it. I'd struggled with the fact that my parents were gone, dead or otherwise, they were gone. My life was different. I wanted to put the whole thing to rest.

She said she understood.

•

Logan and I celebrated the end of this Vietnam picture. We went to Disneyland and rode on the It's a Small World ride. Logan pointed out the Hawaiian dolls surfing and dolls that were supposed to represent Japan, the country where his grandparents were born. There was one doll representing the Philippines.

We went into the Haunted Mansion, waiting in a room with portraits of dead people. Before our eyes, the room began to grow and the portraits of dead people elongated revealing these funny circumstances of how they died, like one prim and proper girl standing on a tightrope while an alligator snapped at her heels. Then we were put into cars on conveyor belts and taken through the mansion. Ghosts danced and flew through the air, making spooky noises. At the end of the ride, an image of a ghost was projected onto us, appearing like it was riding in the cars with us. I laughed.

I knew ghosts didn't look like that in real life. Ghosts aren't seen at all; you just feel them, hovering about, refusing to be forgotten. Ghosts don't have to be dead people—they could be moments of time that come into your mind when you least expect it, haunting you. Recently, I'd been haunted with a memory: the last moment I saw my mother, putting me on a plane and waving farewell.

Dear Monty,   September 4, 1995

How do you say good-bye? You did it so well in
your movies. When Frank Sinatra died in From Here
to Eternity, you wept. When Elizabeth Taylor visited you the very last time in A Place in the
Sun, you were stern, brave, yet sullen at the
same time.

I watched The Heiress last night. Olivia de
Haviland refused to let you into her life, locked
her door, barred your entrance. You were enraged,
bitter.

How do I say good-bye to Mama?

Amada had become a diligent actress, researching her charac-
ters, building their history.

She worked on a play once, *The Caucasian Chalk Circle* by
Bertolt Brecht. The play was based on an Asian story, "The Chinese
Chalk Circle." It is also the story of Solomon in the Bible. I suppose
the story of a mother wanting the best for her offspring pervades all
cultures.

The story was about two mothers who fight over a child. They
bring their grievance to the king. The king decides to split the child
in half so both mothers may have the kid.

He draws a circle with chalk, places the child in the middle, and
instructs the mothers to tear the child apart. The two mothers take
hold of the child and pull. They yank while the child in the middle
screams in agony. One of the mothers cannot bear the child's cries

and lets go; she lost.

The king returns the child to the loser, believing the true mother, the real mother, could not tolerate her child's obvious pain. The king awarded the child to the mother who let go.

I worked with Dr. Chapman on mourning my mother. We played all sorts of games.

"Pretend I'm your mother," she said. "What would you say to me?"

I looked at her warm face; her long black hair resembled my mother's. There was an uneasy silence. Dr. Chapman was solemn about this exercise.

"I...want...to say," but before I could finish, I started to laugh, bust up. It seemed so ludicrous to me to pretend that way.

Dr. Chapman smiled and said, "Okay, maybe that wasn't a good suggestion. How about writing a letter to her?"

I rolled my eyes and said, "I only write letters to Monty."

"Why do you do that?"

"Some people keep diaries or journals—I write letters. It's comforting to me."

"Do you still see him?"

"Not as much."

"Maybe because you're happy?"

•

I went to Echo Park, the first place I'd seen Monty, and had a picnic. I didn't have a picture of my mother. Or of my father. So I did without them. I bought some candles, incense sticks, and a bouquet of flowers, star lilies and chrysanthemums. I bought a bucket of fried chicken, some oranges, a bottle of 7-Up, and a pack of Oreos.

I placed three paper plates, three paper cups, and some eating utensils on the grass, creating three points of a triangle. I divided the chicken evenly and put some Oreos on the plates. I left the oranges on the grass. I poured the 7-Up into three cups and arranged the flowers in the center. I lit the incense sticks and stood them in a mound of dirt.

I took a deep breath and closed my eyes. In my mind, I called out to them, my parents. I asked them to come and eat with me. I asked them to bless the food before me. I imagined their spirits occupying the spaces where the plates were set. I imagined them being the other points of the triangle.

I opened my eyes then ate the fried chicken, knowing they had left luck behind.

CHAPTER THIRTY-SIX
Watching the Morning Mist Burn Away

Dear Monty,   March 15, 1996

Sorry I haven't written in awhile.

I've been consumed with other things. Like Logan.
I like the way he massages my shoulders when I'm
tired. Or the way his hair sticks straight up
when he wakes in the morning. I'm fascinated at
how meticulously he folds his laundry and irons
his underwear. I laugh when he uses a whole tube
of Clearasil when a pimple emerges on the tip of
his nose. I curse him for using MSG on the fried
rice he makes. I revel in the fact that he has a
small birthmark on his left butt cheek.

The last few weeks have been hectic. I'd been an
extra for a few movies and they'd been shooting
early in the morning. I usually meet Logan during
the day and the sight of him energizes me.

I have to meet him in an hour. We're going to see
a movie, one that he worked on.

I'm writing you to let you know that I still love
you, but I love someone else, too.

"**W**hy do you do that?" Logan asked. "It's weird." I'd let
Logan in on some of the things that no one else in the
world knows. I mean, if we're going to be living together, he should know some of my habits. Including my blotching.
"Your letters to a dead guy I can sort of understand, I mean I was

raised to respect the dead, too. But blotches? And always on page 168?"

"It's just something I do," I said.

"Well, it's just plain weird." He smiled his quirky little smile. I loved that smile. So did Amada and Mrs. A. We went out for dinner once. It was the first time I told Mr. and Mrs. A that I liked men. I didn't really tell them. I just made it obvious by informing Mr. and Mrs. A that Logan and I would be moving in together.

"How much are two bedrooms running these days?" asked Mr. A.

"I don't know," I said. "Logan and I will be sharing a one-bed-room."

"That is too small. But I suppose two beds would be cheaper," he said.

"Actually there will be only one bed."

Mr. and Mrs. A looked a little perplexed, then their eyes widened in recognition. Amada almost busted up. She tried really hard to contain herself.

Logan and I found a little apartment in Venice. It was only a few blocks from the ocean.

My favorite times with Logan were in the mornings, before we started our day. We'd take a leisurely walk down the beach, watching the morning mist burn away, revealing a sky bluer than a Billie Holiday ballad.

"Why don't you want to talk about her?" Logan asked.

"I've dealt with my mother and my father. I don't want to discuss them." I try not to think about them. It gets easier if I really try.

"You don't want to talk about them even with me?"

"If I talk about her, I'll remember her. I'll wonder why she never came, if she died, if she lived. Then I'll be really sad. I don't want to be sad about that. I'm willing to be sad about something else. But not about that. I spent a good part of my life wondering where she is. No more."

•

I attached photos to our refrigerator, keeping them up with magnets. Photos from the past year. Logan and I at Disneyland. We bought hats with ears on them. Logan and I in San Francisco. We went up to visit his parents, spent Logan's birthday with them. His parents, Mr. and Mrs. Kushida, wore a forced smile in the picture. They were still getting used to the fact that he's gay. Regardless, our faces beamed. Logan at the Long Beach swap meet carrying a stuffed easy chair that now sits in our living room. My favorite was of Logan, me and Amada at the opening night of a play she did. She worked almost full-time with an Asian American theatre troupe. They do shows around Southern California. It was a family picture really—a semblance of a life.

Logan optioned his first screenplay to a small production company in Hollywood. He was thrilled. I was thrilled for him. Still, money was tight. He got a job teaching cinema classes at City College. I continued to do extra work.

CHAPTER THIRTY-SEVEN
Her Hand Fluttered Like a Butterfly

Dear Monty,   May 29, 1997

Mrs. Billaruz called. I had Logan take a message.
He did.

"What did she want?" I yelled from the kitchen.

"She wants to send you news footage from Filipino
TV."

"Why?"

"She said it was about vigils remembering those
who disappeared. She wants you to call her."

I didn't call her. I don't have plans to do so. I
bought a new address book recently and transferred names, telephone numbers, and addresses
from my old book. I didn't include Mrs. Billaruz
or Mr. Boyd. The only remnant of Amnesty
International I have is a bumper sticker and that
is buried in a drawer somewhere.

Dear Monty,   June 27, 1997

Mrs. Billaruz's package arrived. It's sitting on
the coffee table. I had a real long day working
as an extra for a new television show. I'll see
the video when I get the chance.

The phone rang. I picked it up. It was Mrs. Billaruz.

"My boy," she said, "why haven't you called me?"

"I'm sorry. I've been really busy. I—"

"You haven't seen the tape, have you?"

"Mrs. Billaruz, things have been really hectic," I lied.

"Do you have a VCR?"

"Yes…"

"Play the videotape. I'll stay on the line."

"I'm on my way out," I lied again.

"Play it!"

I took a deep breath, and with the phone secured between my cheek and my shoulder, I played the tape. In the video, a news anchor said there was a vigil in Manila to remember those who had disappeared during the Marcos regime. It was an overcast day. Throngs of people gathered in a park to pay homage to the political prisoners who died or disappeared. Some of them carried pictures of missing loved ones. The camera took close-ups of these people carrying pictures of their deceased.

The camera rested for a moment on a woman who wore a sweater and a plain blue dress. She carried a photo across her chest. It was a photo of my dad. The woman holding the photo was old, her hair a little gray.

But it was my mother.

"Oh God," I said. Mrs. Billaruz apparently said something, but I didn't hear her. I rewound the tape and saw it again, pressing the pause button on the frame that carried my mother's image.

"Did you hear me?" said Mrs. Billaruz.

"What?"

"Did you see what I'm talking about? That is your father's picture she's carrying, isn't it? I don't know if that's her, your mother. Maybe it is an aunt or friend or something, but I wanted you to see."

I didn't answer her. I was transfixed by my mother's image.

Thank God Monty came. I hadn't seen him in such a long time. It was good seeing him again, in front of me, beside the television with a slight smile on his face. I loved his brown suit and black penny loafers. His hair looked great, neatly combed with a sheen that sparkled in the afternoon light.

"Is that your mother?" Mrs. Billaruz said a little louder. I had forgotten she was on the phone.

"Yes. It's her."

"At first, I didn't know. I'd been taping news footage of anything to do with the Marcoses. I saw this. I almost didn't send the video-tape to you. I didn't want to upset you if that wasn't your mother."

"It's her," I said.

"Are you sure?"

"Positive." In the video, the woman did one thing that gave her away, that let me know she was my mother. She placed her hand over her mouth to stifle herself, to stop herself from crying. She did-n't cup her mouth, her fingers hugging her jaw. Instead, she kept it flat, her thumb and her pinky spread out from the rest of her fin-gers. Her hand fluttered like a butterfly. I remembered that. When I boarded the plane to come to the U.S., she cried. And she used her hand that very same way.

"Are you there?" Mrs. Billaruz asked.

"Yes," I said.

"Isn't this wonderful?"

"Yes. Yes it is. I have to call you back, Mrs. Billaruz. Someone arrived. I hadn't seen him in a while. I'll have to get back to you." I hung up.

How long did I stand there with Monty? An hour? Two? I want-ed to touch him. I wanted to touch him so badly. With my mother's image frozen on the television, I wanted him to hold me. I reached for him but my arms went through him.

The sun fell. I was thrilled when Logan came home.

"Hi, today was a bitch," he said. I didn't care. I didn't give a rat's ass about his day or him. I wanted Monty. Mr. Clift had been there for me from the beginning of this ordeal. Before Logan. Before Amada. Two people I loved most. He was the first. I wanted Monty to make love to me. I needed him to make love to me.

I approached Logan, and stared at him.

"Something wrong—" he said, but I cut him off. I shut my eyes tight and kissed him. It was a strong kiss, and he sort of giggled. I summoned Monty, beckoned him to make Logan disappear. I opened my eyes and Logan was gone. Mr. Clift appeared. It was just us. I relaxed into Monty's arms. He in mine. I took off his clothes and kissed him all over. We laid together. He rested in my mouth.

I rested in his.

I loved having my arms around him, holding him tightly. I didn't want to let him go. Then he orgasmed. So did I. He fell away to rest.

I couldn't sleep. I itched. My arms itched. I scratched myself, feeling my nails scrape against my skin. I stopped just before I bled.

I reached over and said, I love you. Mr. Clift didn't answer. Logan did.

I love you, too, he said.

•

I asked Logan to pick me up from the hospital. He had been good about picking me up from my sessions with Dr. Chapman. Logan and I have talked about my time at St. Joan's psychiatric ward before. We've talked in short, vague details. He knew I didn't want to discuss it; he never pressed it.

"I had some things to work out" was what I told him. I never told him about my hurting myself. I never told him how I used to find men and imagine them to be Monty. I planned to tell him someday, but I chose amnesia. It's easier to forget bad things, pretend they never happened. I don't have to deal with things if they never happened. Inevitably, it all comes back, every forlorn, hideous detail comes back.

I had to tell him.

"You hurt yourself?" he asked.

"I used to. I hadn't done it in a long time. But I've been thinking about it lately. Hurting myself, that is."

"Seeing your mother must have really been hard."

"I thought it was over. I thought I had gotten over it." Telling him about spending time with a dead movie star was a little harder.

"You used to see Montgomery Clift? Touch him?"

"Yeah."

"Have sex with him?"

"Yeah."

"Wow."

I was scared. Scared he would think this was too weird. Too weird and leave me. I didn't want him to disappear. He'd joked about knowing people who were psychotic; he'd call a lot of people he didn't like psychotic. His boss was psychotic. People who didn't like his screenplays were psychotic. But his boyfriend?

Logan once told me he wrote "formula" screenplays. He wrote movies where the lovers managed to get together in the end, where the good guys always won, and no matter how poor or disheveled a family was, they managed to afford great gifts for the children at Christmas. He believed all that stuff. He believed in formula; it worked. In a formulaic manner, he said, "I'll stick by you." Good. And I loved him a little more.

•

"Are you sure that was your mother you saw?" Dr. Chapman asked me.

"YES!" Everyone kept asking me that question. Logan, Amada, Mr. and Mrs. A, even Mrs. Billaruz called again for me to state unequivocally that the woman in the video was my mother.

"Don't get upset. Sometimes we see what we want to see, that's all," she said.

"I'm not imagining things."

"Do you think you'll hurt yourself?"

"I hope not." I hope not.

She didn't understand. She just didn't.

•

"Find her," Amada said. "Find her."

She didn't understand how scared I was knowing my mother might be alive. If she died, it would have been easy: she didn't return because she was dead. Alive, I wondered what went wrong.

"Find her," Amada said. "Risk it. Take a chance."

"You don't get it."

"Yes. I do. Do something that takes courage. Something that could have horrible consequences."

"Why?"

"Because that is the only way to be brave."

"I am brave. I've been through a lot—"

"Will you shut up and listen for a moment. Why do you men get threatened when you think your masculinity is on the line? Bravery does not happen once or twice, like getting over a car accident or getting out of a hospital. It is an ongoing effort, facing everything that scares you."

That was the first time I'd realized Amada looked different. Sometimes when you've known someone for a long time, you assume she always looked that way. Sure, she may have a different haircut or she may have lost or gained a few pounds, but she'd remained the same.

Amada's face had changed. Not so much her features, but what was behind those features. Her eyes used to appear anxious, unsettled. Her face used to be a little more full, with softer angles. Now her eyes appeared relaxed, a little more at ease. The angles of her face had become more sharp, defined.

"When I had that abortion," she said, "it took every ounce of nerve I had. I was only seventeen. I corrected a mistake. It takes guts to correct a mistake. There are so few times a mistake could be corrected. And I did it."

"But you almost died."

"I wouldn't have it any other way. People can say whatever they want about girls like me; they call me stupid for wanting to be an actress or dumb for getting pregnant, but I don't care.

"Find her. There was a mistake made, you were sent here, separated from your folks. She was supposed to come, but she didn't. You have the opportunity to correct a mistake. Find her. Find your mother; do this brave act."

I asked Monty what to do. I asked him to show me what to do.

CHAPTER THIRTY-EIGHT
Bookends

There are no more letters. There is just now. There is just me. Logan, Amada, and Mr. and Mrs. A saw me off at the airport. They hugged me, kissed me, said good luck.

I boarded the plane. My letters to Monty tucked into my carry-on luggage. I waited quietly for the plane to rise. I watched the sun meet the moon. I searched for Montgomery Clift among the passengers of the plane. I didn't find him. I have a feeling he wanted me to do it on my own. Everyone on the plane was asleep. I was to land in the Philippines by morning.

I had a little money saved up, but not nearly enough to get to the Philippines and stay for a while. Logan gave me some cash, but it was Mr. and Mrs. A who made it all happen.

"Take it," said Mr. A, shoving a wad of bills into my hand. "It was some money we had."

I tried to give the money back to him but he backed away. I tried to give it to Mrs. A, but she wouldn't take it. She said, "Go see what happened to your mother."

"I'll pay you back."

"Don't worry about it," she said.

They gave me almost a thousand dollars. This would have been pennies to the Arangans ten years ago, but it was a lot now.

I knew why they gave me the money: It was a peace offering. Guilt. Incredible guilt was all I felt. I'd put them through a lot. Amada had put them through a lot, too. We'd seen so much together. I knew we hurt people without meaning to. Like Amada said, So few mistakes can be corrected. If you get the chance to correct one, do. Mr. and Mrs. A were trying to correct a mistake.

How do I correct the mistakes I made with them? I was cruel to them, refusing them in my life. They took me in, fed me, clothed me, and I resented them for hurting my parents—something they had no direct involvement with. They got entangled with the Marcoses because they wanted a life, a good life. They didn't know what the Marcos regime would do later.

"I'll pay it back. I insist," I said.

"You don't have to," Mrs. A said. "I don't care what you say, I still think of you as my son. You should learn a little from Amada. She would never think of paying us back."

"Well, Amada is a little selfish," I said.

"Yes, she is. That's because we raised her that way. There is nothing wrong with being a little selfish. One of the reasons we got mixed up with that Marcos stuff is because we were not selfish enough. We kept thinking that we owed people. We paid back all the money we borrowed and more, but we never turned them down, because we weren't selfish enough. Learn to think of yourself a little bit."

•

In Manila the humidity wrapped around me like a wool blanket. It was a gray day with typhoons in the forecast. Warm winds blew like the devil himself was breathing on us.

I met a friend of Mrs. Billaruz's. Her name was Mrs. Andifacio. She is letting me stay with her while I search for Mama.

Logan had made a still photo from the videotape. I didn't like the photo, Mama on the verge of tears. I showed it to Mrs. Andifacio.

"I don't recognize her," she said. "But there were a lot of people at that rally."

"Could you introduce me to other people at the rally? I'd like them to see the photo."

"Of course."

Mrs. Andifacio's brother was abducted in 1975. She hadn't seen him since. "I dream about him," she said. "I still dream about my brother. Sometimes, I dream about when my brother and I were children, playing or fighting the way children do, then he disappears right in front of me. I think that is the worst part of all of this. When my brother disappeared, so did part of my childhood. We shared memories together like two bookends holding up books. When one bookend is taken away, what was in the middle falls away."

•

I wanted to find a bookstore or library. I had a pen with which to begin my blotching. I took a taxi, instructing the driver to find a library or bookstore.

"Yes, sir," said the driver, a shriveled man.

He drove around the city, passing Manila Bay. Wind had kicked in, clouds rolled through, and waves from the bay smashed against the cement railway, splashing onto the sidewalk.

I had met over half a dozen people who had sketchy memories of the woman in the photo. Some thought they saw her, most had not. Almost all had remarked on the sadness on her face, grief they understood.

I realized how small I was in this world. I was one of many who had family members taken away, never seen again. I have to confess I find comfort in their company. Thousands of people had disappeared, meaning thousands of families were affected. They all had a missing spot in their lives, a black hole in their gut that nothing can fill.

The taxi driver had been driving for half an hour when I thought how funny it was that in a city as big as Manila, there were no libraries or bookstores. Then I realized the taxi driver was literally taking me for a ride. I ordered him to stop and let me off.

"We're almost there," he said.

"Yeah, right," I said, getting out. I threw him two hundred pesos, which added up to about five American dollars. The taxi driver sped away.

I walked around for hours, it seemed, coming across a large cement structure. It was the Cultural Center, one of many buildings Imelda Marcos erected to make her mark on the city. That was what my father died for? Why my mother was not in my life? All that for a dark monstrosity of a building, looming like a fist.

I had been exploring my surroundings, taking long meandering walks through the city. Drizzle dampened my hair, and as I

wiped the drops of water falling onto my face, I took a long look
around. I didn't know what part of the city I was in, but it was dirt
poor. Exhaust from speeding taxis made the air toxic. The street
was lined with wooden houses, ready to fall. If those houses were in
Los Angeles, they would have never been able to handle even the
smallest earthquake.

I came across a long white wall. I followed it until I found an
entrance. The white wall circled the Malacanang Palace, where
Ferdinand and Imelda Marcos had lived and entertained, where
orders were carried out to make people disappear, where Imelda
kept her depository of shoes. The white wall separated the poor
from the wealth of the Marcos regime.

I peered through the gate, and saw the lushness of the property: Green grass carpeted the ground, colored tiles decorated the
palace porch, and a small river ran through the property. On how
many moonlit nights did the Marcos family sit by the river while the
poor struggled outside their palace walls?

I wondered if Malacanang Palace was any different from any
other palace in the world, Buckingham Palace, the White House, or
the Vatican for that matter? Poverty encroaching on the walls of the
immeasurably wealthy, most of us peering through gates wondering
how they lived.

•

I went to interview a friend of Mrs. Andifacio. Her name was
Phelia Buro. I pulled out the picture of Mama, ready for Phelia to
say, I don't know her. Instead, she said, "That's Cecilia."

Cecilia, my mother's first name. Cessy for short.

"Cecilia something…"

"Luwad," I said, "Cecilia, Cessy Luwad."

"Yes. She was in hiding. She hid for quite a while, I know that.
Maybe a year."

"Hiding?"

"People who rallied against Marcos, who made noise, often went
into hiding. She was looking for her husband, asking questions. You
don't ask questions about missing persons and be ignored. She had
to go into hiding."

"How do you know this?"

"She told me."

"When?"

"When we met."

"When was this?"

"I guess in the late '70s, early '80s. When we were in prison."

"Prison?"

"You did not know your mother was in prison for three years?"

I wanted to hurt myself, desecrate my body somehow, destroy what part of me was left. I knew what they did to women in there. I heard an internal howl, a hot scream that pierced my being.

"No," I said, "I didn't."

"She talked about you. She talked about her son. She said you were in the States with your auntie. She was not well when she was released. Not well at all. You are not treated well in prison, some of us had breaking points. When she found out her husband was killed...she seemed a little lost. You know, lost in the head."

"I know what that feels like," I said.

"I know other people who could help, I know people who were detained—we keep in touch."

"Can I talk to some of these people?"

"I can try. Some people don't want others to know they were detained. They just want to forget the whole thing. Or they don't want to talk about it because they're afraid they can get hurt."

"Hurt?"

"Oh yes. People are still afraid that they will be detained again. Many people are still loyal to the Marcos family, you know. You never know who might be listening."

"I understand."

I was amazed at how the network of political prisoners worked. It was like a select club, with membership limited to the beaten, the tortured, the raped.

I met a man who helped my mother when she left prison, a friend of Phelia Buro. His name was Mr. Tombayo. He had been detained for a few months. He took Mama in when she was released.

"My mother stayed here?" I said. I stood in a flimsy corrugated metal home about twenty miles outside of Manila.

"Yes," said Mr. Tombayo. "For about six months. She slept over there." He pointed to a ratty old mattress on the floor. Wind blew in from the broken windows, the frayed yellow curtains billowed in the restless air.

"She moved around a lot," said Mr. Tombayo.

"Was she well?" I asked.

"No. She looked like she would go away in the head. I would talk to her and she wouldn't know I was there. We went to the movies a lot," he said.

I asked Mr. Tombayo if I could be alone in the room. I wanted to be alone in the room Mama slept in. I took a deep breath, hoping to smell her, but no residue of her lingered, only the stale smell of moisture. Then again, I wasn't sure what Mama was supposed to smell like. I had forgotten her scent.

Mr. Tombayo said my mother went on to live in Angeles City. He gave me the names of some people who could possibly help me.

I found a bookstore in Makati, a well-to-do neighborhood near Manila. Dazzling high-rises jabbed at the sky, shiny European cars glistened in the streets. Light-skinned Filipinos sported names of American and French designers on their clothes. I sat in the bookstore for hours, blotching page 168 of every book I could get my hands on.

When night approached, I walked around. A little boy wearing an oversized T-shirt looked up at me. He sat by my feet with shoe polish and rags.

"Shoeshine, sir?" He asked.

I nodded, unable to speak. I couldn't help but think that boy and I were the same person, one individual meeting at different points in his life.

I wanted to speak to the boy who was me, tell him a journey is in store, tell him that he will encounter people, some he will love, some he will regret ever meeting. A search will take place that will consume his life. I wanted to tell him this. Instead, I watched his little body sway as his hands buffed my shoes. When he was done, he sat waiting for his tip.

I gave him two hundred pesos. He lifted his head shyly, his eyes to the ground. He said it was too much money. I told him to keep it. I saw the boy who was me run off clutching the money in his hands, meeting a woman at the far end of the street. He showed her the money. She kissed his forehead, and they walked away together.

Angeles City is a small town at the base of the mountains. I ordered an orange soda from a wooden store near the bus stop. The weather had cleared; puffs of clouds opened up, introducing a sun so hot, it burned. Its rays lit up the golden dirt beneath my feet, reflecting the heat back up. I approached the owner of the store.

"Excuse me, I'm looking for Mr. Gumboa." I spoke in Tagalog.

"Who are you?" the owner inquired.

"My name is Bob Luwad. I'm looking for this woman." I showed him the photo of my mother.

"You're not from around here."

"Yes. I am."

"You don't sound like it."

He was right. I wasn't from around "here." At least not anymore. My accent didn't sound authentic. I was an American trying to sound like I was a native. I had spoken English for most of my life now. When I spoke Tagalog, it had many English words and phrases mixed in.

"I was born in Benguet province, but raised in America." This seemed to appease the owner. "I was told I could talk with Mr. Gumboa. I'm trying to find my mother. I need his help."

"What is your mother's name?"

"Cessy Luwad."

He cocked his head and studied my face.

"I'm Mr. Gumboa," he said, "and Cessy Luwad doesn't live here anymore."

"What happened to her?"

"She left."

"Why?"

"There was no work here. At least no work for her to do."

"Where did she go?"

"I don't know. There aren't that many nice houses around here for her to clean. She didn't know how to do anything else, you know. She may have gone to Manila."

"I just came from Manila."

"Maybe she went into the mountains. Baguio City, someplace like that. Talk to Rosario. She owns the hair salon down the street," he said, pointing me down a dirt road. I saw no sign of a hair salon.

"How far down do I have to walk before I see the hair salon?"

"Only a few hundred feet," Mr. Gumboa said waving me toward a little hut made of corrugated metal. I walked closer and saw a small sign that said Rosario Lope's Hair Extravaganza painted in red. The inside was dim with one light bulb. The dirt floor was covered with thick cardboard; a cheap oriental rug was thrown over it.

"Yeeeees?" a chirpy voice came from nowhere.

"I'm looking for Rosario."

"That is me. The one and only." She looked at me and smiled, garish orange lipstick tainted her teeth.

She came up real close, and said, "What can I do for you, handsome?"

"I'm looking for someone. Cessy Luwad."

"What would a young thing like you be doing looking for her?"

"She's my mother."

Rosario's head jerked. "That can't be," she said. "Cessy's boy is in the States."

"I was. Do you know where she is?"

"She's gone. She lived here for about a year. She slept in the back. But she's probably in Baguio City looking for some rich woman's house to clean. She used to help out, but I had to let her go. I couldn't pay her anymore. I think she was ready to leave. She'd leave for long periods of time, come back. I couldn't use her."

She showed me the room where Mama stayed. It was in the back of the salon, a drafty and dark room, smelling of mildew. A rusty bed in a corner.

"I sleep here now," said Rosario. "Not a lot of people can afford to have their hair done around here."

I went back to the bus depot and took the next bus to Baguio City.

The bus ride was an uncomfortable one, jammed with tourists from Manila and Japan and Hong Kong. The journey up the mountain was slow and careful. Narrow, winding roads up the mountain were handled with great caution. A jeepney whizzed by in the opposite direction with children on its roof.

I looked out my bus window at rice fields and acres of green trees. Caribou lazily strolled through fields. The sky was a baby blue with patches of sugar white clouds. I saw a waterfall cascading down a hill and pink flowers in the golden dirt.

And the children, such beautiful children. The bus passed kids doing chores or walking home from school. Their copper skin glistened and their white-white teeth shone. They wore bright T-shirts—yellow, red, green.

I got off the bus in Baguio. The city had changed from when I was a boy. Buildings stood in places that used to be open lots. The humidity of the town was certainly different from Manila. Cool and misty. It felt like Los Angeles on a spring morning, a great escape from the horrible heat down below.

A taxi driver offered to take me to a nearby hotel. I threw my small bags into the passenger seat and took off to a hotel on the south end of Baguio. Baguio houses rested on the side of the mountain. They reminded me of Silverlake or Los Feliz.

My hotel room was pleasantly furnished. Beige paint covered the walls. I had a small window looking over trees. I didn't remember the hotel being here when I was a kid. Then again, a lot had changed. I lay down on my bed before continuing my search for my mother.

CHAPTER THIRTY-NINE

Ghosts Begging to Be Set Free

I'd spent five days searching the province, going in and out of the city to the nearby countryside. Going everywhere to find Mama. With not much to go on, I scoured the city showing the photo of my mother to almost everyone I encountered: men who drove taxis, waiters and waitresses at the restaurants I'd eaten in, kids playing in the park, strangers waiting for the bus, professors and students at the university, tellers at the bank, security guards at buildings, shoppers in the mall, anyone who crossed my path had the photo shoved in their face. People avoided me, thinking I was a crazy person.

Where would she go? I kept asking myself. Where?

I walked the streets, dazed and dejected, wondering why I did this? Why did I want to find her? To know why she never came.

I fell to the pavement burying my head into my arms, because I knew the answers. My mother attached me to this world. She was my connection—then all of a sudden, that connection was severed. I was left drifting, living my life as an extra, just an extra. What did Amada say about extras? They're nobodies, people who hang around while the real action takes place in front of them.

To prove that I existed, I blotched books. Always on the same page. Page 168: the month and year of my birth. Leaving a mark somewhere that I had existed. Whoever picked up the book after me may not notice the dot, but I knew it was there. In their face, in their life somehow. I wasn't a nothing.

Where was she? Where was she?

I bruised and scarred myself, hating the fact that I was in America, while my parents suffered in the Philippines. I hated that I was healthy, my skin unblemished, knowing, feeling my parents were being hurt, mutilated. I got away. God damn it, I got away.

Amada said I had to correct a mistake. Hurting myself was my way of correcting things that went awry. My life in the U.S. was a mistake. I was supposed to have the same fate as my father or mother: imprisonment, torture. Instead I got away, I was saved. I had the wealth of America on my back, and it felt like an enormous burden.

In the distance, far away, I heard a noise, a bell, a church bell. I stirred. A church! The only place I hadn't checked. My mother believed in God, she must have gone to church. Surely someone there would have recognized her.

A large pink church sat on a hill. I got to my feet. I tried the front doors. They swung open easily. A man polished candlesticks by the altar.

"Excuse me. Could you help me?"

"Yes, my son."

"I'm looking for someone. I'm looking for this woman." I showed him the photo.

"No, I'm sorry. She don't look familiar."

I stared at my feet, wondering what to do. I looked up and saw a painting of the Virgin Mary cradling Jesus as he lay dead beneath the cross.

"I love that painting," the man said. "When Easter comes, the parishioners place flowers and candles around it. A shrine, so to speak. It's remarkable how we Filipinos celebrate Easter. Almost fanatical about it. Wouldn't you say?

"When I was a child," the man said, "we weren't allowed to have any candy, listen to the radio, watch TV for forty days. The entire time of Lent. We showed how earnest we were by sacrifice."

There was a rattling sound as a cleaning woman came out with a bucket and mop to clean the wooden floors beneath the altar.

The man dusted the gold frame of the pietà with a rag in his hand. "This painting was the first thing I noticed when I took over this parish a year ago."

"A year ago?" I said. Perhaps there was someone else here who remembered my parents. "Who was the priest before you? Is he still here?"

"That would have been Father Wandag. He was transferred to Cebu."

"Is there any way I can get in touch with him. It's urgent."

"Sure. But Father Wandag was transferred because he was getting old. Senile. Couldn't remember his name if you asked him."

I heard the cleaning woman spraying air freshener.

"Nuns? Anyone who may have been here long enough to know the woman in the photo?"

"Maybe, but we see a lot of people. On Sunday, we have several masses, one after another, and they're all full."

I decided it was pointless. It looked like I was destined not to know what happened to Mama, left wondering what happened to her, feeling very much like I did when I was nine. I walked to the far end of the church, ready to leave. Then I sent Montgomery Clift a psychic message, Why did I do this, Monty? Why did I come all this way? For nothing.

"Father," the cleaning woman said, "is there anything you'd like me to do before I leave?"

"Yes, there is," the priest said.

I folded Mama's photo and put it into my wallet.

"There is a small mess that needs to be cleaned up. I need you to tend to it," he said in a tone not of employee to servant but dear friend to another dear friend.

"Of course," the woman said charmingly.

I opened the door to the church, planning my way back to Manila, back to the United States.

"Isn't it amazing how much upkeep a church needs, Yuna."

"Amazing," the woman replied.

I turned slowly. Yuna? Did the priest say Yuna?

I watched them blow candles out. I watched the cleaning woman delicately wipe the glass encasing the candles. I approached them. The closer I got, the clearer her face became. Her hair was shorter, she was a little more frail, but it was undoubtedly her.

"Auntie Yuna?" I whispered.

The woman lifted her face, her eyes meeting mine. Fright filled her face, then, as quickly, relief. The crash of breaking glass echoed in the solemn church as the candle she held in her hands fell to the floor. She backed away from me, fainting.

The priest caught her and led her to a pew. I grabbed her other arm and we gently sat her down.

"I'll be all right," she said. "I'll be all right." She fanned herself with her hands, taking deep breaths. She pressed her hand to my face, her palm flat against my cheek. She put her head into my chest, and wept. Was this the woman who used to torment me as a child?

She asked the priest if she could go. He said yes. We worked our way to a main street. She hailed a taxi, got inside.

"I was deported," she said. "One night I got drunk and got lost. The police found me wandering the streets. They decided to check if I was legal. I wasn't. So they deported me, right away." That explained why Auntie Yuna never came home. She was taken away. "I found myself back in Manila. I worked in bars again. I got tired of that. Or they got tired of me. I wasn't pretty like before. I had nowhere to go except here. I was a waitress for a while. I was a clerk at the university. I finally got this job at the church."

The cab stopped in front of a small apartment building, rancid with the smell of rotten food. She led me up a creaking stairway to her apartment. It was small, her bed, kitchen, and bathroom all in close proximity. Her window was open and the mildewed white curtains grappled with the wind, resembling ghosts begging to be set free.

"You look fine," she said. "Have you found your mother?"

"No. How did you know that's why I'm here?"

"Why else would you be here? You didn't come to find me."

When I was a kid, I hated her, wished her dead. All I felt was pity, pity for the woman she was, pity for the woman she became. I noticed her bed, a stained mattress on the floor. Little cockroaches crawled out of thin cracks in the wall.

She sat by her window, the ghost-curtains blowing around her. "I was bad to you," she said. "I spent a lot of years being awful. This is what I get—a rundown apartment with nobody...except maybe you."

I looked away.

"I want to say that I have a nephew. When I return to work next week, I want to tell people that my nephew visited. My nephew from the States visited me.

"I don't want people to think I have nobody. It hurts me to know I have no one. It hurts even more when everyone else knows it too. Maybe we can write letters. Yes? Maybe you can send me a Christmas card, and I can show it to people. You can send cards on the holidays, cards from Los Angeles. I miss L.A., you know.

"Please, Bong, I have no one. Your mother doesn't want anything to do with me."

"My mother?"

She lowered her head and said, "She's here in Baguio City. She saw me working as a waitress in a restaurant. She made a big scene. She asked me where you were. I told her I was deported. I told her I didn't know where they took you. I told her you were somewhere in the States. She beat me right in the restaurant, almost killed me. They put her away for being crazy. She almost killed me."

"Where is she now?"

"She was let go from the hospital. She comes to church sometimes. Whenever I see her, I walk toward her, but she walks away. She won't let me near her. I haven't seen her in church for a while."

"I have to go," I said.

"Bong," Auntie Yuna said, "may I tell people I have a nephew?"

I nodded.

"Maybe we can write?" she said, and scribbled her address on a piece of paper.

"Maybe."

•

I went to church on Sunday, walking through waves of heat. Women carried parasols and fans. We were burning, burning alive. They walked into church to escape the heat, only to find it became warmer inside, a suffocating warmth.

I watched parishioners come and go, hoping my mother would be among them. After a while, all the women looked the same. I was bleary-eyed, thinking the next woman might be the one.

I had it planned out. Once I spotted her, I would follow her. She wouldn't notice me. I would sit next to her on a pew, and watch her pray or do whatever it is women do in churches. We would kneel together, kindred strangers. She would only know me as the-man-beside-her, but she would know there was more to me. Finally, when Mass ended, we would exit the church and in the afternoon light, she would recognize me, and tell me she missed me. Salvation.

But nothing. I waited through most of the masses and she did

not come. Someone else did, though. Someone I had filed away
long ago. Among the Filipinos, I spotted a woman who did not fit
in. She appeared too self-assured, too arrogant. She stepped out of
a limousine, shrouded in black, a veil falling across her face. In
church, she did not appear solemn or humble. She was too digni-
fied for that. As if God were an equal, not a figure to be worshipped.
That kind of attitude could only belong to an American. It was Mrs.
Baker. The woman who arranged my passage to the States, whose
house my mother cleaned, to whom my mother ran for help. Mrs.
Baker, the soldier's wife.

When Mass ended, she walked to her car. A driver held the door
open. I approached.

"Mrs. Baker?"

"Yes."

I peered into her face. Her eyes had a milky film over them, but
they were focused and sharp. She squinted and asked, "Do I know
you, young man?"

"Yes, you do. I don't expect you to remember me. I was only a
kid when we saw each other last."

"You have to be more specific than that. I knew a lot of kids.
Were you that boy who used to steal apples from my tree? Shame on
you, stealing like that."

"No, Mrs. Baker, that wasn't me. My name is Bob Luwad. You
helped me get to America. Do you remember?"

She turned her head to the left, then to the right, her eyes prob-
ing me. "Cessy's boy?"

"Yes."

"Good lord…" She took my arm and led me into her car. "Let's
talk at my home. We can talk while we have tea, some fruit perhaps."

Mrs. Baker's home was much smaller than I remembered. In
fact it appeared to be about the size of Mr. and Mrs. A's home in
Pasadena. A maid brought in slices of mango with a saucer of
bagoong, shrimp paste.

"Ever since my husband died, I haven't the opportunity to share
my meals," she said with a smile. Her smile emphasized the creases
in her face. She removed the veil and streaks of gray ran through
her hair. "Cessy's boy. I had always wondered what happened to you.
Cessy said you were doing well."

"She hasn't seen me in twenty years. How would she know that?"

"Don't know. She told me you looked good, healthy and everything."

Mrs. Baker was slower, a little more settled. She wasn't the glamorous party hostess I remembered her to be. She had come to a point in her life, it seemed, where nothing was a big deal, nothing excited her.

"Mrs. Baker, how would she know about me?"

"She seemed to know that you're doing well. Like she'd seen you in the flesh. She said sending you to the States was the best thing she'd done."

There was no way my mother could have seen me. I figured Mrs. Baker was a bit senile.

"Did you know she was imprisoned?" I said, trying to approach the topic of my mother from another angle.

"Awful. Awful that happened to her. I had it all arranged. She would send you to the States first. Then she and her husband would follow. I had it all set. But she never came back. I waited weeks. I had my husband try to find your parents, but the Filipino government said they had no knowledge of them. Lying bastards. I tried to pull strings, but nothing.

"I wrote letters to every Filipino official I knew, used U.S. military stationery. I got a letter back telling me it wasn't diplomatic to meddle in another country's affairs. Some nonsense about Americans being the visitors in this country.

"Then my husband fell sick. I was crushed when he died. With his death, I lost any political muscle I had. All I could do was pray your mother was okay, pray that you were okay.

"Around six, maybe seven years ago, she showed up on my doorstep. She was looking for work. Couldn't give her a job. My driver takes care of me, does all the things needing to be done around here.

"She stayed here a while, though, till she got back on her feet. She found a job. I don't know where. She stops by every once in a while, drops off cookies or fruit for me. She tells me you're doing fine."

I looked around the house. I didn't know what I'd see— maybe an imprint, some lingering shadow of her. "How do I find her?

Where would my mother go?"

"I don't know where she works. But I know she goes to the marketplace on Tuesdays. I think she told me she shops for her boss there at least once a week."

"What marketplace?"

"The one near La Trinidad, past the Chinese Temple."

"Tuesdays, huh?"

"Pretty sure of it."

I thanked her, went to my hotel room. I wanted to sleep. I wanted the day over with. I wanted to get closer to Tuesday.

•

I awoke to a dark sky, a purple sky with shimmers of light in the distance. Day was coming.

I stood by the entrance to the marketplace, a large clearing near the city. I was there at six in the morning and watched as the merchants set up their wares. Baskets of mangos and bananas, apples and pears, cabbage and lettuce littered the ground. Sacks of rice, different colored rice: red, brown, and white—long grain and short—leaned against tent poles. The smell of fish permeated the air, a punishing stench from dead sea carcasses forced from ocean to land. Shelves were being loaded with local craftwork like cups, penholders, necklaces. On one table, miniature men sat inside barrels; remove the barrels and erections bigger than the men themselves sprang into view.

I watched buses come, carrying women with wicker bags, a flood of women, indistinguishable women. Would one of them be my mother? Late in the morning, a group of women descended the steps of a bus. Most of the women were plump, like hobbling brown pears. One woman, though, in the back, was thin, wearing a pink T-shirt and badly fitted jeans. There was something familiar about her. She seemed like she could be my mother, but I couldn't be sure. As she passed me, I couldn't look at her, afraid to be rude, afraid to lay all of my longing on a stranger who wouldn't be her.

I followed her, watched her chat with the hobbling brown pears, giggling at some joke. I followed this woman I wanted to be my mother. She separated herself from the plump women, wandering toward a mound of cantaloupes, stacked like a pyramid. She thumped the top cantaloupe, the tip of the pyramid, with her palm. She decided not to get it, rising to her feet, massaging her knees in the process. She went to a bin of broccoli across from the cantaloupes, placing a stalk into her bag. She picked up a plum, sniffed it, bought it, then ate it as she wandered through the maze of the marketplace.

She stopped at a booth selling fabric, fingering the yards of multi-layered cloth. She seemed to like a green, a forest green material. I was close enough to see embroidered rabbits hopping on it. Silver threads lined the path the rabbits were hopping on. She dug into her pockets and pulled out small crumpled bills. She counted them. She didn't have enough money to buy the fabric. She laid the rabbit-hopping cloth down and patted it with resignation.

I wanted to speak, find words to bridge us. But it seemed I couldn't. If I spoke and it wasn't her, I didn't think I could search for my mother any longer. It had been so long since I'd seen her, and I didn't think I had the energy to continue looking. Maybe it would be best never to find her and simply let it all alone. Perhaps it would be best if I remembered her young and vital.

"It's pretty," I said, caressing the fabric. I spoke in Tagalog, fully aware of my American accent. I was amazed I said anything.

She ignored me and walked on. The wind blew her scent my direction: it was an antiseptic smell of baby powder and Ajax. I tried to remember what my mother smelled like, but I couldn't. And not knowing the odor from her pores made me sad, reminding me of my purpose: find her, know what happened, seek her out. She was six feet away from me when I said, "Pardon me…"

She turned, facing me. I stared into her face. Yes, it was my mother. Yet, it wasn't. She would have been only 48, but she appeared older. Her once tar-black hair, rich with oil, was faded and gray and brittle. And her face…her face: riddled with lines upon lines crossing one another to form little crucifixes. Her moist skin had become flaky and had a dusty look. But in that face, I saw mine staring back at me; my reflection in a cracked mirror.

I wondered what she saw when she looked at me? The scars from my accident had healed considerably, but they were still there: long tiny grooves stretching from my temple to my jaw.

She tilted her head, her eyes wandering over me. She lifted her bag, shielding herself, it seemed. Her eyes widened, her mouth opened. She knew it was me...and she appeared scared. Then she dropped her bag, the bag carrying the broccoli, and pulled away, tentatively at first, then assuredly, walking backward, eventually turning around, stepping away, away from me, walking quickly, briskly, then running. She ran. She ran from me.

"Wait—" I followed her. "Wait. Please stop."

She turned the corner and was gone. I ran around the corner. I saw her board one of the buses, her small body disappearing into its metal mouth. The folding doors closed. I watched her make her way to the back, sitting by a window. I ran to her, looking up, yelling at the window, "Do you know me? Do you know who I am?"

She nodded, placing her hand against the glass as if doing so would shut out my image.

"I had to find you." I was breathless, trying to keep up with the departing bus. "I had to...Please wait." The bus picked up speed. "I came all this way—all this way. Why won't you talk to me?"

She stared straight ahead. I screamed into the window. "How do I find you? Please talk to me. I'm at the Pine Hotel. The Pine Hotel. Room 21."

The bus sped away. She was gone. Just like that. The second time in my life my mother went away from me.

CHAPTER FORTY
To Quell the Pathetic Tears of a Child

I don't want to leave my room, having meals brought to me. I showered with the door open in case my mother should knock. I wanted a reunion. I wanted hugging and tears, long awkward embraces, not knowing where to place your hands, yet knowing your hands belonged somewhere on this stranger. I wait for her.

I waited for Monty. I tried summoning him into my world, closing my eyes, willing him to come to me. When I opened my eyes, he hadn't visited. I hoped he hadn't gone away, too.

I think I knew Montgomery Clift better than I knew Mama. I thought of all I'd read, all the movies I'd seen. I thought about Monty's role as Noah in *The Young Lions*. Noah: the American Jewish soldier in World War II, forced to fight in Germany. Noah who loved Hope Lange, an American gentile girl. Noah who had seen two worlds: love in one country and the slaughter of his people in another. Eventually the war ends, Noah leaves the dolor of Germany, and returns home. Home is not where his people are, united by religion, or race, it is where he belonged, where his heart and soul felt most comfortable.

I am Filipino, but I didn't belong in the Philippines. If I had been raised in the Philippines, if I had memories attached to the roads and buildings, the turn of the seasons, perhaps I would have the need to stay, but all I have are my first eight years—most of them I don't remember.

Home. Where Logan is. And Amada. Mr. and Mrs. Arangan. Home is where I'm wanted.

My mother doesn't want me. That's why she never came. She ran from me like a gazelle from a lion. All of my years yearning for her seemed to be a waste. I'm forced to question my memories of her, my memories of childhood. Did she really love me? Did she really intend to join me in America? Or did I reconfigure events to my liking?

When she put me on that plane, did she want to send me away for good? Only telling me she would join me to quell the pathetic tears of a child. Perhaps it was her intention to leave me.

I don't know. I don't know anything anymore.

CHAPTER FORTY-ONE
People Who Come and Go

There was a knock. I answered the door. It was Mama. I invited her in. She sat in a chair by my bed. She sat with her hands clasped, her legs crossed, her gaze to the ground, a forlorn gaze as if praying.

What do a parent and child say after all this time? The silence spoke for itself. I looked at her, then at the floor. I wanted to tell her so much. I wanted to tell her I held her close to me for all these years.

I sat across from her, waiting for her to speak. I knew enough to let the parent speak first. I hoped she'd say, "I've dreamed of you" or "I wished we were together" or simply, "I love you I love you I love you." But she didn't. Instead, she said, "I tried to find work at this hotel, but they wouldn't hire me."

"Oh," I said. Then more silence. A long deep silence. If unfulfilled years, unspoken conversations, uncelebrated birthdays and holidays had a sound, this would have been it—a dead sound— nothing moving, nothing said, not a single inhalation of air, just stillness.

Out of nowhere, she began to clean my room, fussing around, emptying the ashtray, folding my jeans, hanging up my shirts, dusting the table, picking up crumbs on the floor. She went into the bathroom and I heard her flushing the toilet. "The family I work for," she yelled, her voice reverberated from the white tiles of the john, "have the messiest children."

Her voice had changed. When I was a boy, her voice was melodic. Whenever I heard it, I knew comfort was not far away. Now it was jarring, tinny.

She came out of the bathroom carrying a plastic bag of refuse. "You don't have to clean," I said. "You're not a maid." I realized my mistake; she was a maid. She was a maid when I was a boy; she is a maid now. She looked away.

I wanted to tell her that I didn't care what she did for a living. I wanted to tell her, You could be a scuba diver for all I cared. After all, what was I? A professional extra. My existence reduced to filling in the background while the real action, what really mattered, occurred in front of me.

"You don't have to clean up right now," I said. "Don't trouble yourself."

"It is no trouble, sir." Sir? "I mean," she said, "please let me do this." She continued to clean. What else could I do but help her? She wiped the window vigorously, as if she were trying to erase the view. I was on my hands and knees, digging out whatever was under the bed, finding dust balls, lint, scraps of tissue, strands of hair, coins. We rearranged furniture, adjusted the angles of pictures on the wall, blew away dust from the lampshade by my bed, fluffing pillows on the couch, straightening the creases on my bed sheets. And when the room was to our liking we stood side by side.

I didn't realize how small she was. As a child, my head reached her chest, easily falling between her breasts when I hugged her. Now her head fell below my shoulders. It used to take both my arms for me to embrace her. Now I was sure I could encompass her with just one.

"Do you know about your father?" she asked.

"Yes," I said.

"Bong?"

I was startled for a moment. I was so accustomed to being Bob that I had to realize she was talking to me.

"Bong," she said, "I meant to find you. I really did." With that, I heard tears ready to erupt in her voice, and I wanted to cry, too, to burst with relief: I found her or she found me. But I didn't cry; neither did she.

We laughed, laughed! It came from deep within my belly. She giggled, then ripped loose an ear-splitting guffaw. And we fell onto the bed, writhing with delight. That laugh. It was the same. Everything had changed but her laugh was the same.

"Tell me, anak," she said. "Tell me, child. Tell me all about your life."

I blushed. I actually blushed! My mother was in front of me. I wondered if I could actually tell her all of my life. What child tells a parent ALL. I suddenly became embarrassed. I certainly couldn't tell her about Amada's abortion or my self-mutilation. I certainly couldn't tell her about my sexual activities.

I had rehearsed my life story over and over, thinking of my letters to Monty tucked away in my carry-on luggage. I wondered how much to reveal. She sensed my apprehension.

"After all I've been through," she said, "there is nothing you can tell me that would shock me."

"My life has been kind of strange," I said.

She cupped my face in her hands and said, "I have been deprived of you for twenty years. Let me be your mother. I'll take you any way you are."

I thought of Mrs. A. I thought of how I argued with her, disagreed with her. The way a parent and child would. Who let go of me in the chalk circle?

I pulled out my letters to Montgomery Clift. She read the first one and I said, "I didn't start seeing Montgomery Clift immediately. I didn't start to depend on him or adore him or desire him or touch him until later…"

She read all of the letters. She had some difficulty with the English, asking me what certain words or phrases meant.

As she read the letters, I filled in the parts in between. She apologized about Auntie Yuna. I told her that wasn't necessary. She shook her head when she read about the foster homes. She put her hand to her mouth when I explained the letters referring to Amada's abortion. She bit her lip, tears ran down her cheeks when I told her about how I hurt myself. She held my hand when I talked about my motorcycle accident, my hospitalization.

I was worried when she read about Logan and the other men in my life.

"Logan sounds like a good person," she said.

"He makes me happy," I said, implying that I loved him, needed him. I waited for her to respond.

"Maybe I can meet him someday." She looked at me. With that look, she let me know it was okay; it didn't matter that I preferred men. I was relieved. I laughed some more.

I told her all of my life. When I was done, and the view from my window was painted black with night, I said: "Tell me about you. Tell me what happened? Tell me everything."

She did. I wasn't prepared for it. This is what she said...

"I will never forget you crying," she said. "Do you remember crying when I put you on the plane? Do you remember that? I fixed your hair before you left. So you would look good when you landed in the States. It was soft hair.

"I put you on that plane and you flew away. I watched the plane jet away, getting smaller and smaller, until it disappeared, becoming the sky itself.

"I found some friends in Manila who were part of the anti-Marcos movement. They hid me away in an apartment in Tondo.

"I had given the name of your father to a priest. His name was Father de la Merced. He located men and women who were detained by the government. There were over twenty detention centers throughout the Philippines. I knew it might take some time finding him.

"I stayed in that little apartment for three days until Father de la Merced told me your father could not be located. He was probably taken to a safehouse, or an unknown prison facility, somewhere near Baguio City. This would make it more difficult to find him. I went from one hiding place to another. During that time, I helped with the anti-Marcos movement, helping others hide like myself.

"I wanted to join you in the States, but I had to know what happened to your father. I knew you would be safe in America. I could not easily surface. I became known as a subversive, someone known for underground activities. The police could identify me.

"One night, someone pounded on the door. Seven men dressed in civilian clothes forced their way in carrying guns, ransacking the apartment, throwing books and furniture around. Then I was driven to Camp Crane, a detention center.

"They told me to tell them what I knew about the Communists. I told them I was not a Communist. They told me that I was only a peasant, and no one would miss me. They said they could just kill me and no one would care. The man interrogating me slapped me across the face. He ordered me to lie on the concrete floor, and told me to take off my clothes. I thought he was going to rape me, but instead they placed a block of ice on my body. They ordered me to hold the ice with my arms.

"The block of ice was on my body for hours. It melted, freezing me so I could not move. My arms were frozen around the ice, numb. I stared at the light bulb above me, praying that my husband was all right. Praying that my son was all right. Asking God why this is happening.

"The ice slowly dissolved, leaving my arms to hold only myself. The melted ice formed a lake around my body. And I wanted to drown in it. But I thought of you. Brushing the hair away from your face, wiping the dirt from your cheek. I knew I could not die.

"We were taken to Fort Bonifacio, outside Manila, and placed into the Butican detention center. Butican is both a maximum and minimum security detention center. Suspected subversives were taken there. Suspected subversives could be anyone: Men, women, children, professors, students, journalists, peasants, celebrities, clergy—anyone who was suspected of being against the government. A fellow detainee told me at least 50,000 people had been detained in centers like these throughout the country.

"I was placed in a room with twenty other women. The room was tiny with rows and rows of bunk beds. A nun greeted us and showed us to our beds. It was pleasant to have a nun comfort us. I asked her if we could pray, and she said yes. She unfastened the rosary beads from her waist and we traced the wooden beads up the flimsy string repeating Our Fathers and Hail Marys, praying for a quick trial and speedy release.

"The nun got up, and I asked if she would return the next day so we may pray some more. She smiled and said she would be here tomorrow and the next day. She said she had been here for the last two months. The nun was arrested for suspected subversive activity as well. Her crime was leading a prayer before a civil rights demonstration.

"I worried about you. I promised I would join you soon, and my heart broke thinking of you hating me for breaking my promise. I would explain it all to you when I am free, I kept thinking to myself. Somehow I'll find your father and we'll be together again.

"I cleaned the bathrooms and mopped the floors. As a maid, I was familiar with such chores. There were some women who were not. They were proud women from prominent families. They had had servants all of their lives, and I had to teach them how to clean. Because they were from wealthy families, less harm came to them and they were often quickly released.

"One wealthy woman, named Diane, asked me how was my English. I told her, 'It is all right. I speak it well enough.' She said, 'Learn to speak it better. Whenever you speak to the guards, speak to them in English. They'll think you're educated. They'll respect you more.'

"I took her advice and spoke only English to the guards. I often had to think what the next word would be or how the sentence should sound, but I did it.

"Father de la Merced visited me in prison and told me that your father had been executed. When he said those words, I drifted away. I wanted to cry because Father de la Merced said he had been dead for several months already. If I had known that, I would have left the Philippines and joined you. Unfair. It was unfair for me not to know."

She became still. Quiet.

"I stayed in prison. They do terrible things to women," she said. "Terrible things."

She could not tell me what happened exactly, but I knew. I bowed my head. I didn't want Mama to see what I was thinking. They did things to her. Those fucking monsters did things to my mother. A little piece of my insides atrophied and died.

I wanted to touch her, but I couldn't. She was less than a foot away from me, but she seemed so far away. Inconsolable. She was a woman I had never known. We developed new lives, new personalities, new beings. Yet she belonged to me. I belonged to her. No matter how many years separated us, we were still each other's. She was my family.

I pulled her close to me and I remember her holding me like that as a boy, that feeling of warmth. She was—is—my family. She sobbed into my chest, a maelstrom of tears at my torso. That was what I was looking for. Someone to give herself to me. Someone for me to give myself to.

I cried. Not just for her, but for me. I thought of Amada and Logan and Mr. and Mrs. A. They gave themselves to me. I didn't realize it at the time, but they did. I was foolish.

"When I left prison," Mama said, "I was not right. Not right in the head. I didn't know what to do. I was afraid all the time. I knew I had to find you, but I had no job, no place to live. I had nothing.

"I saw American children in Manila, tourists or children of soldiers, and I knew they would be taken care of. I felt America would be best for you. I thought Auntie Yuna would be taking care of you good. I watched American movies, and saw how happy they were, so rich. What could I give you? I had nothing to offer you. I wrote letters to Yuna asking her how you were doing, but the letters kept coming back. I had no way of reaching her. I believed you were safe with her.

"I worked at different jobs in Manila, cleaning houses, but it was not steady work. I moved back to Baguio City a year later, and saw Yuna working in a restaurant.

"I asked her where you were. She said that she was deported, and she didn't know where you were. I almost killed her in the restaurant. I went crazy. I could not believe she didn't know where you were. She didn't seem to care. I was put in a hospital, because I almost killed her."

A long smile spread across her face like a road on a map. She started to giggle. She shook her head, and said, "You know our family has always been a little nuts in the head. Your Uncle Virgilio was known to sit for hours, days and just look out, staring at nothing, then he would snap back to life. Just like that."

When she told me this, an incredible peace came over me, caressing me like a velvet cloth.

Her smile turned sour, her lips trembling like a shivering child. "I wanted to die," she said. "My own child somewhere in the States, all by himself. The thought made me sick. I was in the hospital, not well. I was in the hospital, afraid to leave. I would stand in the corner and look out into space. I would watch TV for hours. Sometimes, a nurse would rent a movie for us to watch. American movies. Sometime in my second year, a nurse rented a movie, a scary one. I had seen a lot of scary movies, but I was not scared. I sat there.

"In one movie, I thought I saw you. I thought I saw you in the background. If it was not you, he looked just like you. Or maybe how I thought you would look if you'd grown. You would have been in your late teens. You looked so happy, so healthy. You went to school, and you were so happy…" She went to her bag by the door, pulled out a videotape. It was *Blood Prom at Hell High.*

"I stole this," she said. "I stole it from the hospital. I watched it every chance I could. I knew you were okay. This was a sign you were okay. I knew you were leading a life that I could never give you. If I worked twenty-four hours a day, cleaned every house on Luzon, Mindanao, and Visaya, nothing I could save or buy could ever come close to what you were getting in America.

"Forgive me for not finding you. I thought you would have more to lose if I did."

I will never know how my life would have been different if I grew up with her. I will never know. I just know she was with me, and from that point on, she will always be with me.

I thought of all the people who have disappeared from my life: my father, my childhood friend Robert, my handsome neighbor J and his wife Baby Bounce Belinda, the different foster parents. I guess there will always be people who come and go. Never to be heard from again. There are a few who stay like Amada, the Arangans, Logan. They don't disappear, giving me foundation, giving me strength. Then there are people who disappear who must be found, forcing them to reappear like the sun in the morning. They must be found because they were there when you were—a bookend, keeping the middle from falling away. Like my mother, like my Mama.

Epilogue

Dear Monty,   February 7, 1998

I haven't had the need to write. Then again, I
haven't seen you in awhile either.

I'm arranging my mother's transportation to the
states. I think she'll like it here. I told her
all about Los Angeles. It feels a lot like Baguio
City, actually, cool and by the Pacific Ocean.
Logan and I are looking for a bigger place so my
mother can have her own room. We'll probably live
in Silverlake, it has that artsy feel that Logan
likes so much. I love the homes resting on the
hills, reminding me of Baguio. It's odd that I
traveled so far to live in a place so similar.

Logan is still writing movies, and got hooked up
with some grants. He's made some short films with
the grant money, and started entering them into
some film festivals. He still teaches on the
side, but he likes it.

Amada said she'll help us decorate our new home.
She's still doing theater in town, but wants to
go to school. She's thinking of getting a degree
in arts education or something. Mr. and Mrs. A
are thrilled that Amada wants to go to school.
Mr. A got a job as head accountant for a small
chain of Chinese restaurants, he offered to pay
for some of Amada's school expenses. She said no.
Mrs. A thinks Amada should let them help her.
Mrs. A got a part time job in a jewelry store.

Her first job in America. She said if we ever
want a discount on a diamond, go see her. I told
her diamonds, even with a discount, aren't in my
budget.

I don't want to do extra jobs anymore. Unless
it's in one of Logan's movies. I tell Logan that
maybe one of his movies could really help someone
out. Your movies helped me. I wondered why you
haven't visited. I was rather depressed that you
hadn't come.

Finally, you spoke to me through one of your
movies: Indiscretion of an American Wife. I
caught it early one morning. You looked fantastic
in the movie; love will do that to you. You
played an Italian pursuing Jennifer Jones, a wife
with a husband in America. You rendezvous with
her, meeting her. Both of you love each other,
but know a life together could never be. She has
her life in the states with her family, and you
have another life to tend to.

I wept at the end of the movie. I wept for us. I
love you, Monty. I want the very best for you,
too.

ACKNOWLEDGMENTS

My first novel required the assistance of many people. Thanks to Ayofemi Folayan for encouraging me when I barely had 5 pages. The novelists Aimee Liu and Peter Gadol for reviewing my book. Thanks to PEN Center USA West. (I vowed I would pursue this book to the very end if I were granted PEN's Emerging Voices fellowship.) With Mona Simpson, Cheryl Britton, Jenoyne Adams, Ellery Washington, Sally Weigold-Charette, Sarah Jacobus, Asha Parek, Cynthia Leyva, Harriet Doerr, Judith Searle, Linda Venus, and John Rechy, I was able to establish a firm foundation. A great group of writers: Karen Wallace Sorenson, Lynne Williamson, Linda Bishop, Matthew Rowland, John Polacio, Charles Beals, Alexis Rhone, Mike Gaeta, and Phyllis Gebauer. The staff at Skylight Books: Kevin Awakuni, Christine Berry, Charles Hauther, Courtney Martell, Tim Morell, Kathy Parkman, Steve Salardino, Garret Scullin, Kerry Slattery, Luis Bauz, Karine Rosenthal, Angela Leazenby. Special thanks to Joe Baker with Amnesty International and Brian Garrido. Some books that gave me better insight: *Montgomery Clift* by Patricia Bosworth, *Monty* by Robert LaGuardia, *The Films of Montgomery Clift* by Judith M. Kass, *Motherless Daughters* by Hope Edelman and *A Bright Red Scream* by Marilee Strong. Susan Aranetta, Carol Ojeda-Kimbrough, and Erick Villagran. Al Zuckerman and Fay Greenfield at Writers House—a million thanks! Thanks to my editor Pat Walsh for giving me a chance to share this book with others. Others at MacAdam/Cage I wish to thank: David Poindexter, John Gray, Avril O'Reilly, Dorothy Smith, Scott Allen, and Melanie Mitchell. Joy, Jessie, John, Adele Bayless, Amber Luke, Sandra Zane, and Kim Carver (Ken Rutman). My colleagues at the Asian Pacific AIDS Intervention Team. Lastly, to Montgomery Clift, wherever your spirit may soar, Salamat Po.